SUMMERNIGHT

BRIDGE OF LEGENDS

BOOK ONE

SARAH K. L. WILSON

This is a work of fiction. All characters, places, and events are purely fictitious.

SUMMERNIGHT

ISBN: 978-0-9878502-7-0

Cover art by POLAR ENGINE

Map by Francesca Baerald

Appendix art by Harold Trammel

www.sarahklwilson.com

Direct comments or feedback to sarah@sarahklwilson.com.

For Cale

Always

Legends

Byron Bronzebow

A good-looking hero who carries a bronze bow. Known in history for his care for the poor and needy.

Deathless Pirate

Known for his love of treasure and invulnerability and recognized by his hook for a hand and belt of human skulls.

Grandfather Timeless

Based in the Timekeepers religion he is known for his high hat, long black coat and golden waistcoat. He is Time in human form subjecting all to his will.

King Abelmeyer the One-Eyed

Known for his single eye and broken crown, King Abelmeyer united the five cities of the Dragonblood Plains in the alliance that lasts today.

Lady Sacrifice

Known for her loveliness, innocence and sacrifice for the people, she is usually clad in a white dress.

Lila Cherrylocks

A master thief and trickster. Known for her long cherry-red locks, deft skills, and adventurous spirit.

Maid Chaos

The right hand of Death. Known for destruction, death and the golden breastplate she wears.

Queen Mer

Queen of the Sea and mother to the Waverunners. Queen Mer is known for her revenge upon man in the form of hurricanes and typhoons and for the shells, scales, and seaweed that she wears.

Ram the Hunter

The unspoken Legend. Not mentioned in the Dragonblood Plains except in whispers, he is known for slaying dragons and going insane in the aftermath.

BRIDGE of LEGENDS
YAN
XIN
JINGEN
Districts
Alchemist
Governement
Temple
University
Spice
Artificier
Trade

1: Summernight Procession

Tamerlan

Legends were coming alive.

Or at least, that was how it felt to Tamerlan as he braced himself against the jostling crowd in the rising mist of the morning. Stale water, anticipation, and the smell of feast-day cakes baking filled the air, warring for dominance. He leaned a little farther over the edge of the railing.

"Come on, little fellow! You can't stay there or you'll fall right in!"

He was inches from scooping up the stray dog – a small sharp-nosed black puppy with wild scared eyes. He'd been edged to the very brink of falling into the canal and if Tamerlan couldn't scoop him up he'd fall right in. The canals of Jingen were no place for dogs. Their slick sides weren't made for ease of climbing – especially for someone with four feet.

He pushed a little farther, smelling oranges and roses on the breeze as he hung over the railing. Was that Dathan below?

His fellow apprentice hung from a sign pole below the railing, looking out over the canal. Fool! He would fall right in

"Excuse me, Apprentice," a merchant said, jostling past him, his conical hat knocking two other people in the face as he passed. He smelled of oil and figs and his thick belly pressed Tamerlan even closer to the railing. Quiet curses followed him but Tamerlan kept quiet, his face screwing up with concentration as he finally scooped the puppy up.

"Got you!"

The poor little thing tucked his nose into Tamerlan's armpit, shaking from nose to tail. He wouldn't be able to keep it. Alchemist Apprentices were little better than property themselves. But he could find a safer place than the edge of a canal.

He pressed through the crowd, keeping the puppy held tight to his leather apprentice apron as he searched for a quiet alley. How many more people would join the crowd before the gondola procession passed through the District of Spices? Already street vendors pushing laden box-carts pressed against priests carrying smoking braziers. Goodwives wearing crisp aprons barely managed to keep hold of bright-eyed children in the press of the crowd.

The people of the Alchemist's District were layered over the canal like the tiers of a cake, some looking down from red-shingled roofs, some from high windows or balconies, others from along the rail on the street, and some – like his friend Dathan, below – lined the slick, narrow walkways along the canal.

Tamerlan slipped into the alley, glad to find it mostly abandoned with the crowd so obsessed with the coming procession. There was a set of steps leading to a back door and underneath it, a safe looking shadow.

"Will you be okay here?" Tamerlan asked the puppy, tucking him into the space under the steps. "Just keep your head down and no one will notice, yeah? That's what I do."

He gave the puppy a last stroke, leaving regretfully. In a perfect world, he could bring the puppy back to his lonely room in *The Copper Tincture.* In a perfect world, he wouldn't have been sold as an apprentice to Alchemists, but instead he'd be a librarian or a monk. Something that required a lot of reading and thinking. Something that didn't involve manhandling crates of spices until he thought his mind would go dull from boredom.

He slipped back into the crowd. He should check on Dathan. He'd been late with his duties three times this week and if Master Kurond caught him hanging from a flagpole, he'd be put on short-rations for a month.

He eased through the crowd and down the crowded steps to the canal below, ignoring angry looks and fierce curses. The rock here was slick. Someone was bound to slip and fall in. It wouldn't be Tamerlan. He kept a hold of the rockwork, his eyes fixed on the bend of the canal.

An orange cat slid through the crowd – a bad omen. Tamerlan's mouth went dry at the thought. He wanted no more bad omens. Acid washed up into his mouth and he swallowed it down, ignoring his churning belly. The cat was grabbed by a pair of hands hanging out from a Waverunner boat and pulled inside.

"Just a cat, Apprentice!" a goodwife laughed at his expression. Her face was bright with excitement. "And now a meal for the Waverunners!

He didn't believe those nasty rumors. Just because the Waverunners never left their small house-boats and gondolas didn't mean they ate cats. Or at least, he didn't think so. And if they did, it wasn't important today.

The crowd murmured with anticipation, a thousand voices whispering the same hopes, a thousand eyes dancing with visions of the season. Some enterprising fool was even playing a lute beside the stone steps that led to the streets above, his tunes a litany of seasonal songs, blessing the waxing of summer, the roundness of fertility, the call of the river, and the strength of growing warmth.

There was something about Summernight that made people forget their everyday lives as the days bled into the night, snatching minutes and hours that didn't belong to them until the longest day of the year crowned the season.

Tamerlan made his way carefully through the crowd, trying not to step on feet or elbow anyone. He felt tight and ragged inside. He'd heard a rumor yesterday. Just something in passing. But it had him worried. If the Legends would truly rise and walk the city again on Summernight – as the tale went – then why couldn't they rise now? Why couldn't they come when he might need them? Legends were as useless as wishes.

Enough of that. He wasn't a dreamy boy anymore with the luxury of imagining Legends walking the earth. He was a man with responsibilities – like keeping his friend out of trouble.

If he didn't get to Dathan in time the fool might even break an arm - then he'd be in real trouble. He tried to keep from glancing at the canal. He'd look when the procession arrived. He'd watch then. But what if she went by and he never even caught a glimpse? Or what if it wasn't her at all, but he never found out. What if guilt and grief still ate at his heart a bite at a time? He shook his head, trying to clear it.

"Dathan!" He called to his friend as soon as he saw him. Dathan stood out in the crowd just like Tamerlan did by wearing the uniform of Alchemist apprentices – a thick leather apron and rolled sleeves to reveal arms burned with acid scars. They were all fresh scars. Dathan had only been an apprentice for a year – bought from a destitute farm family in a landhold to the east of Jingen. He'd taken to city life better than Tamerlan had – he was more social – but it was only last week that Tamerlan had to hunt him down and help him finish his tasks before sundown. They'd traveled by gondola on this very canal. Strange how last week felt a million years away.

Dathan was stretched out along the sign pole, trying to get the best possible view of the procession when it finally turned the corner into the Spice District. Tamerlan rubbed sweating palms on his apron. He needed to get his friend down before that procession arrived. What if Dathan saw his relief when it turned out his suspicions were groundless – or watched him break when he turned out to be right? He'd never live that down.

And he *would* break.

He was close already – his nerve endings all alert, his hair on end, his senses sharper than ever. But he needed to deal with the problem in front of him first. Dathan might fall into the canal and drown if he wasn't careful. His tools – strapped to the apron as usual – would sink him to the bottom in the blink of an eye if he lost his grip. He wouldn't bob right back up like the street urchins across the way who even now were diving to find coins in the wrecks of ruined gondolas.

The sound of a dozen throats sucking in their breath made him stand on his toes to look. Had the procession arrived?

No. Just another fool falling from the street above to the canal ledge. A duck quacked loudly and took off, feet slapping the water as he fought to gain height.

"Get off me you son of a -!"

Chaos swirled as some people dove for lost belongings and stooped for coins while others tried to grab for what had never been theirs.

The poor fool who fell was kicked into the canal and left to sputter and grope at the slick stone walls. Unless he found a friendly gondola, he'd have to swim a long way to find an entrance to street level again.

Tamerlan lunged forward, scrambling along the narrow stone ledge – just wide enough for a hand-cart – that rimmed the canal.

"Dathan!" he called. He was prodded with elbows as he passed. He felt the blows – there would be bruises tomorrow – but this was his chance. That was a chance worth gambling on. "Let me help you down! It's not safe up there!"

He tried not to flinch at the cries of pain from the crowd where he passed. He wasn't trying to injure – but he chewed his lip as he watched Dathan rocking on the sign pole. He still hadn't noticed Tamerlan and that perch was tenuous, the sign pole creaking under the weight.

He climbed up the side of the wall, fingers feeling for the cracks between the stone as he tried to reach his friend. The toes of his worn leather boots scraped along the side of the slick stone wall, catching any purchase they could find. Dragon's guts, but it stank along the canal! What was rotting in those murky waters?

"Son of a Legend! Would you stay put?" one of the onlookers cursed, dodging Tamerlan's kicking feet. "First one fool, then another!"

"Dathan!"

"Tam! Look at the view! Come on up!"

And then he was level with the sign pole. Fresher air prevailed here. Peonies and roses in garlands were strung along the rail to the street above for the Summernight Festival. He breathed them in, trying to find calm in their familiar scents.

Today was the first morning of the five-day Summernight festival. Five days of celebrating and feasting. Five nights of mystery and delight.

Today, the city would rejoice.

A burst of raucous laughter spilled onto the street above him as someone left a tavern. Early morning and the celebrations were already beginning. The smell of meat tarts and the local brew swirled into the street before the door was closed again. Tamerlan's mouth watered. He could already taste the holiday cakes he loved so much, but this was not why he was here.

"You've got to come down. Dathan! The sign pole is close to breaking. If you fall – "

But his words were cut off.

A gasp drew again from a thousand throats and cries of excitement quickly followed.

"They're here! The procession!"

Below him, a woman's voice pierced above the rest, "The dragon's tribute! The Lady Sacrifice!"

She sounded almost worshipful. And of course, most of the people here were. They weren't in the costumes of the Legends yet – that would come later in the festival when they ran through the night like the Heroes of Legend reborn – but this was just the first part.

Bells pealed loudly, flooding the streets above and jangling in strung lines along the canal. Some were the dull throbbing sound of the big guild bells, others the tiny tinkle of shop bells, or deep bong of temple bells. Bells would ring throughout the city, District to District as the procession passed through each part before stopping at the Sunset Tower in the center of the

Seven Suns Palace. Tamerlan remembered that from last year, although last year his only thoughts had been filled with drinking in the tavern and eating holiday cakes with Dathan.

This time was different. The Lady Sacrifice had arrived. And if she was who he thought she might be, then all was lost. His eyes strained to try to see down the canal as the boats of the Waverunners – long sleek boats low in the water and painted in garishly bright colors – scuttled out of the way in every direction.

Tamlerlan could almost feel the rumble of the dragon beneath them at the sound of the bells. But that was just imagination. The dragon had slept beneath the city for a thousand years – if it had ever lived at all. Perhaps it was only rocks and carvings and not a dragon at all.

That made more sense than what the religions said. After all, why would anyone build their city on top of a dragon – literally chiseling their foundations into his scales – if he were alive? No one would be that stupid. Though mentioning that to his childhood priest had resulted in having his ears boxed and a second beating from his father when the priest had opened his fat mouth to snitch.

But if the dragon was nothing more than an interestingly shaped mountain, then why would they drain the blood of the Lady Sacrifice over those rocks? Why would they spill her life out, like water splashed across the street and running into the canals, for nothing at all?

Last year, the Lady Sacrifice had been from Pale Lily Landhold and the procession had begun with Pale Lily spearmen twirling their spears and marching in place in the gondolas in careful synchronicity. Everyone knew she was from Pale Lily after that display.

If he saw the Pale Lily spearmen again, he would be able to breathe – or the canasta spinners of Gentle Trees Landhold who had been there the year before, or the bright purple banners of Summer Wheat.

It was none of those.

Tamerlan's jaw clenched as a pair of pale bulls decked in wreaths of red roses stood steadily in the front of a wide canal-boat – a gondola would never fit them. Their corded muscled bunched under their pale flesh and their minders carried pointed sticks and wore blue tabards. Pale bulls were raised in the north – where Tamerlan had been born.

With every new appearance his hands felt sweatier, his head lighter. Could that rumor he'd heard be true?

The flag hanging from Dathan's sign pole began to flap as a breeze rose, pushing the gondolas a little faster down the canal. They couldn't come quickly enough for Tamerlan. With every new glimpse, his heart sunk faster.

"I just want to see the procession. Just a minute more," Dathan protested. His eyes gleamed with excitement. He was two years younger than Tamerlan and two years more wide-eyed.

Behind the bulls were drummers and cantonelle flute players in their own gondolas, being carefully poled forward at an even pace. The flute players spun and danced as they played, the ragged rabbit skins that hung from their belts proclaiming them to be of Long Wind Landhold.

And now Tamerlan felt an icy chill wash over him. He'd grown up in the land of cantonelle players. Their haunting tune, like the song of the water loon, had haunted his dreams when first he was banished to the glorious city of Jingen to serve in the Alchemist's Guild as an apprentice.

"Don't forget your family," his mother had murmured. "Don't forget your ancestors."

And, of course, he hadn't. Not when night after night of prayers and tears brought no relief to the dull ache in his belly. Not in the long days when the smoke of the Alchemists stung his eyes and the acids of their concoctions burned his skin and he wondered again and again why a household of a Landholder might need to sell a son to the Guilds … and why they had chosen him of all his seven brothers.

And he did not forget today, as he watched the cantonelle dancers go past on sleek drifting gondolas. He did not forget when a gondola lacquered in shiny black with a black canopy and walls of flowing black silk over the passenger portion – the gondola of the Lord Mythos, the city's ruler – queued up in the line.

Before the black gondola, a chain of colored gondolas and the majestic dragon – woven and sewn by the people of the Long Wind landhold, in the white and orange colors of their flags, wound along the canal supported by the colorful gondolas. Beneath the dragon were the legs of those who made the dragon dance, but they couldn't distract from the beauty of the rippling creature.

He did not forget when the smell of home rolled off that dragon, blotting out the smell of roses, and springing up in his mind a longing so deep that it almost washed away the fear that thrummed through him closer than his own heartbeat.

It was the last gondola that he had been looking for – the last black lacquered gondola with the emblem of the Lord Mythos on the flowing silk curtains. He almost forgot Dathan's predicament as he watched it creep toward his perch.

Guards surrounded the curtains, practically standing on the gunwales of the gondola in their attempt to encircle the occupant of the dark boat – their gazes shot into the crowd like they were the very fists of the Gods.

It was that gondola that made his blood turn to ice but still left it howling in his ears until he could hear nothing else. He studied it like the face of a lost love as it passed, holding his breath, waiting.

He wasn't going to see. It was going to pass without confirming his fears.

Not a single curtain on the gondola twitched. Not a guard moved a sword or halberd in acknowledgment. Had he been wrong? Had he been anxious about nothing? Perhaps …

But as the carriage passed, someone parted the curtains at the back of the gondola and between the legs of the guards he caught a glimpse of huge dark eyes looking out at him surrounded by thick lashes.

Amaryllis.

He'd recognize those eyes anywhere. They gleamed with the same fear they'd held the morning he'd been packed away.

"You'll be back soon, won't you?" she'd said in a shaking voice. His only sister – his best friend. It hurt him worse to see her pain than to feel the pain himself.

"I don't think so," he'd said, playing nervously with the woven grass ring she'd given him. It wouldn't last long, but it was all anyone had given him beyond cool looks and frosty 'goodbyes.' It still hung from a thread on his bedpost.

"But I can't bear to live here without you," she'd pled, tears streaking her face.

"I need to go, Amaryllis," he'd said. "If I don't, they'll pick someone else to sell. Maybe even you. Besides, I don't think they'll just let me say no." It had taken all his effort not to let his voice shake here. "And I don't think I can stop them."

"Sell? But we're the Landholds here!"

"And you and I are just two of nine siblings. How many Landholds does a place need, Amaryllis?"

"One," her small voice shook.

"One to inherit, one for a spare, one for the church, one for the lair," he'd quoted the children's rhyme. But it stopped at four because no house needed more than four children. The rest were only worth what you could trade for them and in his case, his father's debts had been forgiven. Ten years of debts with a single son. Any Landhold would have called it a fair trade.

And now here she was, her eyes brimming when they finally met his from that tiny gap in the curtains at the back of the gondola. Widening. Pleading.

His little sister.

The Lady Sacrifice.

In her eyes, he saw his world ending.

It felt as if someone was gripping his heart in their fist and squeezing. He could barely breathe, barely think, but one thought registered: how great a price must his father have received for the life of his sister?

2: Advice of a Friend

Tamerlan

Dathan fell from his perch at the same moment that Tamerlan's heart seized in his chest.

Smack!

Dathan landed on someone's shoulder and someone else's back.

"Hey!"

"Dragon-spitting fool!"

An angry fist knocked against his head and a kick to the groin left him hunched over and retching as he leaned against the wet rock wall trying to catch his breath.

Tamerlan hurried down, swallowing the nausea ripping through him at the thought of his sister heading up the canal in that gondola.

He grabbed Dathan by the arms, helping him stand and pulling him into one of the rare lamp alcoves along the canal wall. Curses filled the air and a heavy voice rang in his ears.

"Jingen City Watch. Make way! What's the problem here?" Jingen City Watch Officers weren't hard to spot. Their uniforms were haphazard leathers over white shirts with worn oilcloth cloaks, but they all wore a sewn-on embroidered badge and the same irritated expressions on their faces as if your very existence had offended the Law.

"No problem, Officer," Tamerlan said nervously. If they got in trouble with the Watch, Dathan would see worse than docked rations. "My friend just took a fall."

"Any trouble will be stopped with force by order of the Lord Mythos," the Watch Officer said imperiously stroking the sheath of his long knife. "Keep to your business, citizen."

"Yes, officer." Tamerlan ducked his head, hiding Dathan's slighter frame behind his height and broader shoulders. His friend was still stunned, leaning against the wall of the alcove.

The footsteps tromped by as the Watch left and Tamerlan drew a relieved breath. He took a moment to compose himself. His head was still swimming with anger and confusion.

Not now, Tamerlan. Later. When there was time to think.

"Hey!" He called to Dathan, shaking his shoulder gently "Dathan, are you okay?"

"Yes," the word hissed between his teeth.

"You need to shake out of it, Dathan," Tamerlan said, his voice cracking under the stress. They'd sold her. They'd sold her like a pig for market. He'd never forgive them. "People are watching. They'll report us to Master Kurond. Head up! Walk."

Dathan shook his head to clear it, sucking in a breath as Tamerlan gently led him through the crowd. He pushed away thoughts of his sister, focusing on the smell of dank walls and sun on algae. He was still here on the crowded canal way with the shuffling crowd. He needed to remember that. Needed to remember that he couldn't help his sister from here.

Gondolas filled the canal again, their gondoliers calling out prices to the watchers as if they were here to pay for a ride rather than simply to gawk. A shoal of gondolas was pushed aside by a larger barge laden with flowers and fruit and country folk peering out of the covered boat with wide eyes and round faces.

"That's better," Tamerlan said encouragingly, dragging Dathan along with the mass of people climbing the stairs to the streets above. The fun was over. "Here, follow me."

He pulled Dathan behind him, up the stairs and then into an alley between two swoop-roofed buildings and a butcher's line of hanging chickens. Wash lines crisscrossed over the crowded spaces and an old woman frowned at them from the steps where she stood hanging more steaming wash on the line. A cur growled as they passed, his curling fur greasy and dark. Hopefully that dog hadn't found the puppy he'd stashed in the other alley. This alley smelled of stale beer and urine – the smell of a place neglected – but the dog and woman told another story. He and Dathan couldn't stay here long. These places always looked empty until someone smelled coins or vulnerability and then suddenly, they were very popular places to be.

"Are you out on a job?" he asked Dathan, looking over his shoulder to be sure they weren't overheard.

"Yes," Dathan gasped, still hunched over his injuries.

"There was nothing for the guild on the message tree, so I'm finished mine for this morning. Why don't you give me your job and you can go back to *The Copper Tincture* and recover?"

Visiting the message tree was usually his favorite chore. A chance to hear what was happening in the Landholds – maybe even at home. A chance to watch the barges coming in from upriver and the ship boats coming the other way from the sea, hulls laden with trade goods and wonders from afar. The whole of the world traded with the five cities of the Dragonblood Plains.

But today, with Summernight almost upon them, there had been no messages from without. Orders for Nightbursts had been placed and filled weeks ago and that was the only thing that the Alchemists provided for the celebration – other than oil for the colored flames of the canal lanterns.

"Fine. I have to pick up a package for Master Kurond at the Queen Mer Library," Dathan said with a moan.

Tamerlan looked him over, shrugging uncomfortably. "Can you get home? You're not too hurt?"

"I'll be fine," Dathan said. One of his hands fumbled at a belt pouch.

"Only, you don't look too healthy. Listen, those guards weren't joking. The Jingen City Watch will be on the lookout for anything strange. Summernight is too important to be ruined by vagabonds. Why did you climb that sign pole? You know our Guild Masters wouldn't approve! You could be sold again, Dathan – to someone worse than the Alchemists."

That was always the worry. Alchemy was stinky work and dangerous, but there were worse jobs. Especially in a city like Jingen.

"You're too dirty for the Library," Dathan protested, but he handed the small scrip he'd pulled from his belt pouch to Tamerlan. It would have Master Kurond's orders on it.

Tamerlan looked down at the dark leather of his trousers – scuffed now and dirty from helping Dathan up – and the length of his brown leather apron. It ended just above his knees, the pockets at the waist bulging with tools and devices just like Dathan's. He didn't think he'd lost any - he had the pocket-flaps buttoned – but the apron was dirty and smudged and his crisp white shirt was no longer crisp or white.

"I'll be okay. I have a friend in the Library District who will vouch for me. Are you sure you can walk?"

Dathan nodded shakily before clapping Tamerlan on the shoulder.

"Master Kurond said to have them back to the Guild House as quickly as possible. Thank you."

Dathan was already stumbling out of the alley as Tamerlan unfolded the note.

Tamerlan shook himself. It was hard not to let his mind wander to Amaryllis. She'd always loved rabbits. She would carry them around in the summers and she'd sell their little ones to the local merchants. Tamerlan had never had the heart to tell her that they were bought for food, not for pets. To Amaryllis, rabbits were just long-eared furry people.

Perhaps, if he attended to his work, he could talk to one of the Masters about finding a way to see the Lady Sacrifice. Perhaps they would show mercy.

He looked down at the note.

Dathan,

Go to the University District to the Queen Mer Library and retrieve for us the textbooks "Materials of the Sodden Islands" and "Smoke of the Feral Cults" for use in this week's experiments. Ask for Nabella. Do not tarry.

Master Kurond

The University District was not far, though it felt farther today with the press of the celebratory crowds around him. Tamerlan strode out of the alley with purpose, squeezing between the people gathered there. A man with clothing that screamed of the countryside haggled over a bolt of cloth at one of the market stalls, his entire family pressed up around the stall to the irritation of the shopkeeper.

Tamerlan pressed past them, nearly bumping into the servant of a Landhold from one of the eastern districts, half his head shaved, and the other half cut in choppy waves.

"My pardon."

"Watch yourself, Alchemist," the servant scowled. He wasn't much older than Tamerlan and wearing his festival best.

There was a time when any Landhold's servant would bow and scrape to him but Tamerlan lost that place when he was bought by the guild. He should have paid the coin for a gondola and saved himself from the press of bodies and indignity of insults, but coins were hard to find and difficult to part with.

The press of people in the Spice District bartering at the tops of their lungs or calling to each other as street performers danced between them holding out hats for coin, soon thinned to the stoic, calm crowds of the University District.

Tamerlan breathed a sigh of relief. Here, things were more orderly – kept so by the University Guard, dressed in impeccable white and silver. Tamerlan loved the order of the Library District. Imagine being able to spend your days in logical thought instead of mindless grunt-work? Imagine plumbing the depths of philosophy, the wonders of science, the beauty of literature and music.

He nearly walked into a pair of guards before he noticed them as his mind drifted to what-ifs. They frowned at him when he stumbled to a halt, scanning him carefully before moving on. He'd been stopped by that pair before. They must recognize him as Master Kurond's apprentice. Perhaps, he could use that to gain their trust. Perhaps, he could sneak into their barracks one night and steal one of those uniforms and use it to creep into the Sunset Tower at the center of the city – the place where everyone knew the Lady Sacrifice would be kept until the last night of Summernight when her blood would sate Jingen – the ancient dragon who slept beneath their city.

Tamerlan shivered. Such superstitions had always felt far away. What did they have to do with him? Now, they were too close for comfort. Like a straight-edged razor poised at his neck – one flinch and it might seal his fate – or the fate of Amaryllis.

He was crazy to think of theft and trespass. That was as crazy as dreaming that he and Dathan hadn't been bought and sold. Crazy as thinking he might have time to study and invent instead of grinding away his days in service. Crazy, because it would never work.

He still remembered the man they hung in a cage beside one of the canals of the University District as a warning to anyone who dared steal from them again. He hadn't even been dead when they put him there. Or at least, not at first.

But what other option had they left him? If he didn't at least try, could he live with himself for year upon year knowing he'd been useless, harmless, when what his sister needed was a defender? He wrung his hands as he tried to decide what he should do.

"Did you see the Lady Sacrifice in the procession?" a breathless voice asked him. It was Sian – one of the library apprentices hurrying forward to walk with him as he reached the lower steps of the Queen Mer Library. Her filmy Librarian robes clung to her sandaled feet as she walked, her apprentice belt clinking as the glass beads bumped one another.

"Yes," he admitted, smiling at Sian.

"I wanted to see her, too," she went on, tucking her stray hairs behind her ears. She had a smudge of ink on her nose as she usually did.

Tamerlan usually liked seeing Sian. Her friendliness could warm a stone. Today, with her full lips smiling at him and her round face flushed with excitement – today she looked far too much like Amaryllis. Vulnerable. Precious. Had her parents sold her into apprenticeship?

"They say that if you meet her eye as she goes by," the bright girl said, "you will have good luck all year."

Tamerlan felt his face growing hot.

All year.

Which meant that next year they would drag some other poor fool's sister up to that tower and make her wait five days until they slaughtered her like livestock. He felt his fists clenching, but he couldn't stop them any more than he could stop the angry roar in his ears.

"I have a costume for Summernight. Can you guess who I'll be going as?" Sian asked. She had to skip to keep up to his long stride as he mounted the marble steps of the library two at a time. After a moment, she answered her own question. "Queen Mer! Doesn't that fit, since I work in the Library here? They say she founded it herself. She picked this spot – right near the dragon's ear!" They both glanced at the frill-like rock formation behind the library. It stood higher than even the domed blue roof of the library, blocking the streaming light of the morning sun. "It's going to be so fun! We all – the apprentices – get every evening off this week. I will dance so hard my feet hurt and eat until my belly grows to twice its size!"

He paused for a moment to smile down at her. She shouldn't have to suffer through Summernight just because he was broken-hearted. She was innocent. A gadfly enjoying her single moment.

"I hope you enjoy yourself, Sian."

"Won't you join me?" she asked, attempting to look coy. As if he could see her as anything other than a little sister.

"I'm afraid I'll be busy for all of Summernight."

Now, why had he said that? He was given the evenings off for the festival, too. But he was going to be spending them in a way that Sian shouldn't be near. He was going to find a way to break into that golden tower and rescue his sister.

The thought that had been brewing in his heart since he first glimpsed her through the crowd solidified as he stood on the library steps looking out across the city to the single golden spire in the Government District.

"They say that no one has ever been inside and lived to tell the tale," Sian said, following his gaze. Which was ridiculous. Because what was the point of a tower that no one ever entered? Or that no one ever left. Surely there were guards – or at least servants – who came in and out without a problem.

He was going to enter that tower.

He was sure of that now – as sure as he was of his own name – and when he did, he was going to make sure that they never brought another innocent girl there again. Beneath his feet, he almost thought he felt a rumble of agreement in the earth itself.

3: Scenter

Marielle

"You're too obsessive. That's her first complaint. You take things too seriously, don't like critique, don't understand nuance. The world is black and white to you," Captain Ironarm said, as she read the report in her hand.

Someone had actually *written* those things about Marielle. Paper was scarce and ink valuable and someone had sat with their face screwed up, quill in hand, and carefully penned those words.

About her.

Marielle felt herself sinking lower with every word. She thought she was doing a good job. She thought she was putting her training to use and helping people. She was the best Scenter trainee. She could follow any track. She practiced constantly. She didn't eat strong foods or wear perfumes. She was even careful about her soap. Nothing was allowed to hinder her sense. Her kit was meticulously maintained. She took every citizen complaint seriously.

And none of that had been enough.

She could feel her eyes growing wider with every new item on the list. She chewed her lip until it hurt and silently cursed the anxious sweat the sprouted up under her clothing. The Captain would smell it. And she would know that Marielle was nervous. That wouldn't help her case.

"What do you have to say for yourself?" Captain Ironarm's voice was calm and even.

She smoothed the sides of her salt and paper hair back into the tight bun she wore. It was the only tight thing about her. The rest of her face sagged under the weight of years. She'd been the Scenter Captain here for thirty years. Spent twenty-two as a Scenter before that. Joined up at eighteen when her training was complete – just like Marielle. Just like every woman in the Scenter branch of the City Watch.

"None of us sees color," Marielle said, carefully. She didn't understand the insult. She was proud of who she was. Who cared that Scenters couldn't see colors in a world roaring with the turquoise scent of the sea weaving in with the golden brown of baked bread and the gold of attraction. Green still lingered in this office from Jandela who had been in here before Marielle. She'd let off that burst of envy when she passed Marielle in the doorway. Who would want to trade that to simply *see* colors?

"That's not what the report means," Captain Ironarm said with a raised eyebrow.

Of course, it wasn't. Marielle felt her cheeks heating.

"I understand nuance," she said, her voice huskier than she would have liked. She shifted her stance and the leathers of her watch uniform squeaked. They hadn't lost that squeak yet – they were still so new.

"If you understood nuance you would know that you don't drag a Landhold before the magistrate for public drunkenness – especially not twelve hours after he was drunk!"

"I could smell it on him," Marielle said in a small voice.

"But by then he had slept it off. Magistrate Mendyk marched in here yesterday and demanded – yes, he demanded! – that I remove you from the Watch. Don't look at me like that! It will be a hot day in Thespar before a magistrate – any magistrate, mind! – tells me what to do in my own Watch House."

Her hard gaze was fixed on Marielle, nailing her in place. They should have called her 'ironeyes' not 'Ironarm'.

"Yes, sir." Marielle's voice squeaked more than she would have liked, but she kept her back ramrod straight. The Scenters were everything to her. If staying meant being more careful with Landholds well … well, she could consider that.

"Justice, Marielle, is more important than regulation. Do you know what that means?"

Marielle felt new sweat breaking out across her scalp. If only she could wipe it away with her Scenter's Veil! But she stayed perfectly still, her mind racing. What did you say to something like that? The regulations brought justice. And justice was the most important thing in the world. She settled on her catechism answer.

"Justice is the gift of the Dragonblooded to the after-generations. It makes it safe for men to strive and achieve but curtails corruption," she quoted from memory. She knew her catechism. Every citizen of Jingen did. There were rumors that the other cities had different catechisms, but they were only rumors. Marielle knew better than to think so ill of people just because they lived far off.

Her gaze wandered to the map above Captain Ironarm's desk – a map of the five cities of the Dragonblood Plains with a closeup of Jingen and her districts in the lower left-hand corner. The cities were drawn extra large for effect, looking as if you could spit and reach the next city but Marielle knew it was only to see them more easily. They were actually many days of travel from one another.

Captain Ironarm pursed her wrinkled lips.

"I won't be Captain here forever, Marielle," she said sending a stab of fear down Marielle's spine. The Captain was the anchor of the Scenter Watch. "And so, it's important for me to impart a little wisdom where I can. Some things are right and wrong, Marielle. You know this."

Marielle was nodding.

The Captain turned in her chair to look out her second-story window over the city below. The glass of the window was rippled in the small panes, but you could still see almost as far as the river running through the center of the city where the festivities for Summernight had already begun. Marielle almost thought she saw the Lady Sacrifice's procession moving through the canals.

"There are rights and wrongs according to the catechism. There are rights and wrongs according to the laws of Jingen," the captain said heavily. "You are a good student. You know these things by heart. The moral law. The city laws. I heard you recite the complete Jingen Code the day you graduated from your training. And these laws are good. But there is a greater law in place, Marielle. It's a law that branches out over those other laws the way a great tree branches out over a garden. It supersedes them. It encompasses them. Occasionally … it diverges from them."

Marielle gasped. The captain hadn't just said … had she? She didn't say … Marielle could not even let the thought form in her own mind.

"I don't know the name of this law. You sense it sometimes in the catechism. Sometimes you get a whiff of it when you are reading Jingen Law. But it's something greater. It's alive. It answers to something beyond us."

"The religions, Captain?"

"I doubt it," Captain Ironarm said wryly. "Or at least, I haven't seen proof of that."

"It's not …" Marielle began.

"Speak up, officer."

"It's not the dragons, is it? After all, they founded the five cities. We built them on the rocks of their bodies. Perhaps these laws came from them."

The Captain shrugged. "I don't know about that. What I do know, is that over time a Watch Officer gets a feel for this law – what I like to think of as the *Real Law.* And when it lines up with Jingen law, that's a good thing. It makes you certain and certainty in this world is rare. It's a precious thing in the fleeting moments you find it. But there are other times when things are not so certain. There are times when you can sense the real law, but there's no written code to hold it up. There's just you, an officer of the Watch, trying to find a way to twist the written law so you can enforce the *real* law."

Marielle shivered. She'd heard of City Watch like that. Men who put a bloody knife in the coat pocket of a man they knew did something wrong just before he was stopped by other Watch officers.

"Oh, I don't mean vigilantes," the Captain said, catching the look in her eye. "That's not justice either. No, when you get to know the real law, you can see things that other people can't. Patterns. Ways it's hinting at the truth to you. It's alive. And it wants justice more than anything. I think that maybe the world was meant to be just. But, of course, it's not. And that Law – the Real Law – is always working to bring that back."

A thought occurred to Marielle. She cleared her throat and the captain looked at her expectantly.

"What about if the Real Law says someone is innocent but the City Law says someone is guilty?"

The Captain gave her an odd half-smile. "It's those times that we see what sort of cloth you're sewn from, officer."

Marielle swallowed.

"That's what Anaala means when she says you're too black and white. You don't know the Real Law yet. You need time to learn it and until you do, you need to calm down a little and let more experienced Watch officers lead the way."

Marielle felt her cheeks heating.

"Which is why," the captain said. "I'm pairing you with Carnelian for the rest of Summernight. Listen to what she says and see if you can learn some wisdom. She's been on the streets for long enough to wear out a pair of boots or two."

"And if I can't?" Marielle asked. She couldn't help biting her lip as she waited for the answer.

"Then the City Watch is not for you. There are other things a Scenter can do. We'll find one for you. But until then, go report to Carnelian. She's expecting you."

4: THE QUEEN MER LIBRARY

TAMERLAN

Tamerlan had always loved the Queen Mer library. When it was built, no expense had been spared. The denizens of Queen Mer - carved in white stone – decorated every pillar of the library. Squids with a dozen arms wrapped around the base of the pillars, their arms crawling up the ivory uprights. Seaweed and shells, lobsters and crabs, swordfish and manta rays were carved in the spaces between the shelves and along decorative friezes. Waves crashed in the design of the low barriers and walls.

But today, Tamerlan was not enjoying the library. The long shelves of scrolls, carefully tucked away from the light, didn't make his skin crawl with anticipation like they had in the past. The collection of shelf upon shelf of bound books – a marvel of modern dedication to knowledge! – didn't make him wish for the thousandth time that his father had sold him to the Librarians instead of to the Alchemists.

Today, he just felt empty.

He leaned against the desk at the entrance. No apprentice was considered trustworthy enough to go beyond that point. Certainly not the apprentice of the destructive Alchemists.

A book was laid out on the desk with a careful bookmark nestled between the pages. The Librarian at the door had left it there when she went to find Nabella. Tamerlan's fingers tapped impatiently on the desk. He needed to get out of here so he could start gathering supplies to break into the tower. He'd need a weapon. A dark cloak. What else?

His eyes strayed over the open book, soaking in the words while his mind raced.

The Legends will return someday, or so it was foretold by Jandein. He left instruction for their return. "Greet them with open arms if you wish to taste their power," he said, "but do not trust them, for they shall take your most precious gift as payment for their power, your own will and mind in payment for their great acts."

Someone must have been curious about the Legends with Summernight approaching. Or perhaps they were merely planning their costume for the event.

Tamerlan reached across the desk and picked the book up, letting his fingers skim gently through the pages, careful to touch only the edges so the oils of his skin would not hurt the delicate ink on paper. There were chapters on each Hero of Legend with detailed sketches of their clothing and weaponry. There was Byron Bronzebow with his dashing good looks and prominent bow gleaming in the light. There was Queen Mer, of course, with her queenly poise, her bodice made of overlapping shells and her necklace made of the bones of shipwrecked sailors. He flipped the book open at random and the pages fell open to the Lady Sacrifice.

Nausea washed over him and for a moment his vision wavered. He slammed the book shut on the sketch of her lifeless corpse resting over the snout of a dragon, and a page flew out from the force of it, drifting to the floor.

"Apprentice?" the Librarian called.

With a gasp, Tamerlan snatched up the paper and stuffed it into his apron. If he was caught having damaged a book, he would never be allowed in the Library again. Worse, a report would go to the Alchemist's Guild and he would be placed under curfew at the very least. And if that happened, he would lose his chance to break into the tower.

"I'm here," he called in a voice that sounded more nervous than he would have liked.

"Remember to practice great care in transporting our books," the Librarian said rounding the corner and standing behind the desk again. If she noticed her book was out of place, she didn't mention it, simply handing the books to Tamerlan wrapped in a sealskin. The skin alone – rare and amazing – was probably worth more than he was. "The Alchemist's Guild will be held responsible for any damaged or lost books according to the usual tradition. Show me your hand."

Tamerlan held out his hand. He hated this part.

The Librarian pulled out her ledger, carefully wrote his name and guild into the columns and then snatched his hand in her iron grip. Her penknife whipped out of a pocket and with practiced movements she slit the tip of his finger and pressed the print of it – in blood – on the page.

"Sealed with your blood. Any loss or damage will be recompensed with more of the same. Return the books in ten days."

Tamerlan shivered, but the Librarian fixed him with her slit-eyed gaze. There was no mercy in those eyes. She cared far more for those books than she did for the life of an apprentice. He swallowed, glad he hadn't admitted to the page that fell out of the other book.

"Of course," he said, clutching the books tightly to his chest and fleeing the marble halls of the Library into the district below.

A man dressed as King Abelmeyer the One-eyed nearly bumped into him as he flew down the stairs.

"Watch yourself, boy! It's not Summernight just yet!" The man's eyepatch slipped, and he hurried to correct it, pulling his long crimson cloak around him more tightly and straightening the collar so it stood high around his broken crown.

Tamerlan dodged around him, running into the main street of the University District. Servants and apprentices clustered around the great-doors of the biggest schools, hanging garlands of sweet-smelling flowers and brightly colored ribbons. Laughter broke out from the groups that felt sour against the sick feeling in Tamerlan's stomach.

"Want to help us, Alchemist? We could use the advice of one of the Dragonblooded!" a particularly pretty girl called from where she was hanging her garlands. Tamerlan ran a hand through his pale blond hair – a telltale sign of his ancestry – and shook his head as he hurried past. He heard laughter behind him. Another young man joined the girls as they prepared for the shortest night of the year together.

The girl didn't know it, but he knew no more than they did about what flowers to hang. His Dragonblooded ancestry was nothing but a noose around his neck. Maybe if he'd been sold to the libraries it would have helped. Maybe then, he would have the key he needed to rescue his sister.

He reached into his pocket and pulled out the paper he'd picked up, smoothing out the creases as he carried it balanced on top of his valuable parcel.

It didn't look like a book page – or if it was one, it was old and so covered in annotations that it was hard to make out everything. There were corner designs in a gold leaf – intersecting mazes in strange shapes and a faint coloring along the edge of the page suggested that this book had painted pages. So, it was from a valuable book. He'd heard about these. They were called "illuminated texts" – books so precious that every page was a masterpiece.

Strange. The book he had slammed hadn't been an illuminated text.

This page looked like a recipe.

But if it was a recipe, it was a strange one. There was no distillation or compounding. No details for liquefaction. There were warnings above and below. Whoever had written down the recipe had not wanted it used. And someone had scrawled notes on it about their attempts at making the recipe. They were careful alchemist's notes of how he had boiled the ingredients and then distilled them to a thick salve. He'd also made a granular powder and an alcohol dilution. As far as Tamerlan could tell, they had all failed. And the monster had written about them on a precious illuminated text!

'*Use for dire situations,*' the recipe read.

Tamerlan was in a dire situation.

'*For the summoning of the ancient powers and the bringing of skills not won.*'

He was so intent on the recipe that he almost bumped into a procession of Smudgers. He must already be in the Temple District. He hadn't remembered crossing the bridge over the canal here, but a quick glance at the busy streets confirmed his theory. Tall temples and churches rose up on high platforms, as if racing to reach the gods, the cathedral tops of the white churches of the Timekeepers rose delicately over the low-slung tiled roofs of the jade temples belonging to the Smudgers.

The Smudgers who had cut him off wove in a tight line, slowly shuffling their lap around the district and wedging him in place against the canal rail. He'd timed his visit here poorly.

The crowds were frozen on every side. No one would push through a line of Smudgers. With the smell of sage smoke hanging heavily in the air, one of the Smudgers – an old woman without any teeth – winked at him as they shuffled past. The Smudgers were a popular religion, and the crowd was quiet out of respect for their smoking braziers and waving hands. They spun and almost danced as they wove through the trails of smoke, trying to tint their spirits with its essence.

Sage stood for patience and acceptance. Tamerlan didn't want either of those. He couldn't afford them when the stakes were so high. He would have backed away quickly, except that he'd never believed the Smudgers claims that the smoke could change or cleanse their spirits. All they ever did was steal the best deals on herbs coming in by sea and spout their heartfelt tales to get the fresher ingredients while he was left with second best.

No, Tamerlan didn't need the Smudgers. He needed answers. And he wouldn't find them with the Smudgers or on this piece of crumpled paper.

The old woman winked at him again. Hadn't she already passed once before? In her shimmering black robes, light on the breeze, who could say? All the Smudgers looked the same.

He shivered and stuffed the recipe back in his pocket. No need to draw attention to it.

He needed to focus and not be distracted by the lure of a mystery – even one involving books, his greatest weakness.

He would need all the focus he could find to save Amaryllis. He had just five days until she would be sacrificed.

5: Patrol

MARIELLE

"We're due on patrol," Carnelian said when Marielle joined her in the armory. She was tightening the straps on her leather boots and checking her standard issue dagger and truncheon. The City Watch wasn't meant to kill citizens, but they still went equipped for a fight – even Scenters like Marielle.

The smell of armor polish hung heavily in the air, like a dull yellow haze that would have been imperceptible to a non-Scenter. A string of red smoke wove between the weapon racks like a ribbon. Marielle could have followed it upstairs and found whoever had committed violence last night and then come down here to stow away his gear. Maybe it had been breaking up a fight in a tavern and smashing a few noses. Maybe it had been something much grizzlier. Her nose tingled and twitched at the thought of following the trail. It was hard to have the discipline to stand still.

Carnelian ignored the scent like any non-Scenter would do. "Tighten your straps. Make sure your weapon is sharp, check your kit."

She said that before every patrol. And she smelled the same before every patrol. A hint of cilantro anticipation mixed with the dull brown and dry wood scent of boredom or routine and just a hint of something almost-sweet that Marielle couldn't quite place. It picked at her every time she smelled it, like she should be able to place it and just couldn't.

Marielle checked over her uniform and kit quickly. Her weaponry was sharp and ready – not that she was likely to use it. The rest of the squad protected Scenters like a secret weapon. She'd only have to fight if things went very wrong. Her leather shirt and bracers were properly cinched, belt in good shape, warning bell tightly strapped in its pouch, boots buckled firmly. Her cloak and breeches were regulation and clean. Her Scenter's scarf looped properly in place. It was free of smudges or dirt. Marielle liked clean things. When you were always smelling everything, cleanliness was a gift.

Carnelian leaned in close so that her words would only be for Marielle, "Don't worry about old Ironarm. She's got to go hard – especially with complaints from a superior Scenter like Anaala, but we all know how good you are."

She looked right and left sneakily before giving Marielle a mischievous grin. "The rest of the squad is glad you're with us. We're already in the lead on the arrest lists. With you, we'll keep that lead through Summernight. And I bet big on us. Don't make me a loser!"

She punched Marielle's arm playfully before saying, "Scarf up. We're going to the Alchemist's District to cover off a busy sector there. If you don't hide that pretty nose, you'll be seeing double for a week."

Marielle complied, pulling the scarf over her nose and mouth. That wasn't how it worked. The strong scents of the Alchemist District would give her headaches and even nausea, might even make her pass out, but they wouldn't affect her vision. No point telling Carnelian that, though. She liked the Watch Corporal and she might be Marielle's only ally in the Watch right now. The other Scenters were prickly and the non-Scenters usually gave her a wide berth, nervous of her ability to sniff out anything hidden.

Marielle followed Carnelian up the Watch stairs, reveling in the excitement of the Watch House main floor above them. What might appear to be a sleepy hole for ancient Watchmen, popped and fizzled with vivid colors for Marielle.

A bubble of deceit in greeny-yellow and a whiff of caramel in one corner mixed with longing in ribbon-like pink and a whiff of lavender which in turn blurred into the beige boredom and dust scent of the overly-large officer at the front desk. Desperation rolled through in pulsing orange waves and a ginger scent that burned her nose and violet pride that smelled of pine trees washed off Officer Sten'li as he strutted past with his newly polished armor.

Marielle shivered in delight. She could sit all day in the corner of the Watch House and just absorb the scents ricocheting through it like shooting stars on a clear night. She still couldn't believe she got to work here every day. Field trips into the real world had been sparse at the academy.

"No need to rile the girls up," she'd heard Headmistress Archari say a thousand times.

They were all girls. All Scenters were girls, though not all girls were Scenters. Carnelian was proof of that. They said she had vivid red hair – dyed – to go with the name, though Marielle couldn't tell. Carnelian was giving off a fresh light blue and linen scent as they made their way to the doors. Expectancy. She wanted to win that pot for the most arrests.

Marielle wanted to help her.

"Now, we all want to win, right?" Carnelian said as they exited through the tall doors onto the street. Two large braziers burned there. Word was, the Alchemists provided a special oil that kept the flames blue to indicate a Watch House. Marielle didn't care. Light was light. Scents were where true beauty lay.

"Of course," Marielle agreed. She wasn't really listening. Her nose was following a thousand scents, the scarf barely concealing their potency.

"But even though we all want to win, you need to be sure the crime is being committed in the present, okay? Unless it's a big one. Oh, I get why you wanted to haul that noble in. I wanted to wash that smile off his face myself, but we can't afford those kinds of mix-ups, right? We need only solid arrests if we're gonna win. No time-wasters. You with me?"

"Yes, Carnelian." Was that the smell of a jealous husband? It was so close to the smell of a woman noticing that another woman was prettier than her that they could be hard to distinguish without a purer sample. But she needed to get better at trace samples if she was going to be the legend on the Watch that she dreamed of being.

That was definitely the intent to steal creeping through the breeze. She could smell it – rust-like in scent – but so faint that it was impossible to tell where it originated. She spun around, searching, and was hit with a blast so hard she stumbled.

Desperation. Raw, ragged, pulsing orange and ginger streaked desperation. It slammed against her skull like the haft of an axe. It dug into her eyes like the claws of an eagle. She grimaced, clenching her jaw against a scream and then – suddenly – it was gone.

She struggled to breathe against a thick scarf of wool and a heavy leather glove.

"Hold on. Breathe. Oh, maybe I should move my hand," Carnelian was saying. "You only had one layer on. You should know better than that by now, wet-ears! Two layers at the minimum! Even I know that, and I'm no Scenter!"

"Thanks," Marielle gasped, clutching her own nose and the extra layer of scarf Carnelian had wrapped around her face. That had been close.

Whoever had felt that … well, gods have mercy on them!

And that was the worst part of being a Scenter – knowing the worst and not being able to stop it. Marielle always knew. There was never any doubt for her about intentions or hopes or dreams. She could smell them as easily as burnt toast. As potently as rotting peonies.

She could smell her worst nightmares all around her.

And the most angelic of dreams.

She focused on Carnelian, breathing in that light blue expectancy. There was safety there. Expectancy, cheerful optimism – that was a safe emotion. That was one you could breathe all day without throwing yourself from a building.

"I can see why you stopped," Carnelian was saying. "I can smell the ox dung from here. They should clean up after those beasts."

Marielle nodded her head, grateful for the pretense. She could smell the dung, of course, a faint hint of fecund earth. And she could smell the nearby canal – stagnant water mixed with the scent of life from the people who lived on the barges and gondolas there. Waverunners never left the water. If they set so much as a foot on land it was said that they could never return to their people. Marielle would have called that harsh, but it was their law, and a law couldn't be too harsh if it protected people. Maybe there were things worth fearing on dry land. Maybe they were worth making laws against.

The smells weren't unpleasant or overpowering. Natural smells rarely were. It was emotions and intentions that bowled a person over … or worse. But she didn't want to think of what was worse. Not right now.

She followed Carnelian on the beat. Carnelian knew the city inside and out. At twenty-nine she'd seen everything – or so she said. She was strong – and not just for a woman. She was pure muscle and she smelled often of sweat and swill under those predictable emotions of hers.

Marielle was none of those things. But as they followed their beat, the crowd parted, and it wasn't for her swathed face and big eyes. It wasn't for her waist-length plait of black hair or her slight figure. Oh no, it was for Carnelian's eagle-eyed stare and muscled exterior.

"Gonna dress up on your nights off?" Carnelian asked. She liked making conversation, even though Marielle was a poor conversationalist. "You can't when you're working. Gotta be in the right kit."

"I don't think I will," Marielle said demurely.

"You should. It's not Summernight if you don't dress up and you need to experience a true Summernight. We can pick a Legend who covers her face. You know the Legends, right?"

"Remind me," Marielle asked. Not because she didn't know, but because that golden-brown scent of motherhood she was smelling as she passed the stout woman with the big basket was so overwhelming that all she wanted to do was bask in it for the rest of the afternoon.

"Well, there's the Lady Sacrifice, but her face is clear and noble so we can see her suffering and beauty. And Queen Mer, but her face is lit with gems and a crown. Lila Cherrylocks might be a good fit. She's a master thief and she covers her face with a deep hood." She chuckled. "I certainly can't see you as the Maid Chaos."

"I'm not too proud to be a maid," Marielle said absently. She already knew that she'd never dress as a thief or as Death's handmaiden. She was content in the Watch Officer kit she wore.

"You'll see what I mean tonight. On second thought … maybe we should see how you do dressed as Maid Chaos."

"Ooof!" Marielle sucked in her breath. She'd been so distracted by the mother-scent that she didn't notice until too late that she'd stumbled right into someone.

Not just someone.

That pulsing orange scent – the one that hit her only moments before – filled her nose so sharply with ginger that she fumbled for her scarf. It must have slipped when she stumbled. But no, it was still tucked around her nose and mouth.

There were other smells underneath the desperation. Regular smells that filled the background: spices and chemicals, leather, old books, cinnamon, honey, a gentle love of beauty, and something young and masculine and musky.

She looked up, wrestling against the maddening scent of desperation mixing with the human smells of life and occupation. Her eyes met a pair of eyes standing out light and stark against slightly darker skin. His face was chiseled despite the softness of youth and his figure was strong and lithe under the Alchemist apprentice's apron, but it was the eyes she couldn't stop staring at. Because it was in them that she saw what she was smelling – that desperate cocktail of need and terror.

She reached out to him, not meaning to, feeling strange when her hand steadied his trembling arm. His lips – the top one thin and the bottom full, quivered with some suppressed emotion, but it wasn't anger or irritation like Marielle would have expected. He was hunched over a package wrapped in sealskin – something valuable – but his scent said he wasn't worried about the package. His spiking emotions – popping and flaring with bursts of uncertain color – were about something else. He looked like a demon wrapped in an angel's body – like a man at war with himself.

Marielle licked her lips, trying to think of something to say. Nervous orange and ginger sizzled from him as his gaze caught on her uniform and then swiveled to Carnelian.

"My apologies, Officer," he said in a resonant voice – a voice like a full-bodied string instrument. It puffed out from him with a golden scent that tangled around her in a cloud. She knew this scent. She swallowed, trying to push it away, but the more she did, the more it slid into every crease of her uniform. "I did not watch where I was going."

Carnelian snorted. "Watch yourself, Apprentice. The Jingen Watch has double the bodies on the streets for Summernight, but you could still stumble into people with more … ill intent … than you expect."

He ducked his head respectfully, eyes flicking to where Marielle still held his sleeve. She let go with a gasp. That blasted golden scent! The smell of warm honey and cinnamon of fresh earth and sunshine. How long had it been since she'd smelled *that*? Had she ever smelled it so powerfully?

"Careful, citizen," she said through a dry mouth.

He ducked his head again, his slight smile devastating against the visceral pain of his emotions, and then he was walking away, his purposeful strides sliding through the crowd like an adder through the grass. Now, why had she thought of an adder?

"Pretty, I'll admit," Carnelian said, her gaze on his retreating figure. "But he won't get our tally up today. Nose up, Scenter! Find us a good crime!"

Marielle wrenched her gaze away from the young man, her nose sniffing obediently, but it was no use. Her every sense was still drunk on that golden burst of absolute attraction, the hot honey of it sinking into her like the warmth of the noonday sun. She was certain now that she'd never scented anything like it before. And it was hard not to feel disappointed when she realized she probably wouldn't scent it again. Things like that didn't happen every day and she didn't even know his name.

She shook herself irritably.

"I think I smell violence that way," she gestured at the red swirl heading down the street. It wasn't much to go on, but it was better than pining for someone she didn't even know.

FIRST NIGHT OF SUMMERNIGHT

6: Desperate Measures

Tamerlan

Tamerlan ran a hand through his short hair. He hadn't stopped sweating since he ran into the Watch Officer on the street. He'd seen the way that Scenter looked at him – those lovely eyes, so dark they were almost purple. Her gaze bored into him like a drill into softwood. Had she known? Had she scented his intent?

He'd been so shaken he'd nearly forgotten to bring the books to Master Kurond. So shaken he'd almost been caught when he pilfered the toolroom for a set of lockpicks and the laundry for a dark cloak. If nothing else, the Alchemists were great lovers of variety. Their toolrooms and storehouses had every item you could possibly need – even items for a thief.

There was no weapon, though.

He'd debated with himself about what to do about a weapon. He had knives. Knives for preparing solutions, for chopping ingredients, for tooling leather, for sharpening quills. None of them were for killing a man.

Would he need to do that tonight? Why wouldn't his dragon-cursed hands stop shaking at the thought?

He forced his breathing to slow. He had the evening free for the First Night of Summernight. All the apprentices did. Dathan was already gone. He'd barely stopped to check on Tamerlan before he left. But he had checked. A good friend that.

Tamerlan's thoughts skittered like butter across a hot pan. With an effort, he forced them to focus.

He tucked his last knife – he'd taken all the ones he owned, of every size – into his belt and patted his pockets. Nothing extra to jingle or give him away. The folded illuminated page fell out of his pocket and he scooped it up again. Best to leave it here. If he failed tonight, there was a good chance it would mean he was captured by the Watch. Or dead.

Either way, he wouldn't need a fancy page. He tucked it reluctantly beneath his pillow. Wouldn't it have been nice if this chance page could have been the solution he needed? If it had been a map to a secret tunnel leading to the heart of the Sunset Tower or a page spelling out an old loophole to the laws and customs of Jingen. A fanciful thought, but still one that he clung to. If only he'd had time to try the recipe on it. Maybe it would have granted him extra stealth or power. His fingers itched to gather the ingredients even now. Somehow, he knew that where the ancient scribbler had failed, he would be able to succeed.

The Bridge of Legends, the page said in the runes of the ancients, *bridges the gap between life and death.*

If anyone was perched on the bridge between life and death, it was Amaryllis.

And tonight, Tamerlan would join her there. With her arrival today, tonight this was his best chance. They wouldn't expect anyone to try to break her out the very night she arrived, would they? They'd still be sorting out the guard schedule.

Or at least, that's how it would be at his father's Grandhouse.

Tamerlan just had to hope it would be the same here.

He trotted down the winding stairs – three flights – from his small closet of a room through the floors of *The Copper Tincture*. The smell of something acrid filled the second floor. A tincture gone wrong, perhaps. Or maybe it was meant to smell that way. There were no mistakes in the Alchemist's Guild. Only learning opportunities.

Maybe that was true tonight, too. Not a mistake to try to save Amaryllis. Only an opportunity.

He waited until he reached the ground floor to draw a deep steadying breath – even with enough tension to make his hands shake he wasn't fool enough to inhale that acid – and then clenched his jaw.

He wished he was someone else. Good-natured Tamerlan wouldn't be enough tonight. Tamerlan the buddy. Tamerlan the good-hearted. If his friends had been asked if he could penetrate the defenses of the Sunset Tower they would have laughed.

He would have laughed if you asked him yesterday. But this wasn't yesterday.

If only he could be someone else. Someone strong and brave. Better yet, someone who knew how to break into towers and save girls from fates worse – well, at least as bad as – death. A hero.

He clenched his jaw and quickened his pace.

The sun was sinking over the horizon and even though the costumes weren't really supposed to be worn until tomorrow, there were still some people in the crowds already dressed up. The knots that moved from tavern to inn in laughing huddles contained their fair share. In one he saw a specter of Queen Mer, her face painted a sickly green and hair styled in green clay to look like she was underwater even now. He didn't want to even guess what she'd paid for the clinging translucent dress that swirled around her. More than he made in a six-month if he had to guess.

But that was good. He clenched his fists to steady them until the nails bit into the meat of his palms and hoped he would be taken for a reveler in costume. No thief – or at least, not a real one. Just a reveler like everyone else moving through the sunset streets and waiting for the Nightbursts to announce that the Summernight festival had begun.

It was dark by the time he reached the Government District. Even the darkness didn't help him hide here. Large lamps were already being lit by the city workers. They carried oil up to them in massive gourds carried on poles over their bowed shoulders. And just like every time he'd smelled the fishy scent of the oil, he wondered if it was really true that they came from oilfish out in the sea – creatures so large that a single one could smash a ship in two. Queen Mer herself wasn't so fearsome.

Small lights were lit in colored lanterns on strings along the canals – red, orange and gold for Summernight, though the colors changed depending on the season. Their tiny fires reflected again and again over the water while the haunting sounds of the Waverunner's nightly songs echoed back and forth over the water, the cadence oddly reminiscent of the slowly poled gondolas they manned.

But now was not the time to daydream about the wonders of the world. This was not the night to be sensitive to the beguiling colors of the paving stones that made wave patterns through the square as if designed to look like the sea or to marvel at the smooth stone of the government buildings. Or wonder what it would be like to be a Waverunner and live his whole life in the rocking embrace of Mother Water.

He pulled his dreaming self back, deeper into the recesses of his mind, the sound of Master Kurond's voice echoing in his mind.

"You're smart enough, boy, if you could only stop dreaming. The world is a wonder. But it's only useful to us if that wonder can be tapped and sold."

It wasn't useful to him at all right now. He didn't dare be that day-dreaming Tamerlan tonight.

The Sunset Tower stood at the center of the Government District, perched on the highest point of the city, the crest of the Dragon's Spine. Tamerlan shivered as he clung to the shadows, skimming from one to the next like a water strider over a pond.

The night birds began their wistful songs but here in the Government District, the crowds were scarce. There were no good taverns here. And the view of the Nightbursts would be poor unless you were on the roof of the palace. Or perhaps locked up in the Sunset Tower. Oh, his sister's view would be perfect. He bit his cheek to keep from thinking about it, frowning at the metallic taste that filled his mouth.

The wall surrounding the Tower and the Seven Suns Palace was taller than he remembered.

Of course, he hadn't been planning to infiltrate it the last time he'd been here. The walls, purple in the descending twilight, rose like cliffs, a moat of dank water surrounding them. There were no gondolas in the moat. No fairy lights of their lanterns or murmur of their voices. The fecund scent of still water and algae filled his nose.

He could swim it.

And then what?

He hadn't thought this through well enough.

The guards passed one another on the wall above, calling their signs to one another. All was well and all would be well, and all manner of things would be well.

Maybe for them.

Maybe for anyone whose sister would not die in five nights.

There was nothing for it. He circled, looking for the best place to breach the wall. There was a small door across from him here with a large padlock. He could swim across and try the door. It looked like a storm drain. Even palaces had to contend with weather, didn't they?

And he'd brought lockpicks. He might as well use them.

Quietly, checking his pockets to be sure he hadn't lost anything, he slipped down to the edge of the water. It wasn't a far swim. It was the length of one of the ponds he'd practiced in as a boy and about as clean. He'd swim it. He didn't even need to remove his cloak or boots.

The storm drain would be perfect.

He held his breath and slipped silently into the water.

7: To Catch a Thief

MARIELLE

"That's the fifth pair of thieves we've caught tonight!" Carnelian said, clapping Marielle on the back as they handed the pair off to the patrol wagon. "I knew patrolling with you was lucky. My last two Scenters never would have picked up on a whiff so faint!"

Marielle allowed a small smile at the praise. Dusk swallowed the long shadows around them and bled into night. Howls of delight and the faint sound of music tumbled through the breeze to her ears. But to Marielle the rising of the moon was not a time with less to notice, but more. As the heat left the ground and rose into the cooling air, the scents rose up with it, causing almost a reverse sunset as the myriad colors hovered in the air over the cobblestones.

She caught her breath just as she had a thousand times before. The smell of a city nightrise never stopped bringing wonder to her senses.

"Wind that scarf up if it's getting to be too strong," Carnelian suggested. "Things will die off when we get to the Government District. That's where the route takes us next and those streets are as tan-bland as anywhere in the city – or so my Scenters always said."

Marielle followed Carnelian's lead through the wide arches that led to the Government District and over the narrow bridge that spanned the canal. There might not be the same potent smells here of cinnamon, cloves, or thyme that were in the Spice District or the acrid smell of chemical concoctions from the Alchemist's District, but the Government District had its own bouquet.

Fear was usually strongest here. Sometimes tinged with royal-blue and gardenia scented power and the bronze flecks of morning dew scented hope. Other times it hung heavy on the air, mixed with the bitter mustard-yellow and white vinegar of failure, or worse – that pulsing orange ginger desperation that clung to every ripple like mud to the soles of boots in mid-spring.

Marielle wrapped a second layer of scarf around her face, cinching it to keep it in place. She should be proud of having caught the thieves tonight. She should be exulting in her success – they were certainly going to win the pot that Carnelian was so desperate for.

But that was the problem. Marielle loved justice. Who wouldn't love the law? It was so certain of itself. It divided right down through nuances to specifics. Cleaving through the difference between maiming or injury or theft and robbery. One sentence for one. One for the other. Sometimes divided by a hair of difference, but that hair was written down and codified.

Who wouldn't love a world so stable, so black and white, so definite that it could be written entirely down in laws and codified and enforced?

If only Marielle's own feelings could be codified like that. If only the constant gumbo of scents swirling around her in the fog of night could be so definite. But they never were.

Take that man with the startled eyes she'd bumped into on the street today. He'd been barely older than her. That apron and the alchemical smells surrounding him made his profession plain. And yet.

That pulsing orange ginger of desperation around him had clung like the scent of death. The tiny brazen flecks of hope weaving in and out of it had been matched equally with inky black bursts of licorice despair. He was on the edge of something. Hovering. Waiting to fall one way or the other.

And then take her reaction. She shivered at the memory. She'd been overwhelmed by the golden honey scent of her attraction to him to the point where it bled into the pulsing orange ginger smell and mixed into a cocktail so potent it rivaled the stories of lovers dashing themselves from cliffs for the sheer love of one another – if you could call such a thing love.

And it was puzzles like that that filled Marielle with the very *uncertainty* that she so desperately wanted to avoid. If she was uncertain, then she couldn't predict the future. And if she couldn't predict the future, she couldn't prevent the worst.

And if she couldn't prevent the worst, then she'd be swept away on it like a child swept away by a tidal wave.

No. Marielle was much happier with certainties. And she was certain that tonight they were on these streets to catch people violating the certain and sure code of the law.

They patrolled the dark Government District more slowly than they did other streets. It was hard for Carnelian to see between the pools of light provided by the high towering lanterns still being lit at intervals through the district. She had only her eyes to guide her, scent-blind as she was.

Marielle didn't mind. The architecture of the Government District was all certain lines and precise arcs. Clean cut corners, smooth stone, level steps, and uniform cobbles made her heart glad. Someone had thought this area of the city through. Someone had been certain.

Their patrolling took them around a turn to stride past the palace moat. Crowds were gathered on the roof terraces of the palace under the Sunset Tower and their cheers and calls tumbled down to Marielle. They were welcome to their fun. The ladies bright ballgowns caught the light and even from so far away – even when Marielle couldn't see their colors – they looked like jewels strung for a queen.

"Landholds. I'd like to see them work for once," Carnelian said just as she did every time they passed the Seven Suns Palace. She spat in the same place she spat every time. Patrols were easy with Carnelian. She was so predictable that she was almost a certainty.

But there was something different here in the street tonight. Marielle paused. It wasn't the Landholds clustered above. It wasn't the first Nightburst that had just erupted over the city in a shower of brilliant sparks to the cheers and amazement of the party high above. It wasn't the guard seen meeting on the top of the wall in the light cast by the Nightburst.

What was it?

Pulsing orange spun with gold. Just the barest trace. But combined with that slight alchemical scent of acid …

Yes! The man from earlier. His face flashed into her mind as if carried by the scent of him.

What was he doing in the Government District tonight?

"Don't tell me you've stopped to watch the Nightburst!" Carnelian laughed. "I thought you Scenters were practically blind. Can you even tell that it's bright gold?"

Where was he? The trail was so faint. And yet she couldn't get it out of her nose. She was drawn to it like flies to lit torches. It didn't matter how dangerous it might be, she couldn't stop looking for it.

But that faint smell had faded almost as if it had been swallowed by water.

Marielle spun to look at the moat. There was no scent to guide her. Not if it crossed the water. Water hid scent too well – except for the grass-green scents of life growing in the rancid water.

She was watching for movement. Any flicker. Any at all.

Something moved in the corner of her peripheral vision and her head jerked to follow it. Nothing there.

Where was it?

"There!" Carnelian yelled, her hand pointing in the direction Marielle had seen the movement. "Stop! Stop by order of the Jingen City Watch!"

Carnelian cursed and took off like a dog after a cart, stumbling after just three steps over a curb Marielle saw easily. To her, it was bright yellow where a cur had told the world his life's story.

Marielle dashed past, still not catching the scent of their prey, just hoping Carnelian had really seen something. Her dull curses were fading behind as Marielle's heart pounded loud and feet pounded louder where she sped along the cobbles.

There was a squelching sound and then it was as if the scent of the moat had grown legs and was darting along the streets in front of her.

She chased the scent, her feet light on the cobbles.

This was the heady part. Just Marielle and the scent and the chase.

She ripped one layer of veil off as she sped up, the scent growing sharper and stronger. She could see a man-shape in the smell. A man in a cloak. His cloak tangled around his legs and fell as if he'd shed his skin like a snake.

Marielle stumbled, her nose temporarily demanding she follow the cloak and the man both at once. It took a moment to override the nose.

Follow the man! Follow the man!

Behind her, Carnelian's cry of discovery rang out as she scooped up the dripping cloak. And came then the wild feeling of scents blurring as she sped past them. She fumbled at her waist for the strap of her bell, pulling the clapper free so that her chase would sound itself to the Jingen City Guard everywhere.

Ding – a – ling – a – ling – da – ling!

She darted around a corner, following the scent. He'd clearly hoped to lose her here where he ducked under the footing of a bridge and then turned as soon as he was clear of it down the steps and along the rocky ledge that ran the length of a canal toward the river.

Ha! It was not so easy to lose Marielle.

His pulsing orange scent – harsh on the nose, blurred by her golden hot-honey attraction, was mixing with the canal scent now, pulsing orange ginger leaking into grass green but the bronze of his hope was gone. Flecks of black licorice replaced it. Marielle sucked in a breath, sadness washing in with air.

This was the part she hated. The part where she tasted the pain of the criminal. Because criminals were victims too. Some of circumstance. Most of their own selves.

It wasn't for Marielle to determine which this poor man was. It wasn't for her to wonder if he labored over his work, muscles straining and despair slowly building like sawdust in a mill.

It wasn't for Marielle to wonder if his beautiful features twisted with pain in the night as his mind drifted over broken dreams.

It was only for Marielle to chase.

Justice would be satisfied. Marielle would satisfy it.

She couldn't hear Carnelian's footsteps behind her anymore. It took a moment to realize why. They'd run under the arches leading from the Government District and into the Spice District.

Her quarry was not far ahead now. And his options were limited. The steps back up into the street were coming up and if he didn't take them, there wouldn't be another chance to run up to street level again. She would be able to corner him when the canal reached the river. Marielle picked up her pace, clutching at her side as the ache began to form there. She needed to run more often.

His scent swirled with a sudden burst of periwinkle and celery intelligence and then he leapt to the side toward the canal, leaping into a gondola despite the cries of the gondolier and passenger. Without pause, he leaped again onto a passing barge.

Cursing, Marielle screwed up her face and followed, her first leap into the gondola earned her a slap on the back.

"Out! Out of my gondola!" A man in a conical hat shouted.

"Jingen City Watch!" Marielle yelled, her bell jangling and her nose filled with his puffs of mauve and sulfur irritation. She scrambled to the edge of the gondola, kicking into a leap she wasn't sure she could make.

She barely managed to grab the side rail of the barge, pulling herself into the larger craft to the cursing of the driver and the commotion of his cargo – a reeking mass of goats, their voices baying into the night and their organic smells a pleasant break after so much high emotion.

Where had he gone?

She pushed through the goats, her bell jangling.

"The Watch will hear from me!" the driver of the barge screamed, but she paid him no mind.

She could see where the golden-pulsing-orange scent had leapt to the next gondola, but the gondola was too far away for her to make that leap now. Fortunately, a Waverunner family boat was right behind it in the canal. Marielle leapt from the rail of the barge onto the flat deck of the family boat.

A woman shrieked as Marielle scrambled across the deck, narrowly avoiding a burning brazier where a small chicken was roasting, ducking under the lines of wash and past a gaping child cradled in a hammock. Curses and shouts followed her as she leapt from the boat to a gondola and from there to the next gondola.

She was losing her quarry! By the time she reached the other side of the canal, his scent was already up the steps and into the street beyond. Marielle paused, gasping for breath and then she clenched her jaw and ran again.

Up the steps.

Into the streets of the Spice District.

The sound swelled loud as the revelers ran from tavern to tavern, swinging with laughter from the center fountains in the squares, kissing with a lover in a hidden corner, their eyes sparkling with love or excitement or just Summernight, dancing in long swaying chains through the streets with their songs swelling loud into the night.

There was no way to chase now but with the nose.

Marielle fought through a wall of scent, tangled, interwoven, color layered upon color and sensation on sensation. There! The one single thread she was searching for. She keep her eyes and nose focused on it.

Marielle whipped the last layer of her veil off her face, darting between dancing bodies as she followed that pulsing orange ginger and gold scent. She didn't dare lose focus or she'd lose it in the tangle. It was more than just pulsing orange and gold to her now. She knew it like she knew the scent of her bedroom or of Carnelian. It was as familiar as a friend. If there was even the faintest whiff of it, she would find it.

It was growing stronger. And she was growing giddy at the thought of seeing that face again.

Marielle darted around a knot of men with smiles made bright by drink and jest. One raised a mug to her as she spun by, skidding through the turn.

"To the Jingen Watch! Our faithful City servants."

She didn't hear the raucous laughter. Didn't need to.

She was almost upon him. She could smell it.

The scent fled into an alley and Marielle's heart leapt. There would be no way out!

Her lungs were ragged from the chase, the iron taste of blood coated her mouth, but she willed her legs to push harder, each muscle to do its part.

The scent hit up against a door. Marielle tried the handle. Not locked.

She flung the door open and burst inside before she could catch her breath.

It was a step before she sucked in a long breath of air into her panting lungs.

One more before she collapsed in a heap on the floor.

8: Plans and Hopes

Tamerlan

Tamerlan couldn't get his breath to calm down even now when he was safe in his own room, stripping out of soaking wet clothing.

His hand went to the muscles along the side of his back. He had a nasty scrape there from a fall and bruises on his shins, elbows, and side. He'd never been chased before. Not for real. The only chases he'd seen had been in childhood fun as he chased Amaryllis around the lemon trees or chased his small dog through the fields hunting orangetails and spacklefowl.

He sucked in deep, desperate breaths of the fragrant Alchemist Guild air in his rooms, glad for the tang of metal and the acrid smell of something burning that sank so deep into any cloth or leather that it never left. He shook out his short hair and threw all his clothing into a wet pile in the corner as if throwing them away could rid him of the failure of the night.

Mrs. Shen – *The Copper Tincture*'s washwoman – would have a fit when she saw what he'd done to his clothing. Mud streaked his white shirt and the smell of stale water hung heavy over the soaked clothing.

Tamerlan sat heavily onto his bed, trying to calm his beating heart and slow those deep sucking breaths that threatened to turn to sobs.

He'd failed.

He hung his head into his lean hands and drew in long breaths as he shook, naked, on the threadbare blanket. At any moment the Jingen City Watch might come banging on the door of *The Copper Tincture* and they'd haul him off to the barred wagon to be brought to Lord Mythos for trial. Any minute now.

But the minutes drew out long, like threads being spun from carded wool and soon his breathing calmed, and his heart was only a pounding hammer and not the battering ram it had been moments before.

Tamerlan woke, shivering and naked on his bed. He must have fallen asleep while he was waiting to be caught. He sat up, blinking in the almost-dawn light.

One thing was clear from last night: he did not have the skills to break into the Sunset Tower on his own. He hadn't even breached the walls of the Seven Sun Palace. A frontal assault was out of the question. And he could think of no way to sneak past the guarded entrances. Especially not now. Not now that he was a wanted man. Had his pursuers seen his face? He wasn't sure, but he'd known that one was following him by scent.

She had a scarf around her face. He'd seen that. It was why he'd led her to the Spice District and straight into Maverick's Warehouse where he knew they'd been grinding aniseeds yesterday. He liked their scent, but even he had a headache after his brief visit there. What would that do to a Scenter?

He hadn't stayed to find out. Hopefully, whatever it had done had kept her from seeing where he went. It must have. If it hadn't, then she'd already be here banging on the door and shouting "Jingen City Watch" wouldn't she?

He began to dress. He had a single spare set of clothing. A luxury for an apprentice. A hardship for a boy raised in a minor Landhold's house. He'd given up missing the comfort of his old life. But today he wished he had more clothing. He'd have some explaining to do about the other clothing. Maybe if he told them he got drunk and fell into the canal. But he didn't drink. Life was hard enough without making worse troubles for yourself.

Maybe it was time to try doing something with the skills he had. But what did he have, really? He was a dreamer and a lover of old tales. He could tell you the real stories behind the old Legends everyone dressed as for Summernight. What a useless skill when it came to saving his beloved sister!

He was an Alchemist's apprentice – and a good one. The work they gave him was too easy – boring and dry. But that was a skill of sorts. He knew ingredients and compounding. Perhaps it was time to take that old recipe seriously. It was surprising that no one from the library had come looking for it yet. Someone had been reading that book – perhaps even the librarian. Strange that they hadn't noticed that the page was missing and looked back to see whose blood was marked on their register. Unless the page wasn't from that book at all.

Tamerlan poured water from the jug by his basin into a cloth and washed his face, breathing deeply into the wet cloth, letting the feeling of cleanliness be the only thing he felt as he steadied himself.

Okay.

Good.

Enough calm. Time to set aside emotions and attack the problem again. He felt an almost physical pang at the reminder of his failure. But no. No time for that. He'd wasted one night. And there were only four more left.

He pulled out the illuminated page from under his pillow and let his eyes run over the intricate designs. They looked like smoke rising.

Smoke. Hmm.

He read it again, noting again the way that the reader had tried and failed to use the formula. He shouldn't have written his efforts right on the page. They looked like a terrible scrawl compared to the neat letters of the original page. Defacing books was never a solution.

Tamerlan frowned, feeling the dent form in the middle of his brow that always came when he was concentrating.

If he just read the original lettering, what would it say? It wasn't easy to read the runes. They were in the language of the

Ancients. He'd always found it fascinating, reading the short texts his father's Landhold protected with care. But he doubted many in the city could read them. The Librarians would, of course, and some Landholds here, and of course the Lord Mythos. But very few.

The Bridge of Legends, the page said at the top, the first letter set off to the side in a box with its own smoky design swirling around the letter, *bridges the gap between life and death. Use for dire situations. For the summoning of the ancient powers and the bringing of skills not won. But beware. With the Bridge, comes a curse most potent. Trust not what you see or feel. Trust not your own eyes. The Bridge only opens the path, but what angel or demon may emerge cannot be told until first breath.*

Creepy. And yet couldn't he use an angel tonight to bear his sister away from the golden tower? Even a demon would be better than his own impotence. A demon could possibly be bargained with. Or, failing that, it could distract her captors.

In Tamerlan's mind, he was striding up to the gate, head held high, hair rippling in the wind. His lean muscles clung to a massive sword. The guards shifted their stances but then the screams began as a demon hurled from the sky in a fire-laced mass of black destruction. It tore into the guards like death-come-alive and then, as they fought it, Tamerlan raced in behind him, sword swishing through the air, knocking his opponents aside.

He coughed and looked back at the page.

Aniseed

Blue Ox Horn

Tenleaf, dried

Blood of the black squid

Ravencall

Sagebrother

Shorter mint

No quantities. And if you weren't used to reading ancient texts, or weren't schooled in alchemy, most people would have no idea what some of that even was. Of course, the aniseed was obvious. But no one called Orrisleaf "tenleaf" anymore. And how many people knew to ask for actual squid blood when most purveyors sold only the ink or pawned the ink off as blood when asked?

He tapped the page thoughtfully. It *did* say it was for use in dire situations. And was there anything more dire than this? Sure, there were warnings. Nothing powerful enough to save his sister should be used lightly. But Tamerlan had a good heart. And he only wanted to save his sister. Any gods or fates watching would know that, right? So, he shouldn't worry too much about these warnings, because they'd never wish ill on a brother who just wanted to save a beloved sister. Right?

And even if the worst really did happen, could it really be worse than what was *already* happening?

He'd gather the ingredients today. And then … well, one step at a time.

First, the ingredients.

His heart rate was almost normal when Dathan banged on his door to call him for his morning tasks.

9: Lord Mythos

Marielle

A thousand knives stabbed through Marielle's skull as Carnelian dragged her through the streets by her upper arm.

"I can't believe you ran in there, Marielle! You should have known better! Even *I* know that a Scenter in a house of spices is a terrible idea! And one full of aniseed! You're useless to me now." Carnelian clicked her tongue, tugging Marielle roughly so that she stumbled over an uneven cobble.

She didn't mean it – or at least not the useless part. Carnelian flashed from emotion to emotion like a ship on the sea when she was angry, letting however she felt in the moment vent through her mouth like a chimney. She would go back to being predictable when it stopped.

Marielle let the diatribe wash over her like the rain falling over the city, washing debris from the night of partying into the runnels along the cobbles. Roses and garlands in the streets hung limply in the rain, not battered enough to fall, but too wet to look jubilant.

After the first evening of Summernight, the alleys should be filled with drunken celebrants stumbling home, but the wash of rain had quelled jubilant spirits early and the streets were clear and empty as dawn rose over the hills.

One of the Watch wagons pulled up short beside them. It was pulled by a boney nag too old for the job, a flea-ridden grey, flecked dark from the spraying water of the cobbles. The horse snorted, reflecting Marielle's feelings perfectly. What she wouldn't give for a second start to the day.

The enclosed wagon was shiny from use, the rough lumber used to build it long since worn to a polish. Inside the barred windows, a drunk slumped on the bench and from the driver's seat, a voice called.

"The Captain says to return to the Seven Suns Palace. You two are wanted there."

"Why?" Carnelian was never shy.

"Why's it raining when I want sun?" the officer in the driver's seat asked. "Why's the Captain assigned me duty through all of Summernight? Just life. No one said you had to like it."

And with his sweet words still hanging in the air, he clucked and flicked the reins to urge the tired nag on.

"Come on," Carnelian said, pulling Marielle after her. "Maybe we can find a gondola to take us – if they haven't all put you on their blacklists after that stunt you pulled last night."

Marielle clutched her scarf around her nose, letting the wet of the rain ease some of the burning agony inside her lungs. Her mind felt like someone was turning it round and round and randomly stabbing a knife into it as it turned.

Aniseed.

She really shouldn't have been such an idiot. She should have realized that any thief running into the Spice District must know he was being chased by a Scenter. It was the kind of mistake someone too fresh to have learned would make – someone like her.

She followed Carnelian's stream of curses back to the Government District, letting her head hang with pain and shame as they followed the patterned cobbles. They had not found a gondola to take them. Every one they saw was filled with huddled forms of tired partiers.

Being called back to the Government District couldn't be a good thing. No one called people back to the scene of a failure to congratulate them.

Marielle's heart pounded as she followed Carnelian. She was already flushing. Being dressed down would sting – not because she couldn't handle a tongue-lashing but because she deserved it. She should have been faster. And she shouldn't have been duped. She'd been so badly broadsided with that blast of scent that by the time Carnelian found her, picked her up off the warehouse floor, dragged her into the street, and shoved her head in a rain barrel, the scent of their quarry had long since disappeared, crossed and crisscrossed by too many other scents in a District so fragrant that it could make the nose of a statue scrunch up.

She'd like to blame her foolishness on the irresistibleness of his golden honey scent, but that only made it worse. Like she was a silly girl instead of a Jingen City Watch Officer.

They arrived at the moat around the Seven Suns Palace before Marielle realized it. Carnelian kicked Marielle's boots, clearing her throat dramatically. Dragon's spit, she must be agitated. Marielle's nose was recovered enough that she could smell Carnelian's mood. Dusty mustard and lime poured off her in waves so strong that Marielle was having trouble catching the scent of anything else.

By the time Marielle looked up, she felt her own breath catching. It wasn't just the Commander of the Watch waiting there. And it wasn't just Captain Ironarm with him, either. Standing with them was a man who could only be the fabled Lord Mythos.

She could smell the faint residue of magic on him now that she was concentrating. He hadn't used it in a long time, and yet even this tiny residue was enough to rivet her every sense on him, trying to catch even a whiff of the heady turquoise and gold that still lingered faintly on his body. It smelled of vanilla and lilac.

Marielle had made the mistake of thinking that 'Lord Mythos' was his name for most of her life. It wasn't until she was in the Academy that she realized it was a title. A role. The Lord Mythos was the keeper of the city's myths and laws and her ultimate authority.

And this Lord Mythos was young.

He was surrounded by uniformed personal guards – six of them this morning. But there was no mistaking which one he was. Tall and unnaturally pale, with dark hair curving around his perfectly sculpted face and clean-shaven jaw, he was like a raven among jays.

Marielle – if she had pictured him at all – would have pictured him in decadent clothing and rich jewelry. It was surprising to realize that his black brocade coat was unadorned except for black embroidery on the high collar and around the cuffs. A pair of metal bracers graced his forearms, but even these were a dull steel only highlighted by gilding, not the gleaming ornaments she would have expected. His boots, trousers, and the short cape tied over one shoulder and under the other were as simply cut as a guards' uniform, though on him they looked sharp enough to cut throats.

He studied them through narrow eyes, a ghost of a smile on his lips. "These are valiant Watch Officers who found our intruder?"

Even though his words were quiet, Captain Ironarm straightened with pride and the Commander of the Watch looked pleased. It was something about the tone. As if he could say a flower was pretty and then it would be. As if he could call the same flower a disgrace and it would immediately wilt. His words were power.

"As you say, Lord Mythos," the Captain of the Guard said. "Corporal Carnelian Fishnetter and her Scenter, Marielle Valenspear."

Carnelian bowed deeply, and at the tug of her hand on Marielle's sleeve, Marielle remembered to do the same. Thank goodness for sensible Carnelian. She could meet one of the dragons of legend and she'd never look for a second like that was a strange thing. But then, she didn't have magic tickling the inside of her nose like the sweetest embrace of a lover.

Lord Mythos took a step forward, his black eyes studying them with care. His guards shifted uncomfortably.

"I am Etienne Velendark. Your Lord Mythos. I commend you for fulfilling your duty this night." He stepped forward again, standing right in front of Carnelian. "Rise."

She straightened. She didn't even look nervous. Her head was held high, but it was possible that her usual belligerent stance was more demure.

"My thanks," he said, placing a small purse in her hand. "And the thanks of our city. Continue to serve, and your name will be known in Jingen."

Carnelian flushed. That was high praise. It would have been a powerful promise from a Landhold, never mind the Lord Mythos.

But Marielle was confused. Why was he congratulating them? The infiltrator had gotten clean away.

Lord Mythos stepped in front of Marielle. The faint scent of his magic making her want to lean in to catch just a little more.

"Rise."

She stood. Surprisingly, the Lord Mythos was not much taller than her. He was whip-lean and moved like a man used to physical activity, not like one who spent his time governing.

He tilted his head, pursing his lips at her expression and she felt her cheeks grow hot. Had he noticed her regarding him as a man and not the myth he was meant to represent? It was hard to see that he was only a bare handful of years older than her without thinking of the name he'd given. Etienne. Etienne Velendark. It was a name that caressed the tongue.

"You are the Scenter? Walk with me."

Marielle's eyes grew wide at the request, but the hardening of Captain Ironarm's features when she glanced in her direction told her that even the smallest reluctance would be met with force. Perhaps he still meant to punish her for her failure.

Carefully, with as much self-control as she could muster, Marielle joined the Lord Mythos, walking with him as he led her along the moat, through the quiet morning of the Government District. Dawn burned the mist off the moat, stinking to Marielle of stale water and organic growth, but it was likely a pretty sight to a non-Scenter.

She noticed there was no offer of a purse for her.

"Your eyes are unique," he said as they walked. "You are of Landhold blood?"

Marielle stumbled, recovering quickly as the Lord Mythos offered a solicitous hand to steady her.

"My apologies, Lord Mythos. Your question startled me."

Her face was so hot it must be burning bright enough for Captain Ironarm to see from behind them. And her nose – her nose filled with his scent until she thought she'd have to pull up her scarf to make herself stop drawing it in … in … in.

"Oh?" he raised an eyebrow with a faint smile, but there was an edge of violence under it. The last time Marielle had seen that was when Carnelian lipped off to a guardsman from the Artificer District Watch House. He'd said 'Oh?' just like that and a moment later Carnelian had been on the ground nursing a bleeding nose and a chipped ego.

"I am not of Landhold blood, Lord Mythos."

"Then who were your parents? Do they live still?"

Marielle nearly choked. It wasn't that she was ashamed of Variena. Of course not. She visited. Made sure she was well. They both found it awkward.

"I was raised by the Scenter Guild as a foundling." Best to play it safe with the answer.

"But you know who you were born to." His words were so certain. As if he already knew the answer. Did he? "And you will tell me."

Had Marielle thought her cheeks were hot before? They burned so hotly now that surely they would be ash soon. She hadn't been raised from birth by the Scenters, though it was convenient to pretend she was.

"I was born to Variena, a Lady of the Red Light in the Trade District." Her words were not as loud as she would have liked. Not as bold. And she hated his knowing smile.

"And no idea of the father, I shall assume." His smile was cold. But his eyes looked satisfied. What did he have to be satisfied with? And why did it make Marielle suddenly want to look over her shoulder to be sure that Captain Ironarm was still watching? "And the man you chased last night. Could you find him if you scented him again?"

"I hope so, Lord Mythos." At least he was back to business. She could breathe again. She gasped in the overpoweringly sweet scent of his magic residue.

"You will watch for him. The slightest whiff of him and you will have your colleagues haul him in. Do you know how important Summernight is to Jingen?"

The way he said, 'Summernight' sent thrills up her spine. Awe and devotion mixed in his voice. It made her want to know whatever secret he did that made Summernight so magical. And the way he leaned in close to speak to her, the way he was breathless as he spoke, left her hanging on each breath, watching the perfect curve of his lips for each new word to fall.

"Yes."

"Tell me why, Marielle." And now it was her name that he was caressing with those perfect lips.

She caught her breath just in time. "Summernight is the summer festival when we remember the sleeping dragon on which our city is built. The legend says that he is bound by magic ancient and primitive – a magic now lost. Every summer, a sacrifice must be made to please the ancient magic and renew the bond."

"And if ever we fail?" When had he drawn so close? He smelled of mandarin oranges and rusty iron under that heady scent of magic.

"If we fail," she said, shaping her lips just as his had shaped his when he said the words, "the magic spell will break, and the dragons of the five cities will be let loose on the earth to finally embrace their revenge."

"Yes," he breathed and the way he said it set all her hair on end.

"But of course," Marielle said with a nervous laugh. "None of it is really true. It's part of our civic duty to remind us that in life sacrifices must be made. And it's part of the religions to remind us that the gods demand blood. But it's symbolic. There were never really dragons. And they won't come back if they aren't appeased."

"Do you believe so?" He said it slowly, drawing out every word. His gaze was locked onto hers. She couldn't have looked away if she tried. And in the depths of his eyes was a look like a man bound to a pole ready for the first lash to strike.

"Yes?" How could she be sure? How could anyone? And yet no one had ever seen a god or a dragon. And there were many hundreds of rituals performed in the city for the religions every day. What made this one any more real than any of those?

"Interesting." He pulled back to a comfortable distance and his eyes closed and then opened again and when they opened there was nothing there except for pure professionalism. "I will remember you, Marielle of the Scenters. And I will watch with interest as you find this infiltrator. But find him quickly. Nothing and no one must stop us from celebrating Summernight this year. Do you understand?"

"Yes," she breathed.

He spun, his short cape whipping up with the speed of his turn and flashing a shining satin lining at her.

And then he was striding back to his guards, issuing curt orders and Marielle was trying to make her knees lock so they would stop trembling like dried leaves in the autumn winds. The turquoise and gold-flecked lilac scent of magic left the air around her, leaving everything else dull in comparison.

10: Now or Never

Tamerlan

"Honor the ancestors!" the man said, whirling by in the dusty streets. He was one of the few people not already in costume as the day drew to another close. One lonely Smudger, worshiping as his religion demanded while the rest of the city burst into riotous celebration as the second night of Summernight descended.

Dathan pushed past the wrinkled man, "No offense, but you look like an ancestor already!"

The man ignored him, but he shot Tamerlan a piercing look.

"Do you need wisdom? Do you lack guidance? Seek the spirits of the ancestors! Bathe in smoke with us tonight. Purify yourself. Honor the ancestors."

Tamerlan held up his hands peaceably, trying to smile politely as Dathan pulled him past.

"As if we'd be doing that tonight!" his friend chuckled. "Oh, we missed you last night, Tam! Holden and Jez had a bet going that they could each find someone dressed as Lila Cherrylocks to kiss. It took most of the night, but Jez found one willing and Holden owes him a month's wages!"

"A month!" Tamerlan repeated. He would have been laughing, too, if it had been a week ago. It was hard to pretend to find something so trivial charming right now. In the bottom of the basket he carried were the ingredients for the recipe. Every one of them. It had taken most of the day to sneak them one at a time from the vendors he visited for the Guild, but buried under the lavender he was delivering, were all the items on the list. Someone would notice they were gone – he was sure.

He hadn't even had a good reason to go into Madam Chee's shop for the orrisleaf. He'd had to pretend he was looking for something he knew she didn't have on hand to get her to leave the counter long enough to steal it. And that was a risk. Madame Chee was sure to notice. And she was sure to think it was him. He should have paid. But she'd definitely know it was him, then. And what excuse could he give for wanting his own herbs when they had nothing to do with guild business?

"You need to cheer up. Who are you dressing as tonight?" Dathan pressed.

"Maybe I'll dress as Lila Cherrylocks just to make Holden and Jez choke," Tamerlan said with a smile. Keep up the pretense. Don't let anyone see what's under the surface. There was already enough reason for the Watch to suspect him, to find him, to arrest him before he even had a chance to save her.

He peered after the man carrying the smoking brazier and shouting warnings to turn to the ancestors. Was he a watchman undercover? Could he be watching them now, comparing Tamerlan to the description the Scenter would have given her fellow officers?

He forced a laugh, joining Dathan's snorted chuckles. Nothing to see here. No reason to suspect anything.

They hurried back to *The Copper Tincture*, passing a winking King Abelmeyer with his one good eye. A spy, perhaps? Or only a man preparing for the night's celebrations?

"You're coming to Master Juggernaut's tonight, aren't you?" Dathan asked.

"Juggernaut?" Tamerlan's eyes snapped back from red eyepatch strung across the scarred face of the costumed King. Perhaps that was how he would dress tonight. Something brazen and bold. No one would expect him to be hiding behind that, would they?

"Don't tell me you haven't heard! Every apprentice and most of the masters will be there. The Landholds throw a scavenger hunt through the city every year on the second night of Summernight. You know this, Tamerlan!"

"Sure," he agreed.

"And every year we form teams to try to win the prize. It's not just gold this year. It's access. If we win, we join the Landholds at their Legend Ball in the Seven Suns Palace."

Tamerlan blinked. He'd forgotten all about that. If he was in the palace, he would be one more step closer to the tower.

"The whole city will be after the prize this year. Between the money and the contracts for your guild, a year of credit in the Trade District, and a chance for a real Landhold Ball thrown by Lord Mythos? You could set yourself up for life! Every Guild in the city will be fighting for it, Tam. Not just guilds, either. I heard the Librarians will have a team. Even the Watch is rumored to have a team!"

"The Watch?"

But how could he search for scavenger items and try this recipe at the same time? He'd have to choose. If this worked – if it was real magic like he hoped it was – then he didn't need special access to the palace.

"Tell me you're coming, Tamerlan! You're good at puzzles – when you're paying attention."

"Sure, Dathan. I just need to get into costume first. I'll meet you at Master Juggernaut's."

Dathan punched his arm. "Good! We're winning that one, Tam. And then you and I are going to swagger around a Landhold Ball and dance with girls so rich they bleed gold and so pretty you'd die for a single glance from them."

"I'm not ready to die," Tamerlan said. But tonight he might die. If the magic didn't work, he still needed to rescue Amaryllis somehow and the only other option would be to storm the tower gates.

"You take these things way too seriously! Besides, there's no reason for anyone to fear. The Watch have doubled their patrols tonight. The whole city will be out on the hunt tonight!"

Tamerlan's mind was so focused on what was coming next that the return back to *The Copper Tincture* and dropping off the delivery of lavender flew by, and he found himself in his room. He shut his door behind him, the basket with his supplies in the bottom still clutched to his chest as he leaned his forehead against the door and caught his breath.

If this worked – if this magic really came when called, then he wouldn't go running off like a fool tonight. Not with the whole City Watch on alert. Not with patrols doubled. He'd practice somewhere safe. He'd make sure he had the skills this time before he launched himself on the palace.

But *would* it work?

With shaking hands, he pulled the ingredients out of the basket, placing them on the shelves of his wardrobe. He had more than twice what he needed if he'd calculated correctly. Some to test. More to use when he needed it if the test worked. He had a feeling about this recipe. A feeling of how it *should* go as if he were making a soup he'd eaten a thousand times but never made. Maybe it was in his blood or in the memories passed down from his ancestors. Maybe it was just a trick of his mind.

He didn't need to panic. He didn't need to run around like a boy with a half-hatched plan like last night. He needed to take deep breaths and do this carefully. One step at a time.

He stripped out of his guild uniform and down to his smallclothes. First things first. No need to ruin his uniform if the first experiment didn't work.

His door crashed open and he jumped, dropping the uniform on the floor.

Dathan strode into the room, his steps rolling as he displayed his Deathless Pirate costume, a pile of cloth in his arms. "Great, isn't it? Where's yours?"

He pushed past Tamerlan, looking into the wardrobe. Tamerlan held his breath. If Dathan saw …

He looked around the room. There were no weapons. No rope. If his friend saw the illicit haul, he had no way to stop him from reporting what he'd seen. Could he even stop Dathan if he wanted to? Tamerlan had never hit another person in his life. He didn't want to start with Dathan.

"There's nothing in here!" Dathan spun around.

Tamerlan held his breath.

"You know you can't go as naked-boy, right?" Dathan reached out with his pirate hook and jabbed Tamerlan's ribs. Tamerlan tried not to look too relieved as he laughed.

"I'm twenty. I'm not a boy."

"Sure. Tell that to your beardless face. And then thank Dathan, your rescuer!"

"What?"

Dathan shoved the bundle of cloth at him. "I had an extra costume – Lila Cherrylocks. You're going to be the life of the party! Don't take too long. I can't wait to see their faces!"

He closed the door behind him and Tamerlan threw the clothing onto his small cot and pulled a chair from the wall to shove against the door.

He sat down on it, head in his hands. What if someone else burst in before he finished? He'd thought his heart might seize up when Dathan looked into the wardrobe.

With a shudder, he mentally pulled himself back together. If he was worried about being caught, his best option was to do what he had to do quickly and while everyone else was distracted. The sun was already setting outside.

Voices and laughter passed in the hall beyond his door, steps on the stairs and banging doors as the other apprentices and masters prepared for a night of fun, searching for treasure.

Tamerlan waited until the voices faded and the laughter stopped before standing up again on trembling legs and reaching for the illuminated page under his pillow.

It was now or never.

SECOND NIGHT OF SUMMERNIGHT

11: Bridge of Legends

Tamerlan

Tamerlan pulled out the small set of scales and the clay bowl he'd snatched from the workshops earlier that day and placed them on the tiny washstand in the corner of the room, chopping, weighing and mixing ingredients into the clay bowl. With no quantities written into the recipe, he was trying to add them by feel. But how did you get a "feel" for something you'd never done before?

He was working only on instinct, using less of the more potent ingredients, more of the less potent ones and hoping he was doing it right. When he had the ingredients arranged as he liked, he carefully lit a tiny fire in the grate in his room. It was for winter. No one would light a fire on a heat-clinging night like tonight which meant that if anyone saw the fire, they would be suspicious. Hopefully, the chimney wasn't blocked by bird's nests or the smoke didn't alert someone to what he was doing.

Feeling guilty, he opened his paned window to the outside world. If there was extra smoke, maybe it could help to vent it. He was already sweating, and the fire was just a single licking flame. Sweat slicked his forehead and back as he worked over the fire, building it gently.

And now it was decision time. Should he try to light the ingredients in the bowl with some of the lit wood, or should he wait until there were proper embers to place in the bowl like the Smudgers did?

He should wait.

But as the seconds ticked into minutes, worry wriggled in his belly like an asp. Impatiently, he seized one of the fiery sticks and stuck it into the bowl. The flame went out. The ingredients were too wet – too fresh – to simply light from a small flame.

The fire popped and spat in the grate, mocking him.

But now the orrisleaf was smoldering in the bowl. If he waited much longer, that ingredient would be gone while the others still wouldn't be lit. This wasn't the right way to test a new recipe. He was working too quickly, too hastily. He'd lost his opportunity. And if he used the rest of the orrisleaf he'd stolen and it didn't work, he'd have lost his chance tonight entirely and he might as well be out hunting in the scavenger hunt with the others.

Tamerlan bit back a curse. He could see himself losing the chance, being caught tomorrow for the supplies he stole. Or being caught by the Watch or by Master Kurond.

His breath was coming too quickly. He was panicking. He should grab a hold of himself and calm down.

But instead, he grabbed the bowl of ingredients and threw it into the fire, sticking his head into the fireplace over the grate and breathing deeply. That's all it took for the Smudgers, right? A lungful of this stuff?

Tamerlan sucked in the acrid smoke. It stung his lungs, burning, irritating.

Gasping for breath, he scrambled back, coughing with lungs so raw he thought they would seize up. A sweet but bitter scent swirled around him.

This was a terrible idea.

Terrible.

He tried to straighten, but he doubled over in a fit of coughing, his fingers grasping at the floor, trying to brace himself against the heaving coughs, growing bloody as the nails tore on the stone.

Why couldn't he get a breath of fresh air? The window was open. He should be able to breathe, but as he gasped, wheezing, his lungs couldn't seem to take a full breath. They screamed in his chest demanding oxygen.

What's this charming little hovel?

He fell to the ground, rolling to look at the bare beams of the ceiling as he sucked in shallow breaths. He must have almost blacked out.

It was the only way to explain the female voice that spoke in his mind.

Not the only way.

Tamerlan got to his feet, his movements smooth and graceful. Even his breathing seemed to slow, the hammering of his heart calming. He looked down at his shaking body, dirty from where dirt on the floor had stuck to nervous sweat.

This won't do.

He was moving to the wash basin before he knew why, washing carefully.

Aren't you a pretty man? I don't think there's enough fat to even pinch on this body of yours. And there are muscles besides. What do you do to build these lean muscles, potion-boy?

He craned his head as if trying to see himself from behind.

Oh yes, I like you. But as pretty as you are to admire, we can't go out like this. Ugh. Those aren't your clothes, are they?

Tamerlan looked at his clothing sprawled across the floor where he'd left them. The second set still wasn't clean from yesterday's river adventure. He spun, noticing the clothing on the bed and quickly picked them up, looking them over.

Good stitching. Nice fabric. Hmmm. I wouldn't have expected someone as clearly down-and-out as you to be able to find these, but I do like them – even if they have a bit too masculine of a cut for me. And a long red wig? Really? Fake hair is never as good as the real thing.

He was dressing before he knew it. Why? He didn't want to wear the Lila Cherrylocks costume or go on a scavenger hunt.

Is that what this is? I suppose I should be flattered, but honestly, you're far too broad-shouldered to make a good female. And these trousers are going to be loose in all the wrong places and tight in all the right ones.

Tamerlan stopped dressing. Or at least, he told his body to stop dressing. And yet, his boots were slipping on his feet and the wig was going on his head. Wait! Help!

He was stuck inside his own body as the throaty, sultry voice in his head continued to dress.

I suppose we shouldn't use the door. Too conspicuous. But that window looks tempting. Shall we?

And then he – they? – were out the window like a flash and climbing easily down the stone wall as if Tamerlan just scrambled up and down walls spider-style all the time. Instead of wanting to throw up at the very thought of it.

We are not *throwing up. Get a hold of yourself. You're riding with Lila Cherrylocks tonight!*

Ha! That was a joke! Tamerlan might be dressed as Lila Cherrylocks – dressed like a woman! They needed to turn back before someone saw him like this! - but he was riding in his own head like a passenger while some horrific demon ran his body and chattered in his ears. Who knew what she would have him do?

Party? Steal a few things? Maybe win this scavenger hunt you've been telling me about. What are you looking for?

Tamerlan didn't know and he definitely wasn't going to take her to Master Juggernaut's to find out. First, he needed to see if she really could break into locked buildings. Then, if she proved she could, they'd need to break into where his sister was being held. He could dress like a girl all night if he could do that.

I like the idea of visiting this Juggernaut. He has the list for the game? I haven't been in a scavenger hunt in ages *and I love a good chase!*

No. Positively not. What a waste that would be! He'd done all this to save his sister, not to give a demon an evening of fun.

They were sauntering down the lantern-lit street almost as if the demon already knew which way to find Master Juggernaut. Tamerlan fought against the sway in his walk. He did not walk like that!

I'm no demon, pretty man. I'm who we're dressed as – Lila Cherrylocks – and I walk with a sway in my hips.

It couldn't be true. The real Lila Cherrylocks had been a famous thief and brigand.

Yes.

She'd made her fortune outsmarting the nobles of her time and taking every magical item in the city hostage to store in her haunted catacombs under the city.

Yes.

And then she'd died when a rival feigned love for her and seduced her into a deadly trap.

Indeed.

So, she couldn't be here in Tamerlan's head, controlling his body.

And yet I am. What did you think would happen when you opened the Bridge of Legends?

The what?

They sliced through the streets like a fish through water, Lila sniffing the air and taking in the sights like she was drinking in the city itself, eating its atmosphere, reveling in the excited squeals and hushed whispers of the huddled groups scouring the city with blue rolls of parchment in their hands.

The Bridge between this world and the next life? The Bridge to the heroes of Legend – to me. You opened it wide and called and it just so happened that I was nearby.

It was meant to help him. It was meant to be for times of great need.

Maybe it is. How would I know? I haven't seen anyone use it in all the time I've been a Legend.

Why the smoke, though?

Don't you know that the smoke ceremonies open you up to spirits?

Wasn't that a figure of speech?

Nope. Isn't learning fun?

But it was useless if Lila was just going to use it as a chance to have a night out. Worse than useless when Tamerlan only had a few days left until Summernight. They were wasting one of them.

Ah! Don't you know that Festivals are a time when magic comes closer to the world? All that belief out there – all that hope! – it opens doors that don't open at other times.

And it opened the chance to have my world end.

Are you always such a gloomy companion?

She'd found her way through the winding city streets to *Juggernauts' Alchemical Tonics* as if she knew the way.

It's in your memory.

The massive building, built of green jade pillars and steps and inlaid with brass polished to look like gold, had a wide-peaked roof with corners that turned up at the ends. Ruddy red roof tiles clashed with the green jade. Like Master Juggernaut, it was bold and eye-catching.

Its owner stood on the top step, holding his arms up for silence. They had arrived just in time for him to speak. Dragon spit! Dragon spit and the fires of the underworld! He'd been seen.

Dathan shot him a grin from the crowd, motioning Tamerlan over. Lila moved to join him and Tamerlan gritted his teeth – figuratively. He couldn't even do that in his own body. He couldn't even blush as every eye turned toward him with grins and snickers at his costume. Couldn't even hang his head in shame. She was going to ruin everything.

Look, you're spoiling this for me. How about a deal? You go along with my fun and I'll break into something for you tonight as a 'test' just like you want. Then we both get something out of this. Deal?

What choice did he have?

Well, I could skip the part that makes you happy and just do what I want.

Deal.

Get ready, pretty man! This is going to get good.

I'm Tamerlan.

Like I need to know your name. Her mental snort made him want to weep.

"Alchemists!" Master Juggernaut roared.

Around him, cheers rose.

"Are we going to win this hunt?"

"Yes!" the answer soared from every throat, including Tamerlan's.

Beside Master Juggernaut, even Master Kurond was grinning.

"It's not going to be easy, boys and girls," Juggernaut called out. He was loving the spotlight. "They don't give you a list like this and expect it to be easy! Do we want easy?"

"No!"

Great. Lila was yelling, 'no' right along with the rest. She was loving this.

"Do we want to be challenged?" He made a fist. "Do we want to have to slug our way to victory?"

"Yes!"

"We have until dawn! Collect your parchment from Kaviness. Bring your treasures here at the end of the night. I expect to see every one of them when gold lights the horizon! Now, tell me, who is going to win this year's hunt?"

"Alchemists!" we roared and then Juggernaut was joining Kurond and the other masters, patting each other on the backs and laughing and poor Kaviness who was balding at twenty-two and who jumped if you said his name too loud, was handing out parchment slips to everyone.

Tamerlan grabbed his as Lila made his heart race with anticipation.

"This is crazy!" Dathan said from beside Tamerlan. But he didn't sound disappointed. He sounded eager. "There are hundreds of things on this list. How will the smaller teams even do half of this?"

"I don't know," Tamerlan said, reading the list. It wasn't just common things on the list. There were also some things that could only be acquired illegally.

"A human hand?" Dathan asked skeptically. "Where would we even get that?"

Tamerlan shuddered. But it wouldn't have to be taken from the living. There were crypts beneath the city. There were sarcophaguses above it.

"The Satyr's Diamond? What is that?" he asked, amazement dripping from his tone. "A Grimoire? I don't even think those exist! Are you reading this, Tamerlan?"

Tamerlan was. Lila was reading it, too. He hated how she clutched that scrap of parchment, like she wanted to keep it forever.

This is going to be great. We just need to lose this guy. I can tell you know where the libraries are.

Libraries?

For the grimoire, obviously.

If the libraries made you stamp your blood on the pages to take out a book, what would they do to someone who tried to take one?

Tamerlan clapped Dathan on the shoulder as Lila spoke with his tongue. "I'll get the grimoire. You work on that hand. You're friends with that kid who works for the crypt-keeper, aren't you?"

Dathan looked as ill as Tamerlan felt.

Well, you *are the one who wanted to break into something. Let's go try out my lockpicking and theft skills, shall we? And maybe we can find a grimoire in the process!*

12: Grimoire

Tamerlan

Tamerlan had expected the University District to be nearly empty at this time of night. The only district not to use street lights at all, and the district with the largest plazas and open spaces, the University District was wreathed in shadows made long by moonlight, but it was far from empty.

Groups of people – anywhere from knots of five to single individuals – roamed the streets, checking the doors and windows of the Libraries, seeking a way inside.

"Are you here for the Hunt?" A woman asked from a mysterious booth set up against the Queen Mer library.

The booth hadn't been there yesterday. It didn't look like something the Librarians would approve of. They liked things that fit their rules. The garish colors of the booth and the glowing green lantern set on the front table were not the kinds of things they would approve of. Neither was the young woman with hair pulled back under a high hat, her figure hidden under a floor-length black coat with a high collar. It was partly unbuttoned to show a golden waistcoat and a green scarf around her neck. I knew this legend. She was dressed as Grandfather Timeless.

"I might be," Tamerlan answered, smiling. He should be avoiding attention, not speaking to someone who might remember him later. But Lila had other plans. "Can you help me with it?"

The woman smiled mysteriously. "Time knows no beginning and no end. No master and no friend."

"And does 'Time' happen to know where I can find a grimoire?" Tamerlan asked, leaning in a little closer than he would have liked as a blush crept up on the woman's face. She was young, he realized. Not much older than he was.

"All things are the same to time. What is a grimoire now was a sheep and berries before it was parchment and ink. What it will be hereafter is dust and then maybe brick or road or house. What it will be after that … who can say? Perhaps a seed will sprout and pull from it enough life to rise into a tree. Perhaps a man will eat of the fruit. Perhaps what is a grimoire today will be a king tomorrow." She held out a handful of dust on a velvet gloved hand. "Grimoire for your thoughts?"

It was just religious talk. The Timekeepers were popular around here. And they all said the same thing – embrace the all. Everything is inside everything else. Time is timeless. Life is lifeless.

"Maybe I'll be back," Tamerlan said with a wink, hating himself for it.

The girl laughed and the dust was back under the counter. He wondered how many people had bought a handful of dust tonight. He didn't care if Lila wanted to buy dust as long as she did what she needed to do and stopped wasting time talking to cultists as they swindled hopeful treasure seekers.

As Tamerlan turned away, another group of seekers strode up to the booth, laughing and jostling one another impatiently. One of the girls – dressed like Maid Chaos, winked at him as he sauntered by. She elbowed her friend – a laughing Deathless Pirate and they both doubled over in laughter.

Yeah, yeah. What was a guy doing dressed as Lila Cherrylocks? He knew he looked ridiculous.

So ridiculous that no one saw me swipe the lockpicks from that huckster selling dust.

She stole lockpicks? From a thief?

What did you think we were doing there? Flirting?

Ummm … yes?

Ha! I like men with broad shoulders and not a pinch of fat, Tamerlan. I don't like girls in Grandfather Time outfits.

Tamerlan was still blinking in surprise when he ducked into a thick shadow and rushed up the stairs to the Queen Mer Library. The octopuses and curling waves carved into the friezes around the main doors seemed to be mocking him as he sidled up to the doors – twice his height and carved of stone – and pulled a set of gleaming tools out of a velvet bag in his pocket.

She hadn't been lying. She really had picked the pocket of Grandfather Timeless. And she'd done it without being caught … even by Tamerlan.

See? They don't call you 'Master Thief" because you bake great bread. I earned my reputation.

The picks sank into the lock, maneuvered by his expert fingers and with a series of clicks and a gentle hand on the door handle, the door swung silently open.

Tamerlan gasped as he tucked the lockpicks away and slid into the doorway.

The library was dark. Instinctually, he slipped to the front desk, lit in a circular halo by the round window in the wall of the lobby. Moonlight gilded the desk in silver and velvet black. And on the desk, bright in the light of the moon, was the logbook with his own name and fingerprint on the ledger. His thumb pricked where it had been poked to make the mark.

Tamerlan reached past the logbook to a set of books so massive that they were chained to the desk along its length. He'd never opened one before, but Lila seemed to know her way. He lifted the front cover of the first, his index finger sailing down a list. Closed the cover. Moved on. The next book was the same and then the next and then on the fourth book, Lila paused, noting a series of letters and numbers beside a single entry.

Books of Magic, practical XIV34 Z26 A53

He opened the book further, turning four inches of thick paper all at once, his finger twisting the top corner closer to get a better angle on the moonbeam.

XIV13

He flicked through the pages, licking his finger to turn them more easily.

XIV34

There was a list:

Magic: A Chronicle

Magic of the Neverworlds

Magic Potions: a practical primer

It carried on across both pages and probably further still.

Tamerlan's finger skimmed along until it found:

Magic: Grimoire of the Taslan Empire

He was moving before he realized what Lila had come for, slipping into the library beyond. He'd never set foot so far into the library! The shelves loomed like mountain ranges waiting to be mined for golden secrets and silver sorrows. He felt a thrill of delight just looking at them all. If only he could spend all night flipping through them and investigating what the Library held.

He ghosted along the corridors between them. How did he even know where to go?

Don't you see the numbers on the plaques?

And there they were *B16 D42.*

A little farther.

And farther they went, into the mouth of the library. Tamerlan felt as if he were being swallowed by an ancient beast, a creature of imagination and memory, a creature that would swallow him whole. Perhaps in time, it would spit his body back into the land of the living, but it would never again relinquish his mind.

It was the teeth, he decided. The teeth carved along the tops of the shelves between the glowing, moonlit skylights.

Are you always so fanciful?

He'd reached his destination.

Z26 A53

And now his hands skimmed along the leather-bound books, stroking them like the hair of a lover as his fingertips skimmed their bindings. Thick, thin, rough, smooth, each a repository of a world known only within the pages of that one tome – that one, momentary glimpse into the nebulous mind of the one who penned it.

You're a daydreamer. I should have known. A practical person would never have opened the Bridge of Legends.

His hand snatched a book off the shelf – a small book, no bigger than his hand, but thick as his wrist. On the cover, the title was stamped: *Grimoire of the Taslan Empire.*

Success!

They were already rushing down the aisles back the way they came, Tamerlan wishing he could stay just a little while longer. Lila ready to bring her prize back to Master Juggernaut.

I'm surprised you want to stay. After all, I proved I could break into anywhere. Isn't that what you wanted? Didn't you have somewhere else you wanted us to go?

He did!

If they hurried, there would still be time!

He skidded around the shelf and right into a shadowy figure. He tucked the grimoire into his belt in a fluid motion and then his hands came up, grabbing the figure by the neck and slamming her against the end of the bookshelf.

His victim cried out, her voice sharp and muted at the same time. He was cutting off her breath. He could feel her kicking and fighting against his hands.

Stop! Please, stop! Didn' Lila Cherrylocks have a conscience?

Are you kidding?!

Dragon's blood! What kind of monster was she? He didn't kill innocent bystanders!

I –

And then suddenly his hands were his own. He released the choking girl and her dark hair fell away from her face as she sucked in a breath.

Sian! He'd almost killed Sian.

With a moan of misery, he ran. At any moment, Lila would seize control of him again and when that happened, he needed to be far from here – far from Sian, far from this library, far from everything.

He ran out the front door of the library, stumbled down the steps, crashing into a party of searchers. He didn't see faces or even costumes as he clawed his way free and back to his feet, darting into the night.

It wasn't until he reached the Alchemist District that he realized Lila Cherrylocks was gone. Gone completely.

His chance to steal anything else had fled with her.

13: A Curious Crime

Marielle

"And then he … he choked me … I thought I was going to die!" the round-faced girl sobbed as she told her story. Marielle tried to school her features to sympathy, but it was as hard as pushing a ship up a hill.

She smelled magic everywhere. It tingled, turquoise and gold, vanilla and lilac, and bright sparkles still puffing in the air even though the scent trail was hours old. It made her feel more alive, more real, able to see every ambition come true. It made her senses sharp and every nerve on her body tingle. To call it addictive, would be an understatement.

It was hard to pay attention to any other scent. The scents of Carnelian – the usual rust and spring grass – and the sobbing girl – dust and ink and some sort of shattered hope in a pale blueberry – faded into monochrome in comparison. Though there was a faint whiff of something deceitful about the girl.

"And you can't remember anything about him? You didn't see a face or clothing?" Carnelian pressed.

She was barely holding back her impatience. Like Marielle, she'd already been up all night patrolling, but the patrols in the University District were caught up in something bigger than this. On the other side of the District, a Librarian had been murdered in the night and then dressed to look like the Lady Sacrifice. Something like that required all the Watch Officers and Scenters assigned to this district, as well as the District Guard in their fancy uniforms. So, after a long shift, Carnelian and Marielle had been stopped on their way back to the Watch House and sent to the University District to investigate.

"He was dressed like Lila Cherrylocks. Long red hair and all," the girl said. She kept looking toward the Head Librarian for help, but the severe woman standing by the doors to the Queen Mer Library seemed more concerned about having watchmen in her precious library than about any apprentice.

"It was a valuable book," she stated for the fourth time. "A grimoire. Priceless. It must be found."

"We'll do everything we can to find it," Carnelian assured her gruffly. She didn't care about books, but she also didn't like it when people questioned her competence. Carnelian was all Jingen City Watch.

"Are you sure there isn't more?" Marielle asked the girl – Sian. Yes, that was her name. She thought she could almost smell something familiar under the buzz and pop of magic. But it was hard to concentrate on anything else when the addictive scent of magic swirled in the air. Was that a hint of the pulsing orange ginger and gold she'd smelled on her elusive prey, or was she just hoping that she smelled it again? She inhaled sharply, trying to pull it in, but the magic was too strong. It sizzled through her brain like popping Nightbursts.

"I'm … I'm sure," the girl said nervously.

"He didn't perform some kind of magic?" Marielle pressed.

"No!" the girl squeaked.

Carnelian sighed. "Okay, we'll do what we can, but with the Summernight Festival unfolding around us there will be any number of people in Lila Cherrylocks costumes."

"But will all of them smell of magic?" a resonant voice asked from behind them.

Before Marielle even turned, she knew who it was. Oranges and cloves mixed in with the heady scent of magic. Oddly, his presence seemed to make the magic scent even stronger, thicker, more alive.

"You smell it, don't you, Scenter?" the Lord Mythos asked Marielle.

"As you say, Lord Mythos," she agreed.

Why was he here? If he was going to arrive unexpectedly, wouldn't it make sense that he'd be at that horrific murder on the other side of the District and not here at a simple library for the theft of a book?

"Walk with me, Scenter," he said.

Carnelian shot Marielle a warning glance. Was she warning her not to go or that she had better go?

Marielle swallowed and followed him out of the Library and onto the wide steps that looked out over the plaza below all the way to the hazy sea in the distance. The call of seabirds over the ocean was barely audible as the air slowly warmed to the rising sun.

"You are wondering why I'm at the site of a simple theft," he said, raising a single eyebrow.

For some reason, his given name came back to her. Etienne. When he drew her in so personally, she almost forgot he was Lord Mythos and not simply Etienne Velendark – the young man with the concerned look on his face and a scent both fresh and compelling.

"You can speak. I'm not a god." He smirked at her suddenly-wide-eyes and she felt her cheeks heating.

In the background, she could hear Carnelian trying to assure the Librarian that they would do their jobs while disentangling herself from the dusty woman.

"I might have been wondering," Marielle admitted.

"You can smell the magic here. Recent. Intense."

She nodded. She could hardly smell anything else. He smiled at her nod.

"I can sense it, too. Oh, not like you can, of course," his smile was charming. Inviting. Marielle suddenly wondered about the rumors she'd heard about the Lord Mythos. Sometimes when people were drunk or angry you heard things. 'He loves girls,' they said. Which wasn't so bad except that they followed it with silence or stories about girls who had gone missing. Girls who had never been found dead or alive. "No, I sense the residue the way any magic wielder can. You know that I guard our city, do you not?"

Marielle nodded.

"Do you know that I don't just guard us from trouble without, but also from trouble within? From the disasters that could befall us if we fail in our duties? Or if we stir up trouble in other realms – other realities beyond this one?"

"Are you saying you're some kind of magical guardian of the city? That there are laws for magic, too?"

That would be appealing. Laws made everything simpler.

She could smell a whiff of arrogance – of deep pride – of certainty. It was violet and smelled of pine and mint, but it was hard to parse it exactly from the heady smell of magic clinging to him and flooding the air around him with the caress of promise.

He laughed. It was a sweet sound.

"I suppose you could call it that. And I suppose you could call our traditions laws. And that is why this investigation is important to me. We can't have loose magic running through this city doing whatever it pleases – or undoing it. Do you understand?"

She nodded. Stability was important. Maintaining order made life safe for everyone.

"It's more important even than the break-in attempt at the Seven Suns Palace." He leaned in close, but his look was more than confidential. It was as if he were studying her even now. "I'm relying on you, Marielle. Sniff out this magic for me. Help me bring it to the light."

"I won't fail you." She thrilled with the task. Her job was always important – always vital. Without laws, a city failed. Without laws, the people of Jingen would be stunted and warped. But this … this was bigger, more important still. Someone out there wasn't just breaking the laws of the city. They were breaking the laws of the world. Was this the Real Law Captain Ironarm had talked about?

"Good. I need to tell you more about what we are up against. To help the investigation. I will have instructions sent to your Watch House in the Government District."

Marielle nodded but he was already leaving with a flick of his small cape and a rattle of the scabbarded rapier at his side. With a wave of his hand, his guards materialized from the shadows around the library, surrounding him like a pack of wolves around a magnificent stag.

"I hope you know what you're doing," Carnelian said wryly from behind Marielle.

Marielle turned to her with a lifted eyebrow. The light streaming from around Carnelian's face as she blocked the dawn from view should have made her look angelic. Instead, it only highlighted the way her lip curled in suspicion.

"I'm keeping us on the most important investigation in Jingen," Marielle said. "I'm getting you a win that your fellow Watch Officers will be buying you drinks to celebrate for months to come."

"From where I stand, it looks like you're flirting with death," Carnelian muttered.

But she was wrong. Marielle could tell this was just as important as Lord Mythos said it was. And he didn't mean her harm. He was just as ambitious and devoted as she was. They both just wanted to see the city stay safe and the laws upheld.

They both served something greater than themselves. What could be better than that? Marielle smiled as the minty scent of certainty wafted up from her own pores. She loved that smell.

14: A Curioser Invitation

Marielle

"What is the meaning of this, Marielle Valenspear?" Captain Ironarm was waiting when they returned to the Guardhouse.

She stood in the middle of the main room where the desks were piled with ledgers and ink interspersed with teapots and cups, cans of armor polish and sharpening stones. Only the On-Watch Officer at the front desk was in the room with them. Everyone else was either in their beds or out on the streets. Marielle and Carnelian had missed the change of watch this morning.

Marielle fought a yawn. She needed her blankets. It had been a long night and now a long morning. Captain Ironarm had a small notecard in her hands with gold edging.

"This arrived for you from the Lord Mythos. It's an invitation to the Legend Ball at the Seven Suns Palace tonight. More than that, there is a box with it. A box – I have no doubt – that contains a dress for that same event."

Captain Ironarm's face was flushed and her grey hair looked frizzier than usual. She'd been up all night, too. Didn't she want to crawl under her blankets instead of standing here in the middle of the guardhouse dressing Marielle down in front of everyone? Electric blue sizzled around her as she spoke.

"You," Captain Ironarm continued, "are nothing special, Marielle Valenspear. You are a Scenter – and barely that! Do you think you have the right to consort with Landholds?"

"No, Captain Ironarm," Marielle said weakly. She was too tired for this conversation. She hadn't expected the invitation or the dress. Truth be told, they both made her nervous. What sort of expectations would go along with a gift like that? Marielle was not a girl from the Red Light Streets at the west end of the Trade District and she didn't want to be reminded how close she'd come to that fate.

"And you, Carnelian," Captain Ironarm spun to look at Marielle's fellow officer. "You couldn't keep a better eye on your fellow officer?"

Carnelian's face turned dark, camphor filling the air around her, and Marielle felt a spike of fear. The look Carnelian shot her promised retribution and the garnet scent of rage and pitch told her she had every reason to be fearful.

"I'm a Watch Officer, not a babysitter," she spat.

"You're what I say you are," Captain Ironarm said, her voice hard as a hammer driving spikes into rock. "Just like *I* am what the Watch Commander says *I* am. And he says I'm to do whatever is necessary to avoid offending the Lord Mythos.

Now that the two of you have put us in this mess, it is up to you, Marielle," here she looked back at Marielle, her tone of command ringing, "to meet the Lord Mythos' expectations. You will go to the party. You will do as he expects. You will keep yourself from any further entanglements, and then promptly return to your post. And it is up to you, Carnelian," she shifted her cantankerous glare to Carnelian, "to manage patrol without your partner tonight. Find an unassigned watchman to join you. I think Dacrin is on clean-up duty. You can take him."

"Dacrin! But Captain – !" Carnelian practically vibrated with emotion.

"Cool it, Carnelian Fishnetter. I've heard it all. And you're lucky that's the only thing I'm assigning you. You should know better than this."

She thrust the box and card into Marielle's stunned arms and then strode away, banging the door to her office shut behind her.

Marielle scurried to the stairs. She wanted to read the card for herself and look at what was in the box. She'd been ordered to comply, but she still had no idea what that might mean, and the roiling scents of scarlet anger and vermillion humiliation smelling of burnt wood and camphor hung heavy in the large room.

"You know why the Captain is angry, don't you?" Carnelian asked from two stairs behind her on the staircase. As fast as Marielle climbed, her fellow officer kept up. "You've heard the rumors."

"I've been a bit too busy to listen to rumors," Marielle said, her face hot with embarrassment. She *had* been busy. Scenter training was grueling and started when a child was only seven years old. But that didn't mean she didn't have ears. And on the rare occasion that her mother visited her, the only thing she ever wanted to talk about was city gossip. She had heard.

"You won't be the first girl to fall for Lord Mythos. They say he makes girls fall in love with him and then they're never seen again."

"I'm in no danger of having my heart broken," Marielle argued, speeding up. She was getting breathless. It didn't help that the walls felt like they were closing in. The closer that Summernight got, the more she felt like fate was playing a merry game with her, dragging her down a path she never meant to be on.

"That's what they all say. But they all fall in love. And then they all disappear."

Marielle stumbled on the next step and then froze, spinning to confront Carnelian. "And what? He hangs them up in his wardrobe and keeps them there like a collection of dresses?"

"I never –"

"He eats their hearts to gain their maiden power?"

"I – "

"He uses their souls to fuel his magic while he feasts upon their bodies? I've heard all those rumors and more! Or do you forget who I was born to?"

Now Carnelian was the one with the darkening countenance, both of them gasping for breath. Anger clouded Marielle's vision so that all she could see was the cynical twist of Carnelian's mouth and the emerald musk jealousy of her scent sinking into the walls around them so strong it was almost as strong as the scent of magic.

"I'm just saying that I can protect you," Carnelian said. "I can go in your place. I'll make sure that nothing happens to you."

She looked really upset and a small pleading, worried thread joined the jealousy. A barely distinguishable strain of ochre and smoked paprika in the jade clouds around her.

"I can take care of myself," Marielle said. And she knew it would be true because it had to be. The Captain wouldn't say no to anything Lord Mythos asked for. Carnelian, fueled by jealousy might get in her way, but she didn't think that would stop Lord Mythos from getting anything that he wanted. And she was worried. She was worried because the scent of him still clung to her and every inch of her was desperate to breathe in that magic again.

Maybe the rumors were true. Maybe that scent alone could drive women mad and make them fling themselves from the tops of buildings or take poison because they could not have the magical ruler of the city. But it wouldn't be true of Marielle.

She slipped into her room, ignoring Carnelian's farewell and shutting the door firmly behind her, latching it before she placed the box on her bed and tiredly read the note. It was an invitation, printed on a shiny card.

ADMIT ONE

To the Seven Suns Palace

For the Ball of Legends

On the third night of Summernight.

And then in a fine, flowing hand was penned:

Marielle,

I hope that you have considered my offer and will join me at the Seven Suns Palace tonight. Present this to the guards to receive entry. I have provided adequate attire. Everything will become clearer once you see what I have to show you.

Lord Mythos.

Marielle opened the box, her heart pounding with nervous fear. Inside, laid carefully in the box was a Summernight costume. A filmy, gauzy white dress with a white brushed-silk corset and a pale tulle skirt dipped at the bottom in some light color that Marielle could not see. It swept up to the sides with shining ribbons. The very essence of sweet innocence – the costume of the Lady Sacrifice.

Marielle shivered. Of all the Legends, this is the costume that he sent her?

Was there something he was trying to tell her? Marielle chewed her lip nervously and thought about all the things she couldn't possibly know.

Maybe Carnelian had been right after all.

Maybe she was in real trouble.

15: Noxious Threat

Tamerlan

Tamerlan prepared the concoction carefully, following the directions that Master Kurond had written in his spiky script.

"After you finish with that, go to bed, Tamerlan," Master Kurond said tiredly. "You did well in the scavenger hunt. The whole Alchemist Guild is walking on clouds today. We're the only ones to fill the complete list. Or at least, that's what they told Master Juggernaut when he turned in our chest and list at the Seven Sun Palace. No one else had a grimoire. No, don't tell me where you got it. I still don't want to know. And no one else had Dathan's stroke of genius and managed to turn in a skeletal hand. You're both doing me proud. Mrs. Shen will leave fresh clothes hanging on your door for tonight."

"Tonight?"

"Did you forget? One of our rewards for winning is an invitation to the Legend Ball, and you can hardly go in your apprentice clothing. I went ahead and purchased clothing for all the apprentices. Wear it so you don't disgrace us."

The door creaked behind him when he left and Tamerlan lost himself in the routine work of compounding the ointment from the recipe. Easy enough. And a way for the guild to make money to fund their other projects.

He didn't even look up when the door creaked open again or when a pair of soft slippers whisked across the wood floor.

"Ahem."

Tamerlan almost dropped his stone pestle when he did look up.

Sian!

His eyes went wide, his breath choking in his throat.

"I know it was you," she said in a wavering voice.

Her hood was up, wreathing her face in shadows, but Tamerlan could still see the ugly bruises ringing her neck. Bruises he was responsible for. He made a sound in the back of his throat and took a step forward on impulse.

She stepped back, slamming into a workbench behind her and scattering herbs across the floor.

"Don't come any closer!"

Tamerlan froze. "I won't. I promise. I'm so sorry!"

He felt like he had lost a tiny piece of himself at the look in her eyes.

"So, it *was* you," the words were almost a sob. "I didn't tell the Watch. I don't want you to be in trouble, Tamerlan. I used to think … I always thought … You used to be a nice boy. The kind of boy a girl felt safe around."

"Sian," he said, hands raised defensively. Her every word was a blow. He'd hurt her. He'd almost killed her. "I'm so sorry."

"Don't." She flinched from his words. "I didn't tell them this time, but if I ever see you again outside of Library business, I will tell. I'll tell anyone who will listen. Don't ever come near me again, Tamerlan!"

Her eyes were wet with unshed tears and her voice shook in a way that begged him to still it, to iron out the wrinkles of her crumpled heart. But she was already leaving, her threat still hanging in the air like a noxious smell.

Tamerlan clenched and unclenched his fists in frustration. There was nothing he could do to make this right. He couldn't even apologize. And he couldn't even tell himself it wouldn't happen again, because as soon as he was done compounding this ointment he was going to go up to his room and weigh and measure the rest of his ingredients so he could bathe in smoke again tonight.

Should he stop? Should he think about what might happen if he used the smoke again?

Lila Cherrylocks had almost murdered that poor girl with *his* hands, but she'd also done what she said she could – she'd broken into the Library with ease. It would be just as easy for her to break into the Sunset Tower, especially now that he had an invitation to the Legend Ball. If he chose not to do that, his sister would die. And he hadn't actually killed Sian. He had stopped Lila in time.

He would just have to stop her again if things got out of hand. Until Lila Cherrylocks broke his sister free from the Sunset Tower, Tamerlan would just have to eat his guilt and let it haunt him from the inside while he did what he had to on the outside.

He ran his hand through his hair. None of this was what he'd planned, but with only three nights left, what other option was there?

THIRD NIGHT OF SUMMERNIGHT

16: Legend Ball

Marielle

When Marielle had been a little girl her favorite story had been the story of Queen Mer because Variena had been excellent at telling it. Her mother had draped long scarves around herself like water and seaweed as she told the story.

"The Queen of the Sea is as moody as the sea herself," her mother had said, waving her arms under the scarves like the shifting tides. "And like the sea, she claims the lives of men and swallows their fortunes. Like the sea itself, she rises up to judge wickedness on the earth and swallow up the haughty."

"Like the Dragonblooded?" young Marielle had asked, wide-eyed.

"Some," her mother agreed, "But Queen Mer is not concerned with individual guilt. She swallows a ship for the sake of one man in it. Swallows a city for the sins of just a few. Beware the vengeance of the Queen! Her wrath is great! A woman, little flower, a woman never forgets a wrong done to her!"

And then her mother's eyes would go wide and she would wave her arms like a giant octopus and chase small Marielle around the room until Marielle folded into a little bundle of laughter and delight and her mother would scoop her up and put her to bed for the night while she entertained her guests.

That was the closest that Marielle had ever come to a re-enacted Legend.

Until tonight.

Marielle straightened her scarf carefully. She wasn't used to such a loose, gauzy scarf, but using her uniform scarf wouldn't make sense at a party and the one that Lord Mythos had provided matched the dress.

The dress felt too pretty to wear. It had been too pretty when she put it on in her room – all clinging, filmy cloth like soft silken clouds – and it was too pretty here. Worse, it smelled of magic – just enough that it made her head whirl and pound. The other Scenters in the barracks had shied away when she walked past, shooting her nervous looks – but she didn't think it was the dress that was magical, just the residue that the Lord Mythos left on it.

She'd felt so awkward that she'd left the fancy slippers in the box, leaving her knee-high boots on instead. They were covered by the dress, but she was beginning to regret that decision now that she was so close to the Seven Suns Palace and the wonders beyond. Someone was sure to notice the iron-reinforced soles of her Watch boots.

She stood in the gently rocking gondola with eight other people as it skimmed across the inky water – one boat in a line of a hundred – waiting for its chance to travel through the Water Gate into the palace.

A menacing portcullis hung over the Water Gate and dragons had been carved in the wall on either side of it – a ward, no doubt to keep back spirits. But the humans guarding the gates were even more of a deterrent. Their long polearms were tipped with blades as long as Marielle's arm and they gleamed razor-sharp. The guards smelled of watchful determination, a crisp blue with a hint of peppermint.

Raucous laughter spilled from the gondola ahead of Marielle's as it passed through the Water Gate.

"I don't care if they won the Scavenger Hunt," a woman in Marielle's gondola said with a sniff. "Alchemist Guild members shouldn't be allowed into the Seven Suns Palace.

Compared to the crowd of party-goers in her boat and the others, Marielle's dress was actually quite simple. A man in her boat was dressed as Deathless Pirate with real skulls strung on a rope around his waist and his short-cape slung over his shoulders completely covered in what she thought might be blood-rubies. The feathers in his hat were made of gems and silk and they flashed as if by magic. The woman with him – the one angry about the Alchemists – was dressed as a Lady Sacrifice, just like Marielle, but she wore a white dress sewn all over in tiny bits of mirror and metallic thread that barely clung to her swaying curves. They both smelled of arrogance and anticipation.

Marielle's eyes had widened at the sight of them when she had joined them in the gondola, but they were only the first of many. It turned out that her "elaborate" dress was quite plain in comparison to those around her. Maybe she should have worn the slippers that went with them. If anyone saw her City Watch boots under the dress, she'd look like a fool – though she was a lot less likely to twist an ankle than the woman ahead of her who was dressed like Queen Mer and wore slippers with heels so high that she tottered worse than a ship on high seas.

A loud gong sounded as they entered the Water Gate. The deep throbbing sound reverberating from a long way away. Marielle knew it was the great gong that stood in the central square of the Government District but even knowing that didn't keep her from being startled at the sound.

A loud splash from a gondola behind them suggested that someone else had been startled by the gong.

"I don't know why they have to ring that old gong every Summernight. It gives me a headache," the other Lady Sacrifice complained as their gondola finally reached the landing inside the walls of the Seven Suns Palace and they began to disembark.

Already, just steps into the palace, Marielle was in awe, her eyes as large as they had been in those days when her mother playacted Queen Mer. She had no time for the critical complaints of the Landholds arriving with her. Bright lanterns hung along the water's edge, lighting the water with a thousand tiny lights like the stars in the sky. They hung in long chains from the walls of the inner palace.

Marielle and the others entered through a wide arched door and into the space beyond where painted silks of landscapes were hung with lights fastened behind them, throwing colorful lights out from the cloth and long, dark shadows.

Between the lights and shadows, characters in costume with painted faces mimed the stories of Legend. Marielle recognized Queen Mer with her dripping crown and vengeful countenance – but this Queen Mer wore a dress bedecked with sewn glass beads that reflected the colored lights and flashed with her fury.

Byron Bronzebow stood proud and noble as he redistributed wealth to the commoners – wealth he'd stolen from the Landhold of his city when he challenged him to an archery contest and won. And then more wealth that he stole again when he fooled the Landhold and made him a public disgrace.

The spectacles went on as the crowd grew, slowing down as they reached a pair of shadowed doors lit with flickering torches.

Marielle felt edgy. The wonder of the crowd – a delicate ivory tinged with the sent of warm fir trees – filled her nose, but with it came a thousand smaller scents. Irritation, impatience, lust, anger, hope, ambition. They flooded her senses so that she could hardly take a breath. She pulled up the scarf, letting a single layer wind around her mouth and nose, but even that was not enough to do more than dull the ache of so many humans with so many hearts throbbing their own orchestral strains and clashing against each other like warring swords.

A burst of sparks rained out of the torches and then, from above, a wide sheet descended, the corners tied with silken ropes and suspended from above. A woman lounged on the sheet. Her garb was that of Maid Chaos, the breast-plated warrior with a crown of dying roses who stood at the right hand of Death and while this Maid Chaos was cheerfully eating grapes while brandishing her silver shears, Marielle couldn't help but shiver. Maid Chaos was her least favorite of the Legends. Wherever she went, Death followed.

"Welcome to the Legend Ball on the Third Night of Summernight," she proclaimed. "Take care, for on this night, Legends walk the halls with you and the man you speak to, or the woman you dance with, may be no man or woman at all, but a Legend from the past come back for just one night to bid us a merry Summernight."

"Do you think it's true?" an eager girl from beside Marielle asked. Her Maid Chaos outfit was almost as elaborate as the woman in the sheet, but with a more buxom breastplate. "Wouldn't it be lovely to dance with a Legend?"

Marielle gave her a tight smile, realizing too late that she couldn't see it from under the veil. It would most certainly *not* be lovely. Marielle had a bad feeling that any Legends walking the earth today would need to be arrested before they broke every single city law.

The sheet was pulled back up into the shadows and the doors were flung open. Music spilled from the great room beyond, accompanied by so many scents that Marielle was forced to wind two more lengths of scarf around her face. It wasn't thick enough to suppress so many hopes and fears and disappointments mingling into a powerful deluge that threatened to crush her.

She stumbled to the side, grabbing at a carved pillar to steady her as she choked on the cloying scents. Other bodies, jostling to enter the room, swept her along in their movement until she was in the Grand Hall, the vaulted ceiling soaring above her where hundreds of candles were set in each hanging chandelier and hundreds of chandeliers hung over the room. Just paying the chandler bill for a single night would take more money that Marielle could earn in a year.

She couldn't see far into the room with so many people crushed against her, but there were hints overhead of spectacles to be viewed and intricate devices.

And then suddenly, the other scents were all swept away as a fresh, over-powering smell washed over them, not just overpowering them but almost burning them away. The scent of magic.

"I'm glad that you accepted my invitation, Marielle," Lord Mythos's cultured voice said from beside her.

Marielle looked up, her breath catching in her throat at his perfect dress. Alone, of all the guests, he was not dressed as anything at all. He simply wore all black in perfect, precise tailoring that made everyone else's elaborate costuming look garish in comparison.

"I do apologize," he said, concern lacing his tone, but never touching his icy eyes. "I forgot what a powerful effect an event like this might have on a Scenter. They're about to start the entertainment, and I'm afraid it will only get worse."

He did not look sorry. The way his eyes weighed her made Marielle wonder if he had planned that effect. Had he given her such a light filmy scarf because he knew it could not protect her from the onslaught of scents? Or was she being narcissistic to think that any of this was about her?

"Entertainment?" Marielle asked, cursing herself for her waving voice.

Gleaming bird cages descended from the ceiling, but these were not for birds. They were sized for people.

"It's not real magic – of course," the Lord Mythos said with a tiny smile. "You could smell that immediately, I'm sure." Then where was the overpowering scent of magic coming from? "But with this much belief in the room, this much hope, this many fears, and nerve-sizzling anxieties, well anything might look like magic."

There was a flash and a pop in the golden cages, eliciting small screams and gasps from the crowd and a electric-blue and ivory scent of excited wonder burst up into the air like puffing clouds. Each cage now contained one of the Legends, perfectly costumed.

"It's a game," Lord Mythos said. "My guests will ask the people in cages questions to discover which is the real Legend and which ones are merely play-acting. A magical game in some ways, but it is not why I asked you to meet me here. Come."

He didn't really mean that he thought he had a true Legend in one of those cages … did he?

He strode past her, his short-cape swirling as he passed and his rapier scabbard rattling. He turned back after two steps and raised a single eyebrow.

Oh. Yes. He was waiting for her.

With a start, Marielle adjusted her face-scarf, glad that it protected her from both the scents in the room and the embarrassment of a blush, and hurried after him.

17: UNEXPECTED

TAMERLAN

Tamerlan ground his ingredients with the pestle as quickly as he could, his hands slipping on the rough stone in his haste. He'd overslept. The Alchemists and apprentices were already heading out to the gondolas that would take them to the Seven Suns Palace. Unless he hurried, they would leave without him.

He'd been left a costume as promised – a ridiculous Deathless Pirate costume, complete with purple short-cape, a hook to hold in one hand, and a belt of gleaming skulls. He dressed before he started combining the ingredients. He didn't want Lila Cherrylocks to try to dress as herself again. Maybe if he was already in costume, she'd just accept how he was dressed.

He could hear apprentices leaving, their loud voices carrying up through the open window into his room. He needed to hurry, or he would miss the gondolas and he was counting on them to bring him right into the heart of the Seven Suns Palace. This time, Lila Cherrylocks could enter easily and then she could help him sneak down the halls and find the Sunset Tower.

His heart was already beating faster, his breathing accelerating with excitement and anticipation. It was going to work. He'd already seen her do something just as difficult and she loved parties. She would be easy to work with this time.

This time, he had all the opportunity he needed to steal his sister away from the tower and run away with her. Before he slept, he'd packed away essentials along with food and water and the extra orrisleaf he'd stolen – he had far more than he needed of that. The bundles were in the corner of his room just waiting to be used.

This time, he was ready. This time, he felt confident and hopeful instead of despairing. It was going to work. He could feel it in his bones.

He finished grinding the herbs – he'd used up all of them except for that orrisleaf - and hurried to the grate. He'd borrowed wood from Dathan's room when he wasn't there. It wasn't like Dathan would be needing it in the middle of summer anyway.

Sparking a fire with his steel and flint, he tucked them into his pocket and blew gently on the sparks as they lit the tiny ball of dried grass and twigs he'd prepared. He fidgeted with the silly purple cape as he waited for the fire to grow. Fashion demanded that short capes be worn tied over one shoulder and under the other to give the impression of broad shoulders and chests. A ridiculous fashion.

When the flames finally leapt high enough – their flame in the wood strong enough not to go out when the herbs and powder were added – he dumped the concoction hastily on the fire.

Hopefully, he'd done it right – just like last time. Hopefully, it would work again.

With every nerve tingling, he stuck his head over the fire. He'd meant to gulp in a huge breath of smoke but after a single half-breath he fell back from the fire, his stinging eyes slamming shut as he gasped for fresh air and retched on the smoke. Had it been that strong last time? Coughs ripped through his body, scouring his lungs until he fell to his hands and knees, trembling from the effects. He should have had a bigger breath than that, but when he looked back at the fire, the ingredients were gone, burnt up by the flame. Only woodsmoke remained.

He panted there, waiting. It had been quick last time, but this time there was no voice in his head. He stood up, looking worriedly at the stone bowl. He'd used the same ingredients. He'd done it the same way. What had gone wrong? Was it because he hadn't taken a big enough breath?

No man would wear such a ridiculous costume. Any fool could see you sneaking in the night.

Strong hands ripped off the skull belt and purple cape. And then Tamerlan was kicking the hook to the side and reaching into his wardrobe to find the old worn cloak he'd worn the first night. He shrugged it on as relief filled him. He'd drawn in enough smoke. It had worked.

I suppose the rest of the clothes will do.

But the voice in his head was rasping and masculine, not at all the voice of Lila Cherrylocks. What had he done wrong?

Nothing. When you open the Bridge of Legends you get whoever will come – or whoever can come. You opened. I came over the Bridge. And now here we are. I assume things are dire.

Finally! A Legend who understood!

Your city is ruled by corruption and evil.

Yes!

Freedom is what you need most.

Freedom for my sister.

Freedom for all who live under the chains of oppression.

Sure. But after my sister is saved.

Come. We fight tonight! Where is your bow?

There weren't any bows in the Alchemist's Guild.

We will make do. A weapon will come when we need it.

That seemed like a haphazard way to plan.

"Tamerlan? Are you ready?" Dathan called through the door. "Last call for the gondolas!"

"I'm coming!" Tamerlan threw the door open and Dathan's eyebrows rose. He was wearing a Byron Bronzebow costume. A dashing outfit of close-fitting leathers and a curved bronze bow in his hands.

He looks more of a man than your outfit did, but that bow is a forgery. An arrow would not go five paces from so weak a draw.

Um. Sure. But we needed to go with Dathan now.

"You look just like Byron Bronzebow," Tamerlan said with a smile, surprised that the Legend was letting him speak. Lila Cherrylocks had done all the talking when she took him over.

She's like that. And he's supposed to be me? I wouldn't wear such tight clothing. It makes movement difficult. And I would pay better attention to the quality of my weaponry. A man is nothing without the correct equipment.

"And you look terrible," Dathan said, as they ran down the corridor and the back steps to join the others below. "What happened to your costume?"

"I improved it." This time Byron took over my voice.

"If by 'improved' you mean that you look like a street beggar, then sure, you improved it."

We followed a group of other apprentices through the streets toward the nearest canal, words pouring out of Dathan like a flowing fountain as we went.

"I heard there is gambling so I brought extra coin, and it's customary to dance. Do you know how? And…"

Tamerlan tuned him out. Dathan didn't want replies. He was just nervous about going to the Palace. Everyone was. And now Tamerlan was, too, because he was realizing that it might be harder to break into the Sunset Tower with Byron Bronzebow in his head than it had been with Lila Cherrylocks. Byron was no master thief. He might not have the skills Tamerlan needed.

You were planning to steal? I can do that.

I need to save my sister from the Sunset Tower tonight.

To rub defeat into the face of the Landhold that runs this city?

We could do that. But mostly I need to save Amaryllis.

Bronzebow was concerningly quiet about that.

Could he help?

We shall see when we get there.

Sweat broke out along Tamerlan's hairline. It had been such a foolproof plan!

But it was foolproof no more. He should have broken into the Sunset Tower that first night with Lila instead of insisting that she prove her skills first. Now he was stuck with Byron and there was no way to know if Byron could do the job.

I find your lack of faith insulting.

They stepped onto the waiting gondola, tipping the gondolier with coins, and let the city flow around them. Tiny lights reflected on the water, and around the canal, the sounds of merrymaking filled the air. The canals were filled with people – decadent Landholds and the invited Alchemists were richly dressed as they skimmed along the water heading for the Seven Suns Palace.

In Tamerlan's mind, Byron muttered and grunted with every sight of elaborate wealth in the costuming. And with him directing Tamerlan's eyes, Tamerlan's gaze was drawn inexorably to the darker boats along the sides of the river. The ones that were not filled with elaborate decorations and arrogant partygoers but were instead the modest homes of the Waverunners, or the run-down gondolas peddled by lesser classes. Had there always been so many of them?

"We're almost there, Tam!" The excitement rang in Dathan's voice as he bounced on his toes trying to look into the Seven Suns Palace from their line of gondolas. The gondola two ahead of them was disembarking and there was a flash of rubies from the costume of a man dressed as Deathless Pirate. Maybe it was a good thing that Tamerlan had left most of his costume behind. He'd look like a fool next to a man in rubies. They might even throw him out.

They were almost at the Water Gate of the palace, an impressive gate guarded by men with even more impressive polearms – there would be no sneaking past them – when a loud gong sounded, startling Tamerlan.

But he was even more startled when Byron shed his cloak, slipped off his boots and shirt and leapt from the side of the gondola into the water.

18: Sunset Tower

Marielle

When Marielle had been a small child, the story she had hated most of all was the story of the Lady Sacrifice.

"But why does she have to die," she would ask her mother again and again.

"It's tradition," her mother said. "Someone must die for the city. And it's best to do it in a civilized manner. They don't just grab someone off the streets, they let the people choose. It's a choice. We believe in choice in Jingen. The Lord Mythos purchases the sacrifice of the people's free choice. That makes it different than just killing someone. It's someone who was sold at the choice of the people."

Marielle had gasped. "You can't sell people."

Her mother's laugh held no humor at all.

"Yes, little frog, you can."

"But *who* would sell a person?"

Her mother's voice had been sad. "Someone who has nothing else to sell."

"But you said it was a free choice. What if the sacrifice doesn't want to be chosen?"

"Oh, it's not her choice. It's the choice of the people around her. No one said it was a nice thing, but not everything necessary is nice."

And after that, Marielle had done what every person in Jingen did. She tried very hard not to think about why they had so many parties on Summernight or why they kept their sacrifice locked away in a high tower where no one could hear her screams. And she tried to only think of the bright lights and the pretty Nightbursts and the wild costumes.

But like everyone else in Jingen, she still knew.

***

"The boots are an excellent touch," the Lord Mythos said as he led Marielle to a door guarded by two men with long halberds. They opened it before he arrived, ushering him from the grand hall with its noise and excitement and into a warren of rooms and passages intriguing in their own way.

Marielle's face felt hot. "I didn't mean to offend. It's just easy to turn an ankle in delicate slippers and I'm an officer of the City Watch."

They passed a door lit with low lights and hushed words. Marielle glanced at the opening as they passed. It looked like a game of cards was going on, but the expressions around the table were so intent and sober that she couldn't imagine what might be riding on the games.

"That's not where we're headed," the Lord Mythos – Etienne – said and his scent was of wood smoke and fuchsia. Danger and a warning not to cross him. "And I was not finding fault with you. One of the laws Junfa wrote in *The Clash of Spirits* is this, 'Perfection carries a sting.' He commends the use of a single minor flaw to disarm the enemy and keep him off balance." He regarded her with a smoldering look in his eye that made her insides squirm like river eels. "Consider me disarmed."

Marielle met his gaze, refusing to flinch from the intensity of it. She swallowed, still meeting his eyes.

What did she see in their depths? There was domination there and charm, but something else, too, something hard that made her wonder if he really did hang the dried skins of women he had seduced on hooks in his closet. She should not be away from the main party with him. It was like following a viper into his pit. But would she be any safer there? She had a feeling that if Lord Mythos wanted someone dead he could kill them in a crowded room as easily as a lonely hallway. And he'd get away with it, too.

She clenched her hands at her sides. Being ready for an attack wouldn't be much of an advantage when she had half the muscle power of her attacker, but it was better than being caught completely unaware of what was coming.

"You are wondering why I brought you here in these deep corridors, aren't you?" he asked as they passed a red door.

A man dressed in a closely fitted Byron Bronzebow costume winked as they went by, placing a single finger to his lips before slipping through the door and closing it behind him.

The actions made Marielle's heart beat faster. She had smelled corruption and a sickly green mist as he'd entered. He had something twisted on his mind. Every instinct within her demanded that she open that door and prevent anyone inside it from breaking the law. But what if it wasn't the City Law that they were breaking? What if it was the moral law or the Real Law? She shivered.

The further she followed Lord Mythos into this warren of back rooms, the more complicated things seemed to be and darker the scents that she smelled. The red door was not the last door she thought hid dangerous secrets and not the last one that closed suddenly when they appeared, though often those who were closing the doors winked or nodded at Etienne Velendark.

"The managing of a city-state of this size takes a certain … flexibility," the Lord Mythos said. "I might not like it any more than you do, but that is how cities are run."

If he felt the way she did, he would have already rooted out every infraction in these rooms and sent the people in them back to their homes – or to the jails to be prosecuted and likely executed. His words were empty – a veil to hide his approval of what happened. There were only two stances when it came to breaking the law – opposition, which was always strong and definite, or approval which could be strong or weak and hidden. Agreeableness, keeping the peace, these things were not the same thing as morality.

She gritted her jaw, but now a new scent washed over the scents of rust-red depravity which smelled like blood, pink-purple deception smelling of fragrant lilies, and the foaming yellow-orange of greed that burned the nose like washing soda.

The new scent was all vanilla and lilac and turquoise with little golden sparks bursting from it. It joined the magic of the Lord Mythos, amplifying it, increasing it and overpowering everything else. Like the drunks they pulled from city gutters or kicked into the canal, Marielle stumbled, suddenly in a stupor as if she had drunk too deeply into her cups and now her mind was both dull and marvelously sensory.

"What is that?" she asked, trying not to slur her words. She was not certain that she had succeeded, but the wide smile on the Lord Mythos' face, still open and welcoming despite the predatory flash in his eyes told her that she had failed.

"Magic lets our city continue to thrive and flow like the Albastru River that feeds our canals and allows the gondolas and barges access to every part of the city. Have you ever wondered about why there are so many types of names in Jingen?"

"Names?" It seemed like a strange turn for the conversation to take.

"Some names are of the ancients who were here before, like the name of our city, 'Jingen' or the 'Albastru' river and some are parts of the Smudger religion. Other names sound like they are from another place entirely, like my name, Etienne. Or the words used by the Timekeepers' religion. Or your name, Marielle."

"The cultures of the mountains came down and joined the people along the river many generations ago," Marielle answered by rote. "That the whole would become more than the sum of its parts."

"That is the catechism," the Lord Mythos remarked as he led her to a dark staircase that led upward, winding around huge gears bigger than the house Marielle had grown up in.

He grabbed a candle in a candleholder from the wall beside the staircase and began to lead her up into its spiraled tangle. It made Marielle's skin crawl. It made her want to turn and run. And yet, with every step the scent of magic grew stronger, pulling her feet down step by step.

The Lord Mythos kept talking, unaffected by the magic swirling around them. "In the time of the dragons, men had to form strange bonds. And when the dragons were finally bound, we were forced to stay near them to keep them ever held in our thrall. The Dragonblooded of the mountains – people like you with violet eyes, and often with pale blond hair – and the people of the plains and sea with their dark skin and curls. They made blood-oath together, formed the five cities and vowed to keep our promises together. For every year, to renew the bond and keep the dragons captive, the blood of a Dragonblooded must be spilled."

Marielle clenched her jaw as he spoke. She didn't believe the old legend about the dragons. Everyone knew the cultures had melded and that the five cities had been formed and everyone knew that someone died for tradition every year, but no one really believed those tales about dragons. They were just things people had made up a long time ago to justify how they did things. They were no more real than the stories of Queen Mer or Byron Bronzebow. Tales for children to teach them bigger things. Tales to delight or horrify. Tales to explain the inexplicable. But not truth. Never close to truth.

Probably, they'd executed a criminal the first time they "sacrificed" the "lady" or perhaps it had been some barbaric way to force one group under the heel of the other. It had been so long since the first time no one knew what really had happened, and no one had to be told that the official story was just that … a story. Something interesting for the religions to talk about and paint on their walls or set in glass. Nothing of real value to anyone.

Nevertheless, he'd asked her if she was Dragonblooded when he met her. He mentioned it again now. That was worrying.

The staircase curved around something and then began to head downward again, skirting more large gears wreathed in shadow.

"I thought you already had your dragon sacrifice," she said through gritted teeth.

"We do," he said. "Sold of her family's free choice. We are below the Sunset Tower right now. Below the spot where she awaits her service."

Marielle felt a stab of pity mixed with horror. Above them, some poor girl waited, knowing that her family had sold her like an ox to be slaughtered. It could just as easily be her. That was what Lord Mythos was hinting. Did anyone mourn that girl? Was there anyone out there who wished it didn't have to be this way? Anyone other than Marielle?

Even in her magic-drunk state she felt torn by the thought of the unknown girl. A tiny voice in the back of her head suggested that if she was so troubled, then why didn't she offer to switch places with her? The rest of her mind received that advice with trembling fear, begging Marielle to ignore it.

"Then why have you brought me here?" Marielle asked and she was proud of herself that her voice did not shake with fear, though her chin trembled a little.

"There is magic missing."

"Missing? Are you suggesting there has been a theft? Of magic?"

"I'm suggesting that somewhere in the city someone is performing magic and that what he or she is doing has drawn some from the supply I have built here. We siphon it off carefully and store it for the needs of the city, but magic is drawn to magic." That explained the way his magic seemed amplified around this other magic. "And so, some has escaped its confines and gone to find that other magic. I think someone wants to steal more from my store. And that cannot be allowed to happen, or the next time that a tidal wave threatens the city I will not have the power to turn it aside. The next time a fire rages and homes and people burn, I will not have the magic to quell the fires. The theft of the grimoire in the Library – by someone in the Alchemist's guild. Did I mention that they turned it in for their prize? And the attempt to break into the Seven Suns Palace – these things are all tied to what I am sure is a plot to steal the rest of the magic from this store."

The had finally reached the end of the stairs – Marielle thought that perhaps they were just a little lower than ground level – and now the magic was so strong that the scent made Marielle reel and cling to the wall. She felt as though she might be sick.

"And now we reach the spine of the dragon. See his scales where your boots stand on the floor?" the Lord Mythos asked.

Oddly, the stone here did almost look like scales – if dragon scales were twice the size of Marielle curled in a ball. But rock often formed strange shapes and patterns and the room was small, much smaller than she would have imagined, though by the echoes the ceiling was very high. Dark stains splashed over the slick rock of the 'scale' puzzling Marielle for a half-a-heartbeat until the smell of old blood rose up from them.

"And this is where you slaughter your sacrifice," she said coldly.

"One could say so. Follow me."

He led her to the other side of the room where a railing was set up even though the wall was only an arm's width away.

"Look down," he said as they reached the rail and suddenly the reason for the rail seemed to make sense.

The floor fell away in an arch as if the rock were rounded and this wall didn't quite meet the rounded arc of the rock. In the narrow drop between them, a bright light filled the space revealing a drop so far down that Marielle could not see the bottom.

Magic swirled heavy in the air – so heavy that Marielle was almost blinded by the scent, but underneath it was something else – something faint, something she couldn't quite place.

"I know that Scenters can't see colors," the Lord Mythos said. "So trust me when I tell you that the light you see in that crevice is bright red. It's the breach in the dragon's scales and the way to tap his magic. It's the wound that must be kept open by the added sacrifice."

Marielle had heard of something else that might explain an open, roiling bright wound like that. Something else could explain the way it felt hot and the way that the rock around it was smooth and dark. She had heard tales of volcanic openings before. She was not such a fool as to think that they were wounds in the back of a dragon. Everyone knew they were made of lava bubbling and boiling from the belly of the earth.

"And I am showing you this," the Lord Mythos said, "to help you in your investigation of the crimes in our city. Because if you fail to solve this crime – if for some reason the Lady Sacrifice is not sacrificed on Summernight, or if so much magic is drawn away that her sacrifice is not enough, then I want you to know that I care more about this city than anything else. Do you understand that, Marielle?"

The gleam in his eye was hypnotizing, like looking into the eye of a snake.

"Yes," Marielle said, her head whirling from the scent of magic and her vision swimming with it.

"And I know exactly where I can find a backup sacrifice, Marielle."

A wash of cold ran over Marielle as his meaning penetrated through the fog of her magic-drunk mind.

"And I've been told that Variena – that's the name of your mother, isn't it? – is open to negotiating a price for just about anything. I wonder what her price would be for your blood?"

Marielle did not know, but she was just as certain as Lord Mythos was that with Variena, anything could be negotiated for the right price. Something pulled at her like a string leading from her belly to the floor and it felt as if all her blood was rushing to her feet.

For the second time in the week of Summernight, Marielle's consciousness fled, and she dropped heavily to the floor.

19: BYRON BRONZEBOW

TAMERLAN

By the blood of the dragon, move!

Byron was yelling in Tamerlan's head – as if he had any control over his own body. Ha! He was nothing but a ghost haunting his own body.

Byron leapt from the gondola, grabbed the top of a pole held by the surprised gondolier beside them, swung in a full arc from the pole, his feet slicing through the air like a knife, and then rolled into a flip while airborne to land on a third gondola. His feet slapped on the wood of the boat as he ran from stern to nose, kicked up on the bow and leapt to the peak of the ferro, balancing there for the barest sliver of a second before kicking off to summersault forward through the air to land on the deck of a houseboat pulled against the canal wall.

They were going the wrong direction! They needed to go to the palace! This was their only chance to get through those doors with an invitation in hand. No guards to stop them. Nothing to turn them around!

First, we right this wrong.

What wrong?

He was already scrambling up the sheer stone face of the canal wall, his fingers and toes finding cracks to climb that he hadn't even known were there.

He reached the top of the wall, climbed onto the street rail and began to run down the narrow rail with the balance of an acrobat, sprinting into the darkness in the exact opposite direction he wanted to go. What could possibly be down here?

This.

Below him were two Watch Officers. One of them – a red-headed woman with short hair – seemed familiar. They both held axes in their hands, grim expressions on their faces.

In front of them, a Waverunner family boat filled with water while the family desperately tried to pull chickens and heirlooms and bedding from the boat as the water filled it. They hung from the sides of another house-boat, the people in the second boat all speaking in a loud jumble while someone wailed at the top of her lungs.

"It's our home! Don't you understand?"

The red-headed guard was speaking. "You are hereby in violation of City Law 214-a stating that all boats in the City of Jingen shall – "

Tamerlan's mind was flooded with a much louder voice.

SEE? Injustice! They take from these people their homes and livelihood. Those are The Forerunners of the Retribution!

We just called them Waverunners.

The sacred people of Queen Mer. They are relentlessly peaceful. Killing them or taking anything from them used to be a crime punishable by death!

They weren't the only people who had been pulled up to the small jetty where the City Watch Officers stood. A small craft that looked like a gondola but was smaller, narrower, and sleeker was pulled to one side and the other guard held up a writhing boy who stood on the deck of the sleek craft a long oar in his hand.

Tamerlan leapt from the wall, landing between the guards.

"Unhand the boy!"

"On whose authority?" the red-headed woman asked, her eyebrow arching arrogantly.

"The authority of the Real Law," he said. Where was Bronzebow getting this stuff? He sounded like a story.

"We're the law around here," the redhead said coolly. "There's no room for the boy on that houseboat. Take him to the Watch House."

"Please!" the boy begged. He was maybe fourteen or fifteen. "If I leave the water I can never return. Please!"

"You should have thought of that before you forgot to pay your watercraft tax," the guard said, pulling at the boy.

Tamerlan's jaw snapped shut and he gritted his teeth as his fist balled at his side.

No! This was a bad idea! Don't do it!

And then his fist crashed into the guard's jaw and the guard's hand dropped the boy at the same moment that the houseboat suddenly sunk the last few inches into the canal with a loud *glop.*

The guard cursed, but he wasn't fast enough. Tamerlan grabbed his truncheon from his belt with one hand, seizing his cloak with the other and pulling it over his head before whacking him hard on the skull with the truncheon.

There was a moan of pain and then Tamerlan spun just in time to duck under the swinging fist of the red-headed guard. She spat at him, drawing a wicked knife from her belt, but he shoved the other guard at her so hard that they both staggered over the edge of the jetty and into the murky canal water.

"Boy!" the boy was calling him, gesturing urgently. He was small and thin, his skin covered by nothing but a pair of baggy breeches tied around the waist with a bit of red rope. "Come on, boy, before they get you!"

"Be safe on your way, good citizen!" Tamerlan said, rolling his eyes internally. No one talked like that. No one.

I do.

But as Tamerlan straightened, chest thrust out, a look of satisfaction filling his face, the guards began to pull themselves back up onto the jetty.

"You'd better not be there when I get up on shore," the red-head warned, ringing her watch bell above her head.

From the distance a second bell replied. Reinforcements were on the way.

"Come on!" the boy called. "They get you and you'll be locked up till they send you sinking!"

And he was right. A favorite execution style was to tie a man to a rock and sink him into the river.

Tamerlan shivered.

He shivered. Not Byron Bronzebow.

The blood drained from his face and his head was suddenly light. He knew it was bad that he hadn't managed to breathe a full lungful of the smoke.

The Legend had already fled his mind.

He looked around, frantic as the first guard climbed wetly up the side of the jetty, throwing murderous looks at Tamerlan. With a half-disguised yelp, he dashed to the boy's boat and leapt aboard.

"Hurry!" he called.

"That's what I'm, saying, boy!"

They darted into the night, the craft so fast that every stroke of the boy's oar took them four times further than any other boat.

"Your names and faces will be on every Watch House notice board in Jingen!" the redhead called. "Justice will be served!"

They skimmed along the water, heading toward the river, dodging spills of colored lights along the way. With so much traffic, their boat was soon lost in the shoals of gondolas going to and from parties all over the city.

The boy clung to the shadows, even shooting the locks along the canal like rapids in a river, ignoring the shouts and raised fists of the lock workers. From the spine of the dragon where the Seven Suns Palace was to the river, it was all 'downhill' but even still it was a wild ride when they shot over a full lock into one already at the lowest point, the bottom of the boat slapping the water when it hit.

Tamerlan clung to the ferro at the front of the little boat, stretched out across it like a rug along the floor. The boy seemed to know where he was going. All Tamerlan could hope was that he really did.

Nothing had gone according to plan and now he had only two nights left to try to save Amaryllis before it would be too late.

20: Scent of a Name

MARIELLE

It had been gray the morning that Marielle's mother had taken her to live in the Scenter Academy. Marielle's emotions had been the spring green of anticipation, leaving a taste on her tongue like cilantro. Her mother's had been the soft pink and orange blossom of infatuation.

"Why can't I stay with you," Marielle had asked.

"You're a big girl now, honey frog. You're big enough to learn and grow. Scenters have good lives. Useful careers. You have more options. You won't have to live behind a red door."

"But you aren't going to live behind a red door for much longer, are you?" Marielle had said.

"Not if Hez'ng does what he promises," her mother said with a smile, the melting pink of her scent, sweet as honey cakes, drifting through the air.

"Why do you love him so much?" Marielle asked. "Jazmeer's mama says he is not a nice man."

"Oh, honey frog, we can't choose who we love. Someone who other people might think is bad could be just the right fit. Someone other people can't see as precious might be just life and water to you. You just see the good in them, the human part no one else can see, and you just can't live without it."

"But you can't bring me with you when you go live with him, can you?"

"The Scenters will be good for you, honey frog," Varienna had said, kissing Marielle on the forehead. Her scent told Marielle that her mind was already back on Hez'ng and the future they would have together.

Marielle had gone to live with the Scenters, but the next time she saw Varienna that scent was gone, and the red door was back. And Varienna never spoke again of love – or at least not in connection to herself.

***

Marielle straightened her tunic for the third time as they waited at the door of *The Copper Tincture*. She still felt rumpled, hours after dressing and hitting the streets with Carnelian.

"Remind me again why I found you in bed still dressed like a partier?" Carnelian asked with a smirk.

Marielle blushed. She'd fallen asleep in the pretty dress when she'd stumbled home and cried herself to sleep. There was no hiding from fate in Jingen. She of all people knew that. There was nothing a Scenter couldn't sniff out, nothing the Watch couldn't unearth, no place that rumor did not touch or that prying eyes did not see. If, in just two days time, the chosen Lady Sacrifice was not killed and her blood sprinkled on those warm rocks Marielle had seen, then they would come for Marielle. And there would be no stopping them.

She had shivered all night from the cold and from that thought, tossing and turning, sweating with fear and horror. All these years, she'd known what they did to girls on Summernight. All these years, she'd tried not to think about it, but it was coming for her now – or it would if anything happened to stop the sacrifice of the girl they'd bought in the countryside.

Had she been sleeping like Marielle? Had she been tossing and turning in her bed as the hopes and dreams bled out of her long before the life did? Had she cried every tear until even tears abandoned her? Marielle had clung to the sweaty sheets, shaking like a leaf, knowing right down to her bones that there was no way she could hide from this and no way she could outrun it. If she failed to keep the Lady Sacrifice safe from whoever was stealing this magic, then she was going to die in just two days.

"Remind me again why we're out during the daytime when we are on Night Watch?" Marielle replied. She was too tired to let Carnelian push her around. She hadn't slept a wink last night.

"You're sure that the scent led here, right?" Carnelian asked with a grimace. She'd dragged Marielle up out of bed, barely waiting for her to dress before marching her out to a jetty along the canal in the Government District and demanding that she catch a scent there. "I don't lose criminals. At least not for long. And those two escaped from right under Dacrin's nose while you were out galivanting!"

Carnelian had been there, too. But it wouldn't be very wise to point that out to her. Just like it wouldn't have been wise to mention it on the jetty where Carnelian had raged about the fool she'd been partnered with and how she'd slipped out of first place on the tally board because he'd let some shadowy figure get away.

"It's up to you to track him!" she'd demanded, shoving Marielle forward as if she wouldn't have been able to smell that scent from across the canal, never mind right on the jetty.

But that was the problem. She smelled *two* scents.

One, was the heady, intoxicating scent of magic – the scent from the Library and under the Sunset Tower – the scent that the Lord Mythos insisted was the key to keeping his ceremonies safe. The scent her very life hung from like a last petal on a dying flower. Lilac and vanilla, turquoise and golden sparks.

The other scent was the one she'd smelled before: bright and golden like hot honey but mixed with a ginger popping orange and in this case, a soft lavender of compassion. And stranger than finding both scents there – distinct and yet together – was the feeling that despite the addictiveness of the magic scent, what she really wanted was to follow the gold and orange and lavender.

"Of course, I'm sure that this was where the scent led," she said, admiring the carvings in the door of *The Copper Tincture*. They told the story of Xe'li and her desperate desire to stop time, how she drank a tincture of copper and was youthful for a thousand years. But the day she told a lie, her youth fell away and she crumpled into dust. And now, as Marielle ran a finger over Xe'li's intricate robes, she was lying too. Because she hadn't taken Carnelian to where the golden scent led – streaking away from the conflict like an arrow from a bow, but rather to where the turquoise and gold of the magic had come from. The lilac scent of it still hung in the air like a banner.

"If it is, they'll be able to identify the picture," Carnelian said.

"Picture?"

"Dacrin's good with a pen." Carnelian pulled a folded parchment from her pocket and shoved it at Marielle.

She was still unfolding it when the door opened, and a smiling young man greeted them.

Marielle felt her eyes widen at the picture in her hands. Dacrin *was* good. He'd drawn a perfect likeness of the face she'd seen in the crowd when she first caught a whiff of that intoxicating golden honey scent. Her eyes traced the face in the sketch, trying to burn it into her mind.

Carnelian snatched the parchment away from Marielle.

"Jingen City Watch," she said to the young man in the doorway. "Do you know this man?"

She handed him the parchment and the young man took it in trembling hands.

"Is he hurt? Dead?"

"Not that we know of," Carnelian said curtly. "What's his name."

"That's Tamerlan," the man said. "Tamerlan Zi'fen of the Zi'fen Landholds. He's an apprentice here."

Marielle swallowed. It was as if the name made the scent more real. He was a real person. An apprentice here at this Alchemist House. And somehow, he had brought magic from this place but lost it on the jetty when he fought with Dacrin and Carnelian.

Where did magic go when it left? Did it waft away like smoke, or melt like ice, or did it still linger like the scent of death? Perhaps, they were about to find out. She felt excitement frizzling through her like bubbles in water. They were about to finally get some answers.

"We need to speak to the Master Alchemist here," Carnelian said.

"And we need to see Tamerlan's room," Marielle added, trying to look calm when inside she was anything but calm. The residue of magic washed out the door all around the young apprentice's scent of ochre and smoked paprika worry, overpowering the smell of metals and chemical mixtures in the Guild House beyond.

"Of course," the young man said, looking shaken.

He led them into the Guild House, past a stylish anteroom, and down a long corridor to a room where things in glass bottle bubbled and smoked. Marielle had known to expect the smell – she'd wrapped the veil around her face four times to try to combat it, but it still rode over every sense so that she had to stay outside the room, clutching the wall for support as Carnelian went inside to speak to the master.

She was still shaking there, her head pounding and her nose on fire with the acidic scent of the place when Carnelian and a Master Kurond came out of the room and he began to lead them back through the corridors to a staircase.

The Guild House walls were white plaster, uneven but clean. Metal twisted into interesting shapes served as art hung on the walls and heaps of tools and fragrant herbs and oily bottles lined shelves anywhere there was room to set them up.

"Don't mind the clutter," the man said as he led them. He was fit for a man of his age – mid-forties – and he strode through the halls like a king in his castle. "Things seem more turbulent than usual with the Festival going on. You're certain that Tamerlan has committed some crime?"

"Not certain," Carnelian said. "Not yet, at least. What we know is that the trail led us here and the man we saw looks like your apprentice."

Master Kurond wiggled his fingers impatiently – a man not used to waiting – and Carnelian handed him the charcoal sketch of his apprentice.

"It does look like Tamerlan. Did he return to his bed last night, Dathan?" he called behind him. Marielle jumped at the sudden shout. She hadn't realized that the dark-haired apprentice was still following them. He smelled of *The Copper Tincture* with a small hint of cranberry guilt.

"No, Master Kurond," Dathan said, his young face crinkling. "I've been worried, but I thought maybe he just had too much to drink."

Master Kurond waved a dismissive hand irritably. "He's not a drinker, Tamerlan. Worth every penny I paid for him. He does his work conscientiously. He gets along with others. He's well-mannered and well-groomed. He has an excellent memory and good deductive skills. Everything you would expect from a Landhold's son and everything required in an Alchemist's apprentice. With application, he could run his own Guild House someday."

They had reached a small door and already Marielle knew it was Tamerlan's. The residue smell of magic poured from it in waves of turquoise and lilac and the golden vanilla-scented sparks danced like the tips of waves on the river under the noonday sun.

The powerful, addictive sweet hot honey and cardamom scent filled her up like a cold drink of water on a hot day – the smell of the man she had run into on the street, all clean masculinity laced with tarragon and lavender, cinnamon and honey. It was lavender compassion mixed with orange pulsing desperation, a sparkle of flashing cleverness and a deep, throbbing strain of bronze hope rolling through the rest like a banner on the wind. It was too much.

Everything inside her was drawn to it. Everything she knew told her that letting this anywhere close to her spelled disaster. She was not here to enjoy a scent. She was not here to fall in love.

She was here to catch a master criminal – a thief of magic and a threat to her life.

“Here’s his room,” Master Kurond said. “I doubt you’ll find much there. He doesn’t have many possessions.”

He opened the door and Marielle pushed past Carnelian to be the first inside. Her partner crooked an eyebrow cynically and stayed by the door to speak to Master Kurond.

“Bought from a Landhold, hmm? Any chance he might try to steal a boat to run back home?” she asked him.

Marielle went over to the washstand. Nothing there. Just a simple comb and basin. The wardrobe held a single set of clothing – well worn – and a Lila Cherrylocks costume. Her heart sped up. Hadn’t the girl at the library claimed she had been attacked by a man in a Lila Cherrylocks costume?

She pulled her scarf down and buried her nose in the folds of the costume, trying to get past the magic scent, and then trying not to be bowled over by Tamerlan’s enticing smell. But under all of that – yes! – there was a hint of books and seaside winds. Dust and stamps and vellum. It was the smell of the Library District.

"I doubt he would," Master Kurond said. "He had opportunities here. Memories there – but none good unless I miss my guess."

"Any other reason he might have to attack two guards and steal a gondola?" Carnelian asked.

By the fireplace, Marielle noticed a mortar and pestle. They were empty. The fire grate was a different matter. Most grates were clean in mid-summer awaiting use when the weather turned cold again. This grate had a fire in it recently.

"A gondola?" Master Kurond sounded surprised. "He'd have no use for that. The guild will pay for a gondola if that's necessary."

"And the guards?" Carnelian pressed. "Any reason to attack them out of nowhere?"

Despite her light-headedness from the heavy magic smell – heavier here at the fire grate – Marielle could smell the smoke. Strange. That wasn't just wood smoke. There were herbs and other things in there. Was that orrisleaf? She hadn't smelled that in a long time. And a little aniseed. She shivered. He'd led her to an aniseed shipment when he'd wanted to overwhelm her before. And now here it was thick and heavy in the air. Interesting.

"Depends on what they were doing," Dathan said from where he stood out of Marielle's sight.

"What is that supposed to mean?" Carnelian asked with a warning note in her voice. The boy had better shut up. Carnelian was spoiling for a fight.

"He's soft-hearted. If they were hurting someone or being unfair… " his voice trailed off.

"I think you have things to attend to, Dathan," Master Kurond said carefully.

Marielle ignored them, studying the room while she could.

The golden scent of Tamerlan was strongest on his bed. She sat on it, letting his scent fill her up and feeling just a hint of guilt at how much she liked it. She would recognize it now anywhere she went. Even the smallest trace and she would know it was him. She spread her hands out over the blanket, fingers spread, breathing in every last trace of him – a whirl of color and scent and emotion stronger than anything she'd ever felt – stronger even than the addictive smell of the magic.

Carnelian and Master Kurond were still talking and she wasn't listening to a single word. Her mind was popping and fizzling with a scent so overpoweringly *right* that it made everything else in the world feel wrong. She wanted more. She would follow that scent anywhere.

Stop, Marielle! You are a Jingen Watch Officer, not a girl with her hair up for the first time!

Something crinkled under her palm. She pulled the blanket back. A small page of paper was there. Carefully, she tucked it behind her belt. She'd look at it later.

"Got his scent?" Carnelian asked.

"Yes," Marielle said, feeling like she was lying. Did she have his scent? Could you keep the wind captive? Could you nail down the sun? Could you hold back the years and unwind the hours? Could you make what was outside you come inside and what was inside come out? She had his scent like you had a memory – not nearly as powerful as you wished it to be and fainter the more you grasped for it.

"Then we'll go for now. Tell us if he returns," Carnelian said as they left.

It was all Marielle could do not to stay. The scent called to her as she followed Carnelian, but tucked away in her belt was something just as interesting – the folded piece of paper. Perhaps it would be what she needed to find this Tamerlan and prevent him from stopping the Summernight sacrifice before it was too late.

Because no matter how addictive his smell was and no matter how compelling the trust of his friends or his story of being sold into apprenticeship was, if the Lord Mythos was right about Tamerlan and he really did want to stop the death of the Lady Sacrifice, then Marielle was the one who would be sacrificed tomorrow night.

She shivered.

There was nowhere to run from that and no way to hide.

21: Queen Mer's Son

Tamerlan

Tamerlan awoke huddled in the bow of the sleek little gondola. Waves rocked the boat with an almost comforting motion. It defied his troubled heart and tangled emotions. What sort of world was it where simple things like the motion of water could feel so good when everything else about life hurt like a shard of glass wedged in your flesh? Every thought tore at that shard, tugging against the wound and shooting jagged throbs of pain through him like waves of fire.

He was running out of time. And he'd almost been caught. What if Byron had slipped from his mind even a minute sooner? What if he had done something even wilder than saving the boat of a kid? He'd smoked the recipe in the hopes of finding aid for his sister, but there was no controlling the Legends. There was no way to determine what they did when they arrived or how they did it. Byron had been willing to help, but he hadn't been able to pass up the chance to help someone else, too. Lila had been willing to help, too – for a price. And both times had been just too short for what he'd needed.

Maybe that was the key. Maybe he needed to smoke a deeper, greater lungful – or several lungfuls. What he needed was to have them take over his body for longer. And he needed the Legend who came to be Lila Cherrylocks. She was the one with the ability to break into things and she could be reasoned with. At least a little.

"What you gonna do now, boy?"

Tamerlan startled as the boy sat up from the stern of the gondola, blinking at him in the growing morning light. Was he really calling Tamerlan 'boy'? The kid was fourteen if he was a day. Maybe fifteen if he was a slight fifteen.

"You burned your boat to ash last night, boy."

Tamerlan blinked at his rapid speech. He'd dealt with gondoliers before. He'd seen Wavereunners from afar. But he'd never really talked with them for long and the boy's rapid speech – intonations different from what Tamerlan was used to – was not what he was accustomed to. He squinted, concentrating at the next burst of rapid-fire speech.

"You're not welcome back on land, boy. You don't have your own boat. You don't have a future. No Jingen for you. Where will you go? Where are your people?"

"I don't have people," Tamerlan said quietly, realizing it was true. When the guild found out what he'd done he wouldn't be welcome there. They'd cut their loss with him and buy a new apprentice. And his family had sold him. He wasn't ever going back home again. "Where did you get this boat?"

The boy grinned, flashing perfect white teeth. "This boat is mine. All mine. I designed it. I built it. My home."

"You built this? It looks different from other gondolas."

He nodded sagely. "Faster. Sleeker. Smaller. 'No good for houseboat' they say. 'No good for passengers' they say. Who says I want passengers? Who says I want a house? I want to be fast. I was fast last night."

"You were very fast," Tamerlan agreed, standing up in the boat.

Around them, the other people under the bridge began to stir. They'd tied the gondola to a line hanging down from the Spine Bridge at the west end of the city. It linked the Alchemist and Artificer Districts for traffic that didn't move well on barges or gondolas. During the days, it was filled with stinking carts, stomping horses and angry drivers. At night, the lamps along it were lit and traffic was mainly carriages or foot traffic.

They'd found it easily in the dark of night, joining hundreds of others who lurked under the bridge – small boats tied to hanging lines, and hundreds of hammocks, some huge woven baskets that made small huts dangling on ropes from under the bridge.

The sounds of people waking and rolling up hammocks filled the air.

"I didn't know this place existed."

"You never see the bridge before?" the kid gave him a long look, twisting his mouth like he was speaking to an idiot.

"I've seen the Spine Bridge. I just didn't know that people lived under it at night."

"You don't know much, boy."

"I think I might be older than you," Tamerlan said mildly. "And my name is Tamerlan."

"Names are earned," the boy said. "Why did you save the boat last night?"

"Did you want it to sink?" Tamerlan asked. He was beginning to like the boy. He was less shaken by the night before than Tamerlan was, and yet he didn't seem to have any family or friends to rely on. It was just him and his little craft.

"Fool. Boat sinks, I die. There was no room on the other boat. And if I leave the boats, I die."

"What do you mean?" Tamerlan asked. "Because your people won't let you return to the boats? You could still live on the streets."

"Nothing away from the water is real," the boy said, rolling his eyes. "You leave the boat, you join the dead."

"I'm real," Tamerlan said.

"You see yourself last night? You were like a spirit of the dead springing up. You tore through the enemy like a demon of the night. I think maybe you're only real now because you slept on the boat all night."

The kid rummaged through a cloth bag that had been hidden under a panel at the back of the boat. He pulled out a tunic that was slightly less grimy than his pants quickly pulled it over his head. His thin body was crisscrossed with scars. Tamerlan felt a tug at the sight. He knew what those felt like.

"That's a theory, alright," Tamerlan said. And in fairness, he hadn't felt very real the last few nights. And he wasn't even sure what real was anymore. He could have sworn he dreamed of Lila Cherrylocks last night. But he didn't know if it was a dream of if he had really heard her laughing at him in his mind.

"So, where will you go now, boy?" The boy was tucking his cloth bag back into the recesses of the hidden panel.

Tamerlan clenched his teeth, thinking. Where did he go, now? He had to try again. He'd have to go back to the Guild House and see if he could grab some of his things there. And he needed more ingredients. Those he could get around the city today if he was careful. If he wasn't seen or caught.

He had to hope that Master Kurond didn't know he was in trouble with the law. If the Alchemists knew and they found him first, they'd punish him in their own way before they gave him to the City Watch. He flinched at the thought of the acid they used to etch a mark of shame on the backs of the hands. He'd seen that before. Old Jand who hauled waste from the Guild House was marked like that. He'd been caught stealing from the Guild. And that would only be the beginning. Worse, their punishments would take time and time was the one thing he didn't have.

"If I haven't earned your name, is there something I can call you until I do," he asked the boy. "It feels disrespectful to call you 'boy.'"

The boy snorted. "You can call me Jhinn, boy."

Tamerlan bowed respectfully. He might not be a Landhold anymore, but if being sold had taught him one thing, it was that all people preferred to be treated with dignity.

"Do you know a place where we could hide a few things, Jhinn?"

Jhinn grinned. "For a price, maybe."

"Okay, for a price."

Jhinn gestured at the line hanging from the bridge. "Untie the boat. We'll talk price while we go."

Tamerlan untied the boat, his mind on the list he was forming of where he could go to buy or steal the items he was going to need to smoke again. He'd need a lot of them. He'd need to stockpile. If it mattered how much he actually breathed in, then next time he needed to breathe in as much as possible and he needed to keep on doing it until he got what he needed. And for that, he was going to need a lot of spices and a place to keep them.

"It needs to be somewhere that I can store a lot of things," Tamerlan said.

"Valuable things?" Jhinn asked.

"To me."

"Ten percent. You keep them in my place. I get ten percent."

Maybe he wasn't as young as he looked.

As they skimmed along the morning water watching the white river birds fishing along the edges of the reed clumps, their long legs scissoring through the water, Tamerlan let the cool morning breeze and the warmth of the sun on his face lull him for a moment.

It would be okay. He just needed to change his plans and adapt. He hadn't lost his chance. Next time, he would smoke a lot and next time, he would get a better Legend for the job.

And now he had an ally. Sort of.

And that was something, wasn't it?

SUMMERNIGHT EVE

FOURTH NIGHT OF SUMMERNIGHT

22: To Catch a Law Breaker

Marielle

Marielle shifted on the three-legged stool. It was hard to stay still when the scents slipping in through the window were so enticing.

Oranges and sweet buns, roast pork and sweet peppers, fried cakes and puffy pastries – every mouth-watering food you could buy in the nearby streets and inns were there. And mixed in were the freesia, roses, and mandarins hanging in garlands on the streets, all forming a sparkling tangerine and warm brown sugar symphony on Marielle's vision. Her mouth watered.

Excitement and delight spiked in reds and electric blues smelling of electricity and sweet apple. On Summernight Eve, the tradition of Jingen was to dress as the Legends and give gifts door to door. People filled the streets below with baskets and barrows and carts heaped with baking and treats, fruits and trinkets. The more a person could afford to give, the better luck in the year to come. Tomorrow night, on the shortest night of the year – Summernight – the year would begin afresh and with it, the luck that came from giving.

Marielle would have no such luck. She wasn't lying in wait to give anyone anything. She was waiting here to take – take a man's freedom, his future, his life.

Master Kurond had been very accommodating, allowing Marielle to sneak in when the other apprentices were preoccupied with dressing for the evening. No one had seen her arrive. No one had seen her sit quietly on the stool and with the sun setting soon, it wouldn't be long until dusk fell and with it, Marielle was certain that Tamerlan – the golden scented apprentice – would return to his rooms to retrieve anything he'd left there.

He would probably want the book page Marielle had found. Or at least, she was hoping he would. It seemed valuable. And people rarely hid things under their blankets unless they were personal to them. She felt for it in her belt. It was still there.

Her every sense was focused on the window. By the scent trail, that was how he'd left. It would make sense that he would return that way, too. In a world where everyone else thought in circles, Marielle couldn't help but think in a straight line.

The door to the room creaked as it opened and Marielle jumped, rising from her seat so quickly that the stool wobbled. She fumbled for her truncheon and then froze when the man walking in the door was not the one that she expected.

"Marielle Valenspear," the Lord Mythos said, entering with a swirl of magic residue and a puff of plum arrogance.

"L – Lord Mythos!" What was he doing here? He was hosting a party tonight – one for the Landholds of the city and the Guild leaders. He'd even invited Marielle to it again, sending her a second dress.

"This is not where I expected you to be tonight, Marielle."

Marielle felt sweat breaking out along her spine. "You said it was vital to find the person who tried to break into the Seven Suns Palace."

"So it is," he said, quirking a single eyebrow. That single change to his face changed the entire thing, taking him from sober and angry to mysterious and possibly intrigued.

Marielle tried to explain. "So, I'm making it my top priority. I'm waiting to see if the apprentice of *The Copper Tincture* returns tonight. We followed his scent here. He's the one who tried-"

She was babbling. She felt like a fool. But when those eagle-eyes swept over her, they rattled her. Those were the eyes that might be the last ones she saw if she failed.

"You remember what's at stake here." It was a statement, not a question. It was almost as if he had read her mind. He leaned in close, so that his eyes were level with hers and only inches away. "Because I haven't forgotten, Marielle."

His gaze should have been intimidating. It should have made her quake with fear, but instead, it was the Lord Mythos who looked vulnerable.

"I believe in the law, Lord Mythos. I believe in defending it. That's why I'm here and that's why I sent Carnelian in my place to report to you at the party tonight."

He waved his hand like that wasn't important but something in his eye gleamed in a way that contradicted the gesture. "I don't need a report. I know how things are progressing."

She cleared her throat nervously. Best not to have any misunderstandings. "Then why did you invite me. Why did you send me a fancy dress?"

He scoffed. "It's not enough that I might want to see you? Would that be such a crime?"

His eyes were haunted with something, like he was being stretched between two trees and the ropes were growing tighter.

Marielle swallowed, careful with her words. "Do you really have to kill that poor girl on Summernight?"

His lower lip trembled when he replied. How old was he? He was barely older than she was, she thought. And right now, he looked younger still.

"It takes blood, Marielle. It takes blood to save us all. And if I don't give it – if I fail in my duty – so many more will die. The streets will run with blood and the dead will wash up along the shore for months."

He ran a hand over his face like he was wiping the thought away.

Marielle shivered. He really believed this mystic stuff. He really believed the old catechism. Marielle didn't think that she'd ever met anyone who truly believed – who didn't just say the words by rote, mouthing the traditions because that was what was expected.

"You believe in the law," he said. "You feel it in your bones. It pulses through your veins. Each day is purposeful because you love it, because you defend it, because it makes the insignificant things you do – the steps of your patrol, the care of your uniform, the glance you lay over every citizen – it makes all that full of meaning. Isn't that true?"

And when his eyes met hers, she felt like he really did understand.

"Yes," she breathed, feeling her pulse drumming in her cheeks.

"That's how I feel about Jingen. I live to defend this city. I spend every moment of every day thinking about her health and prosperity. I would die – gladly! – in her defense. Can you understand that?"

He had grown paler as he spoke, his hands gripping the hilt of his rapier until they were white-knuckled.

"Yes," Marielle said. Because she really did understand. If Lord Mythos – if Ettiene Velendark - loved Jingen like she loved the law, then no wonder he was so obsessed with the Summernight sacrifice. Her love of the law filled her up. It called to her on dull days and shone brightly when she'd feared she'd lost her way. It made her warm inside with a fire that didn't stop burning. She could quote every law of Jingen. They ran through her head when she polished her boots and brushed her hair. They tickled her memory when she rode on a gondola or watched the water lap in waves around the waterlilies. The law was life. And it kept all things and people in Jingen safe as long as it was followed. And she loved that she was a part of that.

And if Etienne felt the same way about this city, then she respected that. More than that, she understood him.

He was looking away now, looking out the window to where the sun was growing dimmer. Perhaps it was a colorful sunset. Marielle would never know, and she wouldn't care because not seeing the colors of sunset meant she could see the colors blooming up from Lord Mythos, the crimson and birch smoke of passion and the deep rose of obsession, bursts of creativity in peacock blue with the scent of peaches and something almost like the gold of attraction sprouted up from him in splashes of intensity. And mixed in it all was the heady clove and mint smell of him mixing and strengthening.

He turned back to her, hawk-fast, his eyes dark with intensity. "For the first time in my life, I feel torn, Marielle. I must make sure that the Lady Sacrifice does her duty. I must not let anything stop it."

"Then why wait until Summernight?" Marielle asked. "Does one more day make so much difference?"

"The timing must be precise," he said, shaking his head. "If it is not done at midnight on Summernight, it will be for nothing."

Marielle swallowed.

He turned back to her, eyes haunted. "Do you think I revel in it? Do you think I desire it?" His voice lowered. "My own cousin died as a Lady Sacrifice while I watched. It haunts me to this day."

Marielle's mouth was too dry to swallow.

"But this time, Marielle – this time is worse." The look in his eyes echoed his words.

"Why? Haven't you done this before?"

He scoffed. "Every year, I do this again. But this year there are fewer choices for the Lady Sacrifice, Marielle. And you are one of those choices." His voice grew so quiet it was barely above a whisper. "And I do not want you to die."

His whisper tickled her ear, raising the small hairs along the back of her neck.

Flattering. But why her? He barely knew her.

Marielle's eyes narrowed as she watched him. But it wasn't fear that filled her. It was a gut-wrenching horror that someone else was going to die and that likely, she was the one person who could stop it. Because if Marielle offered to take her place, wouldn't she be a perfectly acceptable replacement?

She should say something. She should offer herself in the place of the other girl.

But no matter how many times the thought echoed through her mind, she couldn't voice it. It was as if her very voice was betraying her. It stuck in her throat like a fish bone.

"I must leave," Lord Mythos said eventually. He was looking at the door, but he bowed his head over his white-knuckled grip as if he was trying to keep a hold on himself. "Catch this thief. Neither of us can live with the alternative."

He left without looking back at her, his short cape swirling in the wind of his passage. The door shut softly behind him and with it, the warmth seemed to leave the room. Marielle wrapped her arms around herself and sunk back into the stool, but now she felt haunted as if one of the Legends really had come back to life and was standing there jabbing at her with a stick.

She could end someone else's pain if she was bold enough. But while it sounded noble when she thought it the first time, she didn't know this girl. She didn't know anything about her. Maybe she wasn't a good person. Maybe she didn't deserve to live any more than Marielle did. But what filled Marielle with shame was the realization that even if she did know her and even if the Lady Sacrifice was the perfect paragon of all virtues, Marielle's tongue would stay silent. She didn't want to die. And she wasn't ready to give up her own life for anyone else – even an innocent victim of an ancient tradition.

The minutes ticked by far too slowly and with every one Marielle smelled her own bitter disappointment as it filled the room like a brown haze and hung over her head like a cloud, tasting of sharp turmeric.

She was a terrible person.

23: A Gamble

Tamerlan

"This is more stuff than you need, boy. Dried up plants and stinky goo. I would never promise a place for them if I knew what you wanted to hide." Jhinn shuffled the ingredients deep into the hull of the small skiff, packing them down under an oiled canvas.

Tamerlan carefully arranged the smaller bunches of ingredients he'd kept for tonight, stuffing them one at a time into a small leather satchel at his side.

"When you told me that you had a hiding spot, I had no idea that you meant it was another boat," he said.

This boat was smaller than the sleek gondola that Jhinn steered everywhere. Stubby, but with a low profile, the top completely wrapped in oilcloth, this little boat wasn't made for people. It was made for supplies.

"What do you think happens if the city gets attacked? What if we have to run fast? I have a plan. You have stinky plants."

Jhinn did have a plan. He'd taken Tamerlan out of the city and down the river to a little dip in the bank under the roots of a pair of Da'shal trees. The tiny craft was tucked in there, filled mostly with water in skins and glass bottles and dried foods wrapped in oilcloth.

"Thank you for letting me keep my supplies here," Tamerlan said. "I don't know why you're so kind to me."

The boy rolled his eyes. "I don't know why you want to store stinky plants like they're made of gold. But I do know why I helped you. And not just because you saved my boat." He paused. "I can see your friends."

"Friends?"

"The two people looking over your shoulder all the time. The one with the long red hair and the one with the bronze bow. They want things from you. They haunt you. No man should live like that. My people have ways of dragging unwanted spirits out. You want to find a Spirit Singer? I can take you."

Tamerlan swallowed. Jhinn could see Lila Cherrylocks and Byron Bronzebow when he looked at Tamerlan? That was concerning. He'd never believed all the talk about the Waverunners being from another world but talk like that made a person think it might be true.

"It's a generous offer," Tamerlan said. "Thank you."

"No, not generous. Necessary. You can't let spirits take you. They use you for their own reasons. Evil."

"I need them right now. I need to save my sister, and without the spirits, I'll lose my chance."

Jhinn clicked his tongue, shaking his head. "Where will you go with your sister when you get her free?"

Tamerlan flushed. "I hadn't thought that far ahead. I'm just trying to get her out of the Sunset Tower."

Jhinn sighed. "You have no plan, boy? You're lucky you met me. When you have your sister, you bring her to Jhinn and I'll get you out of Jingen, yeah?"

"It's a generous offer," Tamerlan said with a smile. "Too generous. We'll be wanted fugitives. That will bring trouble for you."

The boy shook his head, waving his hands dismissively. "I already have trouble. I already lost my family. I'm already mocked for the boats I build. I always wanted to go look for the People of Queen Mer. Maybe now is the time. Bring your sister. We'll go together."

"Sure," Tamerlan said gently. The boy was big-hearted and far too generous. Tamerlan wouldn't involve him if he didn't have to. But what if he had to? "We'd love to go with you."

If he lived that long, it would even be kind of fun.

He'd read about the People of Queen Mer, of course. They had set out from somewhere in the north in the years that the Dragonblood Plains were first building the five cities. They had been sent by prophecy to find a story of some kind and told by the same prophecy that they must not leave the water until it was found. Most of them had passed by the five cities intent on their search, but some of them – their boats battered by the waves and in need of repair and their stores low – had stayed in the five cities, working as gondoliers or ferrymen to try to make enough money to resupply and finish the journey. Either the gondola business wasn't as lucrative as it looked, or they'd simply decided to stay because even now, generations later, they had not continued their search for the story.

"Okay, it's a plan. And now you go and get what you need from your rooms, yeah?"

"Yeah," Tamerlan said, smiling slightly. He hadn't smiled this much in … how long? "Let me take a turn with the oar."

Jhinn frowned, handing it over reluctantly. "Gentle. No need to sink the boat on your first try, yeah? I could use a nap."

They changed places and Jhinn settled in a hole-ridden blanket in the prow of the boat while Tamerlan worked the oar in the back. It was hard not to give in to the waves of panic that rolled over him when he wasn't talking about something else, but he tried to focus on the sun setting and throwing brilliant colors over the waves. He tried to focus on the rhythmic *splish* of water running off his oar as he skimmed it over the waves before dipping it back in the water to pull against the water. The work was good for him. Doing anything mindless was good, though anxiety ate at him from within like a thousand beetles chewing, chewing, chewing from inside his belly, consuming him one tiny bite at a time.

He had to go back to his rooms. He hadn't been able to get his hands on more orrisleaf and there was some in those packs he'd made for himself and his sister. Getting the packs would be a good idea, too.

And Jhinn was right. He needed a plan beyond just grabbing her and running. If they left the five cities with Jhinn, no one would even know who they were. No one would have any reason to come looking for them. They were unimportant. Just two spare children of a Landhold family – not special in any way. They could even take up the life of the Waverunners, living boat to boat. It wouldn't be so bad. Tamerlan liked stories. He could spend his life looking for one.

His thoughts were jagged as he rowed, quick bursts of memories of reading stories to his little sister while he was supposed to be cleaning the stables. He'd look up from the story to see she'd done all the work while he read.

But the memory was marred by the stab of worry ripping through him and reminding him of the chewing beetles. He wouldn't ever read to her again unless he succeeded.

He'd failed too often.

If he were only someone other than Tamerlan the dreamer – if he were a soldier, or a true Landhold, or anyone with experience – maybe he would have saved her the first night. Maybe he wouldn't have sunk to using the Bridge of Legends. Or, if he had, then maybe he would have been able to control the Legends instead of letting them control him.

He clamped down on the thought. 'What-if's' wouldn't help. He was Tamerlan. He couldn't be anything else. Tamerlan the hard-working apprentice. Tamerlan who lifted and moved heavy things and built muscle that way, but whose mind was always somewhere else dreaming of what could be and what had been many moons ago. He could use that if he was clever enough. He could use a fit body and a dreamy mind if he could just figure out how to put them to his advantage.

He was coming up on the Alchemist's District now. He hadn't eaten all day and that was a good thing. The nausea gripping him would be worse with food inside.

All he had to do was to sneak into *The Copper Tincture* and get the orrisleaf. Then he could smoke again and go save Amaryllis. He'd left the window to his room open. He could go that way. No need for anyone to see him come and go. It was a gamble, sure, but a gamble worth taking. If he was just careful. If he could just focus. If he could just find a way to steer everything right this time, then he would finally succeed and he and Ama and Jhinn would row off into a distant future of sea and stories. He could already smell the salt on the air as he tied the gondola to the jetty and shook Jhinn awake.

"I'll be back soon."

"I'll be sleeping," Jhinn muttered irritably.

"Thank you for everything."

"Don't get caught by the Watch."

And then he was slipping through the dusk shadows and toward *The Copper Tincture,* slipping between costumed groups of people as they carried baskets and pushed carts, laughing and pronouncing blessings on anyone in their path.

"A candied plum, hooded one?" a woman with round cheeks and bright eyes dressed in a shabby Maid Chaos costume asked as he passed her. "It comes with a blessing!"

"Another time, Maid Chaos," he said politely, ducking around her and into the shadows again. The streets were packed with people and he stood out in his simple clothing. He should have thought to try to bring a costume. He dodged from shadow to shadow trying to avoid curious eyes and proffered gifts as politely as possible. He was breathing hard by the time he reached the dark alley beside the Copper Tincture.

He shouldn't do this. He should find the orrisleaf somewhere else.

Just do it. Stop overthinking everything.

Had that been Lila Cherrylock' voice in his mind? He shook his head to try to clear it. He was imagining things – obviously. He hadn't even smoked, so there was no way there could be a Legend in his mind. He wiped his sweating palms on his trousers and tried to forget the voice in his mind and concentrate on the job ahead. He'd need every ounce of focus to get this right and not get caught doing it – if anyone was watching. There was no guarantee of that. He stopped his spiraling thoughts before he changed his mind.

Time to roll the dice.

He climbed the stonework carefully, grateful to see that the window to his room was still open.

Almost there.

Almost there.

His foot slipped, but he recovered, pushing hard with the other foot and flipping himself over the window ledge and into the dark room beyond.

"Gotcha," a melodious female voice said, and a hand gripped his arm in the darkness.

24: For a Sister

Marielle

Marielle's mouth was dry and her hands shook as she held her dagger to the neck of the man she'd caught.

It had worked.

It was him!

His scent was so strong that she could almost taste it – warm honey, lemongrass, cardamom, and tarragon all mixing into a heady scent that threatened to sweep her away. Her vision was temporarily blinded by the burst of gold his presence brought with it, tinged with the turquoise and gold residue of old magic and the throbbing pulse of his orange and ginger desperation. Through it all, in a bronze tinge as different to the gold of her attraction as honey was to sunbeams, was a single thread of hope smelling like morning dew.

Marielle gritted her teeth, fighting against the pull of his emotions. She didn't dare to succumb to it. If she did, all would be lost.

She shoved him against the wall instead, drawing her truncheon in a smooth motion and setting it against his neck as her dagger eased back. She pushed against the truncheon – not enough to choke him, but enough to pin him to the wall. She still couldn't believe it was him. It had been such a long shot!

"Tamerlan Zi'fen?" she asked. "You're under arrest by the Jingen City Watch."

He moaned and the sound of his voice set every hair of her body on end as if she was a tuning fork and he'd sung her note.

"Please," the one word spilled from his lips like a pearl from a string. "Please don't do this."

"Don't stop you?" she hissed. "You are in violation of Jingen City Law 34 subsection V – no citizen shall attempt to enter through a locked door belonging to a private citizen, a guild, a government building, or foreign entity. Do you deny that you tried to break into the Seven Suns Palace?"

"No," he said. His voice was exactly as she'd expected – deep and husky. It thrilled her. It made her think of what sorts of things he might whisper to her in this dark room if they weren't enemies and if she didn't have him pressed against a wall with her truncheon.

"You are also in violation of Jingen City Law 21, subsection II – no citizen shall steal guild property, Jingen City Law 34 – again! – Jingen City Law 9, subsection IV – no citizen shall threaten the life of another citizen with violent action, including but not limited to, choking, beating, containing, assault with edged weapons, assault with – ”

He cut her off. “Could I just admit to you that yes, I stole the book at the Queen Mer Library and threatened Sian.”

“You’re admitting this?”

Righteous anger welled up in her. He admitted his crime. No matter what attraction existed, it was clear what came next. She would march him to the local Watch House and turn him into custody. She would testify to his crimes before the Lord Mythos. It would not be comfortable to condemn him to death, but the law was clear and easy to understand, and so was her role. She would take no pleasure in it, but she would carry it out. And she would watch him sink.

“Could you light a candle?” he asked.

“What?”

He sounded so calm even though his emotions popped and blazed. That orange and ginger pulsing of his desperation was the strongest of all. She shouldn’t light the candle. He must be planning something behind all those emotions.

“I can’t see your face,” he said gently.

Why did he have to be gentle? She was threatening him with justice for his crimes! She had a truncheon to his neck! He shouldn’t be gentle. He should be raging and threatening or weeping. She’d seen both. She’d never seen gentle. She’d never smelled the azure and aspen scent that swirled around him when making an arrest.

"What can a little light hurt?" he pressed.

He had a point. But if she let up with the truncheon, he might escape. She put the tip of her long knife back to his throat, shifting her weight nervously.

"Feel that point? I keep it sharp in accordance with strict regulation."

"I have no doubt."

Was he laughing at her? He seemed to find the comment funny.

"If you want a candle, you'll need to light one with the edge of this knife at your throat. It's my insurance that you won't escape."

"Sure, sure. Just let me walk to the washstand, please."

There had been a candle there. She remembered that now. And flint and Firestarter. She kept her knife pressed to his throat as he struck the flint, sparking the starter grass and cupping it carefully in his hands as he blew on the tiny flame, nursing it to life.

The flickers of light send a glow over his face that highlighted his high-born good looks. He looked like the pictures of the Dragonblooded you saw in books or statues around Jingen. Like the warriors from the mountains of old, spilling down onto the plains to fight dragons.

He lit the candle and then held it, looking at her with widening eyes.

"Don't think that just because I'm a woman you can take advantage of me," Marielle said. "I am a servant of the law. I will give my life to uphold it."

"And you love good," he said, his dreamy eyes seeming to see more of her than she planned to give. She pulled her scarf over her nose and mouth in defense. "In ancient times there were warriors of light and justice who were dedicated to doing good and honoring their god. They were called Paladins. Are you a paladin, Officer?"

"Marielle Valenspear," she said, letting the veil drop again.

"I didn't know that Watch Officers were so beautiful," he said, his eyes running over her face and hair like he was trying to memorize them.

Marielle stiffened. If he thought he could charm her with sweet words about paladins and comments on her looks, he could think again. She was no red-door woman ready to please a man for a price. She felt her cheeks heating. She shouldn't have thought that. It was insulting to her mother.

"Are you also compassionate?" he asked, licking his lips like he was nervous to ask the question. His lower lip was fuller than the upper lip – shaped in a way that made Marielle think of kissing.

"We're *justice*," Marielle said. "The Hand of the Law."

"What would you say if I told you that tomorrow they are going to sacrifice a girl who doesn't deserve to die. They're going to spill her blood out for a dusty old ritual. They're going to take all her smiles. They're going to steal all her tears.

They're going to rob from the world all the ways that she would have made everything around her more beautiful."

"I know that," Marielle said, and her tone might have been harsher than she wanted because ringing in her mind was the thought that she could stop it all if she was just willing to give up her own life instead. "That doesn't change the law.

Tamerlan smiled slightly at her – just one corner of his mouth lifting sadly. "Did you know that she's my little sister?"

The words hung in the air between them as he leaned in closer, ignoring her blade, his words quiet and gentle – almost delicate.

"My first memory is of her tiny steps toddling after me. My first heartbreak was followed by her childish hug. I think sometimes that maybe she's the only one who's ever known me. And pretty soon there won't be an Amaryllis anymore and I'm pretty sure that if that's true, then there won't be a Tamerlan either." He glanced into the shadows, a haunted look flashing over his face so quickly that Marielle couldn't have sworn she'd actually seen it at all. "Is that justice?"

"It's the law," she said, but the words felt hollow, like for the first time in her life they didn't matter like they used to. Because it wasn't the Real Law. It was the thing that Captain Ironarm had warned her about. It was that moment when you realized that the City Law didn't line up with the Real Law at all.

"What is the law, Marielle?"

"I read you the codes that you broke. Do you want to hear the section about the obtaining of sacrifices and implementation of the sacrifice system?" her voice grew fainter with every word.

"I do not," and now his voice had steel in it. "What I want to know is this – you serve truth and justice. You love the law because it lays out the right way of things like a straight line through a maze. You are devoted to it because it sets out a wall to defend the innocent and lays a trap for the guilty. But tell me this, Marielle, is this real justice? Who are you defending when you are complicit in stealing my sister's life? Where is truth in the lie that she is worth less than anyone else in this city? Where is the justice in taking from her what isn't yours to take? Tell me *that* Jingen City Law and subsection."

"I can't let you break the law," Marielle breathed, but she didn't know anymore if she meant it. After all, who was she to say that her life was worth more than this Amaryllis? Was there anyone who would think their life had ended if *she* died? Lord Mythos had said he didn't want to kill her. And Carnelian would miss the results she brought. Her mother – Variena – would probably cry. But when they gave her the redemption money for Marielle's life, she would spend it. Variena was a survivor. "If I let anyone break it, then there is no law. And if there is no law, then no one is safe."

"Who is safe right now? Is Amaryllis safe? I'm not asking you to let me break the law," Tamerlan said, clearly taking a deep breath to compose himself. He bit his lip, stretching it between his teeth as he thought about his words. A sheen of sweat had broken out across his brow and he ran his calloused hand through his short light-colored hair. He probably didn't realize how that made his muscles bulge with the movement or how that drew her eyes.

"Then what are you asking for," she asked, a little breathlessly. The dagger point by his throat had dropped without her realizing it.

"I'm just asking you not to stop me – not tonight. Just one more night, Marielle. Please?"

His big eyes were liquid as he pled, like he was on the verge of tears, and the way his emotions bubbled and rolled like the sea in a storm, he could very well be.

She shouldn't say yes. She knew that much. Saying yes was a betrayal of everything she'd ever believed about what was right and wrong and what mattered. She was a servant of the law. She was made of law from core to cusp.

And yet.

And yet it was only her own selfishness that kept his sister in that tower at all. If she marched to the Sunset Tower tonight and demanded to be taken in Amaryllis' place, they would take her, and it would be her life at stake. And no one, not a brother or a friend or anyone else, would bother to fight to keep her alive.

She didn't have the courage to give herself for a stranger. Not even a stranger with a beautiful, angst-ridden brother. She swallowed the sick feeling of shame that filled her.

Maybe Captain Ironarm was right. Maybe what you did in that moment between the Real Law and the City Law told you who you really were.

She took a deep, shaking breath and lowered her knife, sliding it back in its sheath.

Tamerlan danced back deftly, ducking out of her range and scooping up a pair of oiled-jute packs and jamming a mortar and pestle into the top of one of them. He paused for a moment, like he was considering something, and then with a nervous half-smile, he ducked in close, kissed her cheek and breathed a gasping, "Thank you."

He was across the room and leaping out the window before her breath steadied again. Gone before the gooseflesh erupting across her cheek and down her arm settled.

She'd made a decision.

And now she'd live with the consequences.

25: Rampage

Tamerlan

Tamerlan huddled in the shadows of the canal, grinding the ingredients carefully. He was almost ready. This time, he had the lock picks and a knife in his belt. When Lila Cherrylocks – or even Byron Bronzebow – came for him, he'd be ready.

There was a loud peal of laughter overhead from the street above and someone threw a coin over the railing into the canal. Jhinn reached out with careful precision and caught the coin inches from the water.

"I think they threw it in for good luck," Tamerlan said mildly.

"Yeah. It's my good luck now, boy."

Tamerlan chuckled quietly. "Okay. I'm going to go up to one of the braziers up there and smoke this stuff. I'll be back in a few hours."

"Yeah. Sure. I'll be here."

"You don't have somewhere else you need to be?"

"I'm paid up for the night!" Jhinn held up the coin he'd caught. "See? The waves are interested in your progress. If you grab the sister, you'll be glad I'm nearby."

Jhinn nodded, pouring his mixture into a small scarf – he didn't want to lose his mixing bowl – and carefully climbing from the gondola to the stone ledge that ran along the canal. With careful steps, he followed the ledge to the stairs that led up to the street above.

The Temple District was alight with merriment, people in costume racing from temple to temple to give out small carvings and tokens of their faith – good luck for the year ahead. The elderly and small children had gone to bed hours ago and now as the night grew late, the scarier costumes appeared. A Deathless Pirate with his face painted like a skull lurched along the street followed closely by a Lady Sacrifice dripping blood as she walked. What might look like a virginal costume in the day, looked horrific in the darkness and with the added effects of makeup.

Tamerlan's stomach turned, leaving his mouth dry. It all felt too real when he remembered that his sister would look just like that tomorrow. He skirted the costumed merry-makers, dodging a group of Smudgers promising a spirit of pleasure if he took a whiff of their smoke. He didn't need that. He had his own spirit to consume.

Fortunately, the Temple District had open braziers outside many of the Temples. The key was to find one that no one else would share. Tamerlan still didn't know what would happen if anyone shared his smoke and he didn't want to find out tonight.

"Here for a good time?" a Lady Chaos asked, lurching into him with a wide grin on her face and a tottering step. She'd either been smoking the Smudger's pleasure smoke or drinking too heavily. Her blue eyes were glassy with intoxication. Tamerlan leaned her gently against a nearby wall and passed quickly. Hopefully, she'd find her way home safely. He didn't have the time tonight to help her on her way.

Her blue eyes had reminded him of the purple ones that had watched him so sharply back in his room. Why had the Scenter let him go? Why hadn't she dragged him to the nearest Watch House? He had thought she would.

Her compassion – surprising as it was – was like a golden gift from the heavens. In any other circumstance, he would have found a way to pay her back – in friendship if nothing else. Tamerlan liked people who believed in things and if anyone really believed in the law, it was that woman – Marielle. And yet, she'd cared enough to break it. Even her name rolled easily on his tongue. Marielle.

He shook his head. Now was not the time to wonder why she'd given him that gift. Now was definitely not the time to let haunting snatches of her beautiful face flicker through his mind like glimpses of a sunset between the rooftops. He should be using his chance while he still had it.

He snuck around the side of a Smudger Temple. The front of the building bore a sign stating: *All Spirits Welcome Smudge House.*

A group of laughing people still shy of twenty-years-old ran up the steps, nearly tripping over their costumes to lay gifts of plants and leaves at the door. Good luck for them in coming months and years.

"We should take some, too," one of them laughed. "I bet someone else left something valuable!"

Another one, dressed as One-eyed King Ablemeyer stopped him. "I don't want to be on the Smudgers bad side, do you?"

"Ooooh! The spirits will get you!" One of the girls waved her arms like an angry spirit.

Tamerlan half-smiled at their fun as he pulled out his scarf. The brazier at the back of the Temple was burned down to embers. But embers would be enough.

He looked around. No one was watching.

Time to roll the dice for the second time that night. It had worked out the first time, hadn't it?

He dumped the ingredients from the scarf to the brazier, immediately shoving his head into the puff of smoke that erupted from the hot coals.

Breathe! Breathe, Tamerlan! He sucked in great gasps of smoke, reeling from it. He coughed and sputtered, hands on his knees, but this was no time to stop – not if he wanted to save Amaryllis. Gritting his teeth, he stuck his head into the smoke a second time and breathed another lungful of smoke, sucking the acrid blackness into his lungs like it was lifegiving air. When he thought he might pass out from it, he stumbled backward, landing roughly on the cobblestones, his head spinning.

Mine! I want him! That was Lila Cherrylocks! He'd succeeded!

Tamerlan's heart was racing, the blood already flooding into his brain. He'd done it!

I don't think so, thief. I'm taking this pretty man for a stroll around town.

There was a feeling of something *puuushing* in his brain and then Lila's voice was gone, replaced by a voice as hard as a whipcrack and as dry at the bones in the crypts.

The moon is up. I hear the sounds of life around me.

Tamerlan grabbed his belt knife from his belt and stalked away from the brazier without a single look back.

Whatever spirit this was seemed to be focused and intense. Good! She could get him to Amaryllis. This didn't seem like the kind of person who let things like castle walls or guards stop her.

Nice try. Flattery will get you nowhere. I am the handmaid of death. I am the last thing a screaming victim ever sees.

Tamerlan's skin crawled, as he tried to draw back from his own hands and feet. But he couldn't run from his own body. He couldn't stop gripping that belt knife even if he wanted to. Why had she drawn it? Why was it gripped so tightly in his hand, the blade running along his arm like he knew what to do with it? Why were his feet stalking toward the front of the Smudger Temple?

There was a shriek of laughter and a girl dressed like Maid Chaos ran from her group and stumbled into his arms.

"Ha! And who are you dressed as?" she asked drunkenly. Moonlight reflected from her Maid Chaos costume. "It doesn't look very fun."

And then Tamerlan heard his own voice saying, "Death is not fun."

The blade flicked out and then her blood splashed hot across his face as she fell choking to the ground.

No!

No, no, no, no, no!

He tried to scream but his own voice was inaccessible to him. His voice was too busy laughing – and it was *his* laugh. It felt like it would never be his again, as if it had been stolen – snatched from his throat like the life from that poor girl's body. Her eyes glazed over as he left her like refuse abandoned along the street.

No! He did this to save Amaryllis, not to kill anyone, certainly not an innocent victim!

His body raced forward, toward a knot of screaming people in costume. He had never guessed he was so fast or so strong as he tore into them, the small knife flicking into vulnerable places and past upraised hands and terrorized eyes.

Tamerlan desperately tried to shut his eyes, but they would not close as image after image of fear and death and horror burned across them like acid thrown across metal. His internal screams rang in his ears alone. His body was running down the street, already soaked in blood up to his elbows.

He turned over braziers as he ran – was he really so strong? He'd seen it take four men to move them into place! – letting the fire spill across the cobbles or light the edges of fleeing people's costumes aflame. Smoke billowed into the night almost as fast and thick as the shrieks that accompanied it.

He raced down a horse as it fled, slicing his hamstring with a single motion, knocking him off his feet with the lamp post and then cutting his throat as he screamed into the night. An easy spin and slash and the carriage driver fell, clutching his ruined throat.

And now Tamerlan was sobbing inside as Maid Chaos used his body to cut the horse's leg from its body. He raced down the street, brandishing the leg in his left hand, his fingers wrapping around the bloody bone, swinging the leg so that the metal horseshoe struck blows to anyone in his path as he howled out curses and mad prophecies.

"Before you see two more dawns your city will be destroyed! Plead for your salvation! Cry for your unmarked graves!"

There was no way to run from yourself. No way to hide. No way to dull the sights or sounds or smells.

All his life, Tamerlan had trained himself to notice the beauty around him, to see every tone of color, to hear the smallest sound, to take in the barest flicker of a scent and now this … desecration … of everything he was made him wish every one of those moments away. If he'd only chosen to dull his senses, perhaps he would have been able to do that now instead of being forced to taste every moment of this hellish descent into madness.

He swung and slashed, cut and burned, murdered and mutilated his way through the Temple District, nowhere near his sister in the Sunset Castle. Nowhere near what he'd hoped for, planned for, begged for. He'd convinced the Scenter to let him go. He'd sworn it was for the good. His sense of shame at betraying her was nothing compared to the overwhelming, sickening guilt he felt with every heartbeat as Maid Chaos worked her way from street to street, from panic-eyed look to desperate scream, from falling victim to slain defender.

If only someone would kill him. If only someone would slide a sword through his ribs or slash his throat, but no one was as fast or strong as Maid Chaos. She seemed to wrap herself around him as if she were here even more fully than Byron Bronzebow or Lila Cherrylocks had been.

Because I am. I am greater than those fools. There are no shades of grey with me. And certainly, no white. I am black as the night, black as the pupils of my screaming victims.

Perhaps he had gone mad, for it seemed that they fought priests, seizing their staves and polearms and fighting with one in each hand before turning on Watch Officers who ran into the fray, bells jangling on their hips.

Perhaps one had even been sweet Marielle. In the chaos, who could tell who had fallen?

I can tell.

In all the death, who could keep track of how many lives had been lost?

Me, again. I'm very good at this.

The world had gone mad. It was a hurricane of evil, a slaughterhouse that never ended.

And so it has been since the beginning, since the minds of men invented me to blame for their evil deeds. When you see trouble, look for the woman, they said. I have shown them trouble a thousand times a thousand, and I will show it to them again and again, world without end.

He'd lost hope hours ago. Lost sanity soon after. He was nothing more than a gibbering mass of agony as the hours passed and they leapt up into the roofs, burning temples and killing priests and slaughtering anyone whose path intersected with theirs.

The first light of dawn was breaking on the horizon and they were back where they started passing the *All Spirits Welcome Smudge House* – only this time they were on the tiled roof instead of the city street, the canal just behind them.

I fade.

She leapt from the roof into the canal and Tamerlan closed his eyes but not his nose, letting the cloudy canal water fill his lungs. Death would be close. Would it wash him of his last hours? Could even the fires of death erase the guilt of what he'd done?

He let his body sink into the water, not fighting it, not trying to stop it at all.

Something clamped onto his shoulder, dragging him upward through the water. He was pulled up into the air and his lungs gasped for breath on their own. Traitors.

Hands hauled him upward as cursing filled the air.

"What did you do now, boy? That whole Temple District on fire! You burned more than your boat this time!"

Tamerlan sank into unconsciousness, desperate for the relief of insensibility it brought. If only he could wake up as someone else. If only he could never have been born.

26: Shaking Shame

Tamerlan

Tamerlan woke, shaking uncontrollably. A rattling like dice in a cup filled his ears. His teeth. That was his teeth chattering together. He shook his head, trying to dislodge the blood-soaked thoughts, but nothing could block them out. It was dark where he was and wailing sounded out from above him. He tried to sit up, but something hard hit his back.

"Stay down!" Jhinn whispered fiercely. "Keep down. I'm taking you somewhere safe."

There were shouts from above and a gondola passed by. Someone on it was wailing.

"My Danica! My sweet Danica! Only sixteen and gone!" and then the voice had passed in the swoosh of the oars.

Tamerlan wrapped wet arms around his head and sobbed silently until it felt his chest was cleaving in two and his heart was spilling into the hull of the little boat. The gentle beating of the water against the hull wasn't soothing this time. It was more like the drums of war being beaten in triumph when the enemy marches by the piles of the dead.

What had he done?

He shied away from the flood of memories. He knew exactly what he had done. He was soaked with the blood of his victims. He had seen their last thoughts flash over their eyes as he took their lives. And he'd been powerless to stop it.

He was a monster. Worse, a devil.

"Stay still. We're almost there."

It seemed darker under the canvas tarp. Perhaps the small boat had docked under a bridge or a building. Some buildings along the canal had little channels that ran right under them so that supplies could be unloaded right into their storerooms.

Or perhaps it was merely the blackness of his soul covering over his living eyes. The light was too good for him. Warmth too much to ask for, now.

There was a dull *thunk* and then the canvas ripped off him.

They were somewhere dark and wet stonework was overhead. Jhinn stood over him and before he could move, a bucket of frigid, stale water was upended over him. He shivered against the deluge.

"Strip and then we'll do it again. Throw your clothes over the side."

The boy was smart. If he was caught with a bloody Tamerlan it would be more than his boat that they would take.

"You shouldn't be with me," Tamerlan said through chattering teeth as he stripped out of his clothing, throwing it over the side one article at a time.

Jhinn pushed the clothing under water with his oar, stuffing it under the edge of some rock. "You saved my boat. I will help save your sister. It's fair."

"You should leave your boat and go, Jhinn. You don't want them to catch you." Tamerlan threw his belt knife over the side. His hands throbbed with every movement. They were crisscrossed with cuts where the handle of the belt knife had slipped in all the blood and slid the blade too far down. It had cut Tamerlan's own hands with every slash through the flesh of someone else. He looked at his palms. The flesh was ragged and bleeding.

Another bucket of water surprised a gasp from him as Jhinn poured it over him.

"That's better," the boy said. "And we don't leave the boats. I already told you that. Here. Bail the water out of the bottom."

He shoved a rough wooden bowl at Tamerlan to bail with.

"You don't leave because the things on land aren't real," Tamerlan remembered. If only that was true. If only last night had been a nightmare. But it wasn't. It was almost more real than this moment was. He shivered as revulsion filled him. Revulsion at himself. Deep, bone-deep shame at who he had become in a single night.

"And because the land is the place of the Satan. He roams up and down and to and fro, looking for who he may devour."

Tamerlan's wry laugh was harsh in the silence of wherever they were. Superstitions. Old dogma. As useful as the pink-tinged water he was bailing over the side.

"Laugh all you want, boy. You think there's no Satan out there? Then why did you fall off that roof covered in blood and shaking so hard your teeth sound like the clink of coins? Why are your eyes haunted? Why did I hear the wails of many mourners as they came to collect their dead? Try and tell me that's not the Satan."

Tamerlan clenched his jaw at the overwhelming pain of the thought. There were parents up there collecting children. Lovers collecting their beloved. Children their parents. And he had ruined all their lives. If he hadn't smoked the mixture, if he hadn't opened the Bridge of Legends, none of this would have happened.

But you didn't know, a part of his mind kept telling him. But he should have known. After all, hadn't he threatened Sian's life? Hadn't she seen what he was capable of when he was possessed by the Spirits of the Legends? Not all Spirits were Byron Bronzebow. And to his horror, not all spirits were even Lila Cherrylocks.

No, they aren't.

He was going mad. He was hearing her voice in his mind.

Mad?

Jhinn slid one of the rocks in the wall aside, pulling an old jute sack from the depths of it, and then another, and then another and then closing it again.

"Put these on," he said, shoving the sacks at Tamerlan. "It's a Seven Suns Palace guard uniform – blue cloak and all! – I found it hanging on a washing line over the canal and I thought that something like this might be important to have someday."

Tamerlan nodded. "Thank you."

He opened the sacks and began to dress mechanically. They were a little loose in the waist, a little tight against his broad shoulders. But they were the right length. Even the boots fit. And the cloak was warm, warmer than he deserved. When he was finished, Jhinn gathered the sacks, stuffing them in the little compartment behind him with the bags Tamerlan had brought him.

"No one will ask questions of a Palace Guard. We can leave this District before the City Watch come. Some people say they can smell you like a strong curry. We don't want them smelling you, boy. I bet you stink of the Satan."

Tamerlan nodded, trying one more time to send the boy to freedom. "You should not be with me."

"Where else would I go?" Jhinn pulled a small canvas kit from his hiding spot in the stern of the boat, unwrapping it to reveal a needle and bandages. "Let's fix those hands. You're torn like a sail after a storm."

Tamerlan felt like that. Torn. But unlike his hands which Jhinn could stitch, the rest of him was unrepairable.

"I just wanted to help my sister." It came out close to a sob.

"You haven't failed yet, boy."

"Tomorrow night they're going to kill her."

"Then you have all of today and tonight. That's not failure yet. Unless you give up."

Tamerlan drew a stuttering breath, sucking in his tears. Jhinn was right that there was time, but he didn't dare smoke again. Not when it could mean the lives of dozens of people. He felt like he was a deck of black and white cards – more white than black – but he'd been shuffled and all the black were on top. Any play he made could only be black, black, black until they'd all been played. There weren't enough hands left to find a white.

"I can't go back. I can't do it again."

"You were willing to die for your sister," Jhinn said. "Right? That was your plan?"

"Yes."

"I don't have a sister."

"That's probably for the best," Tamerlan said. If this was what love did to a heart, then no one should ever love again.

"I think you need to ask, what is she worth? Is she worth your life?" Jhinn asked as he pulled the needle through Tamerlan's shredded palms.

Of course, she was.

Jhinn wasn't done. "Is she worth someone else's? And if she is – how many lives is she worth? If I could pull my parents back from the breast of Queen Mer … if I could do that … there wouldn't be a price too high to pay. There wouldn't be a limit I would put on what I would do."

"I can't even get the Legends to go in the palace with me," Tamerlan said. Why was he considering this? He shouldn't be talking about it. Talking only made it feel possible and it shouldn't be possible. "Every time I try, they go their own way. But I need them to fight and pick locks and do the things I can't once I get in there."

"Try asking a hard question next time," Jhinn said, tying a deft knot. "That one is easy to solve. You sneak in the palace in that pretty uniform I just gave you. Then you call the Legends when you get there. Can it work like that?"

"I don't think so. I throw the mixture into a brazier or fire and breathe it in. If I did that in the palace, it would draw a lot of attention and it might affect other people, too. Who knows how many Legends can cross the Bridge at once."

Jhinn laughed. "You're a fool, boy. Another easy solve. Just wrap the mixture in paper and smoke it when you're ready – real simple. No big smoke. No one else affected. Just you. And you would waste less of it that way, too."

It was a brilliant idea.

And a terribly dangerous one.

And Tamerlan should not be considering it at all. He kept thinking of what Jhinn said – what was his sister worth? And then seeing the images of what he'd done last night flash through his mind. Shame and hope mixed in a foul brew that nauseated him at the same time that he clenched his newly repaired hands in determination.

It wasn't too late to save Amaryllis.

If he dared to try again.

There was a clinking sound in the distance and Jhinn motioned to him hurriedly. "Strip down again and put your clothes in the bag. Hurry!"

"I just got dressed!"

"Hurry!"

27: Cold Regret

Marielle

Marielle woke to hurried footsteps and the door slamming open, hitting the wall. She shook herself, straightening and wiping her mouth. She hadn't meant to sleep here, but after Tamerlan had snuck away she couldn't just go back to the Watch House. Without him in hand, she had to wait the night out in his room. It still smelled like him.

"No luck, I see," Carnelian said, the glow of the dawn streaming into the room around her. "Looks like we both missed the excitement tonight but come on. Captain Ironarm wants every Scenter in the Watch on this investigation and you're going to help me turn my dry streak around."

Marielle stood, wiping at the corners of her eyes.

"No time for that," Carnelian said, grabbing Marielle by the arm and pulling her behind her. She smelled of cilantro anticipation. "We're already late. I was at that decadent party all night in your place. What a waste of time! Nothing happened there and everything happened out here."

She was so full of pent-up energy that she practically bounced as she stormed through the quiet halls of *The Copper Tincture*, leading Marielle back out to the streets beyond.

"It's a good thing you fell asleep," Carnelian said. "Because there won't be any sleep for anyone tonight."

"What happened?" Marielle asked as Carnelian shoved a flask onto her hands. "It's too early for drinking."

"It's water. Take a swig. Try to get your wits about you. We're about to walk into hell."

"In the Alchemist's District?" Marielle took a swig of the water, using a tiny splash to clean her face and then handing it back to Carnelian. She felt like she was five steps behind her friend already.

"No, the Temple District. By the time I left that Landhold Party and all the frills and lace, it was all over except the sobbing."

"What was all over?"

"Someone has a grudge against the religions of this city, let me tell you. Ho! Gondola!"

A small gondola rowed by a teenage boy streaked past them without so much as looking at Carnelian's outstretched hand. A lump of oilcloth filled the front of the gondola and the whole thing stank of a slaughterhouse. Marielle drew her veil up, flinching from the heavy scent of death even as Carnelian hailed another gondola and dragged her into the small craft.

"Temple District," Carnelian ordered, paying the man a coin. "And right quick."

There had been something else under the scent of all that blood. They were already into the center of the canal, the small gondola disappearing around the corner when Marielle realized what it had been. Under the cloak of blood and death and terror had been a residue of magic, potent enough to cut through blood – and that was saying something! – and just the faintest hint of honey, lemongrass, and tarragon.

It couldn't be … could it?

"Marielle? Pay attention!" Carnelian was snapping her fingers. "We need to be on the alert. Last night someone – some crazy love-forsaken devils – slashed and hacked and bit – yes, bit! – their way through the Temple District. Can this thing go any faster?"

"Hurrying, Officer," the gondolier said deferentially.

"Every Watch House is on alert. Half the temples are gone – burnt to the ground! Timeless Cathedral is half-gone. There's just a tower and a few buttresses left. And the whole thing is blackened. Most of the Smudger Temples went up like ready torches. Doesn't help that they have so much fire everywhere. They're still dragging out the dead but there are hundreds, Marielle. Hundreds."

"Temple District," the gondolier interrupted.

"Keep going until you see the Watch," Carnelian instructed. "We missed it all, Marielle. Everyone did. There were hardly any guards set on the Temple District. We had them focused on the Government and Library Districts after all the threats there. And the ones here didn't get a chance to raise the alarm. With the Seven Suns Palace Guard and everyone of any importance inside the palace – well, it wasn't until the fires took off an alerted us all."

"Who was stationed at the Temple District," Marielle asked quietly. She finished braiding her hair out of the way. She needed it swept back so she could focus. She could already smell the terror and horror rolling from the burnt District like slices of raw red vinegar and stomach-acid icterine. Nausea filled her as the first members of the City Watch came into view. They stood along the rails of the street above directing traffic as gondolas came and went, packing the dock and the edge of the canal ledge.

"One at a time, take your turn. Everyone will have a chance," the voice of a portly Watch Officer droned. He'd done this a hundred times. "No pushing for position. Oars stay in the water, repeat, in the water. You hire the one that's there, my lady. No holding up the lines, please."

"A lot of the Officers were other places, pulled off this beat," Carnelian hedged.

"Who wasn't pulled off?" Marielle pressed softly as they waited for their turn to dock.

"Xi When, Tiya Ka'lina, Casabara Tavereaver, Linnelin Taskervale, Jin Ch'ng, Lia Tasmarina," Carnelian said just as softly, her usually firm face softening in acknowledgment that it could have just as easily been them last night. "They say Lia might survive. Maybe. She had a belly wound. Those can be unpredictable."

Marielle shivered. She was beginning to catch whiffs of what was up in the streets above. Gore and viscera was the primary smell. That and smoke from the fires. Water – stained red and dark with soot and ash – ran from the streets down to the canals in slow trickles, staining the water in grisly whorls of what had once been life and faith.

"Keep your nose up, Scenter," Carnelian reminded. "I think you're the best, and I plan to use you to catch these hounds of hell."

Marielle tried not to look at the dark burdens being carted away on the gondola that left the dock. They varied in size and length, but they were all about the same shape – the shape of dead people wrapped in black-dyed jute.

"Here we go," Carnelian said tugging Marielle out of the gondola as they finally bumped up against the dock.

"Double your rate to carry my girl home," a red-eyed woman said to their gondolier. Behind her, two grim-faced workers carried a dark jute-wrapped form.

Marielle ducked her head in respect to the mother. She could smell the bone-deep grief in the woman like the smell of red wine and thyme. It was a washed-out blue color.

Carnelian hardly seemed to notice the civilians on the dock. Her body was bent forward, head leading the rest like a hunting dog scenting for its quarry.

"This way."

She tugged Marielle up the steps and into the chaos on the street above.

People were everywhere. How strange in a place where so many had died last night – where so much violence had ruled. But they were here. Ash stained and grimy, blood to the elbows or with those heart-wrenching jute rolls in their arms. Tear-stained and hand-wringing or sharply barking orders to bucket lines, they choked the street and spilled into the charred wreckage. Monks and priests in robes the deep saffron of the Smudgers, or the pure white of the Timekeepers, sifted through the wreckage, pulling out what could be salvaged.

It was hard to believe this had only happened a short time before they arrived.

Someone whistled – a piercing sound like a knife to the ear – and Carnelian tugged her to a knot of Watch Captains. Captain Ironarm was there with arms crossed over her aged chest, looking more wrinkled than ever in her exhaustion.

"You're on investigation, Carnelian, Marielle. Find what you can. Check with Anaala. She's started interviewing survivors. Then see what you can sniff out."

Carnelian saluted briskly and Marielle joined her a half-second later, but her eyes lingered on Captain Iron Arm and the other Captains. Oddly, they all smelled the same. Usually in a group like that there were ambition and infighting, wariness, mistrust, loyalty, comradery and so much more all rolled up into one. But today they all stank of a world-weariness so thick it hung heavily on them, mixing with exhaustion and absent hope. She wished she could wash it away, like the ash running into the gutters and from there to the canals.

"Anaala's that way," Carnelian reminded her, dragging her away. Would Marielle be so tired of the world when she was a Watch Captain someday? Would Carnelian? "It's not our job to fix this, Marielle, so don't get hung up on that. It's just our job to find the people who did this and bring them to the Lord Mythos to be executed. Simple."

Marielle nodded, but she had a feeling that there was nothing simple at all about this. And her feeling was growing worse by the moment as the turquoise of magic stood out in little pools of powerful lilac scent and burst around the ash and blood in blossoms of vanilla, threading through the fear and death and the chaos of the night. If Maid Chaos herself had walked these streets, she couldn't have seeded more tumult in the city.

The magic clouded her mind, drawing her attention from one spot to the next as she followed Carnelian. She could almost smell the direction that these people had gone when they tore through the District killing everyone in their path. But there was a little problem. The path Marielle smelled couldn't possibly belong to more than one person. There were many scents, sure, but they followed only one trail. No single scent broke off on its own. There were no places where it branched or converged.

Many other scents intersected with the magic and crossed over it or crossed the path afterward. She smelled the brilliant last moments of the victims of their attack, their last scents like bright flashes in her mind, as if they had tried to dump every last emotion out at once while they still could. Over and around those scents, the smells of the mourners and rescuers, the healers and Watch Officers, the priests and the Smudgers, all wove one over the other, building the form of the scene layer upon layer in a weaving of scent. Those scents – normal scents – were simple enough to filter out, especially with the scarf over her nose, but it was the lead scent that would not make sense.

If it had been more than one person, they must have moved in lock-step with each other. A military unit, perhaps? But she didn't think so, and her suspicions were slowly carving a hole in her belly. Because under the smell of violence and fear was the smell of magic and under the smell of magic was a whiff of something that Marielle had smelled before. The faintest whiff of gold mixed with orange ginger – that smell she was beginning to know so well – the one laced with leather and acid, old books and cinnamon, cardamom and lavender and warm honey – the smell of the man she had let slip out the window last night like an innocent smile slipping off the face of a murderer when he was caught red-handed.

She shivered, suddenly cold.

What had she done?

"Officer Anaala," Carnelian acknowledged when they drew up beside the Officer. She had a hand on her hip as she spoke to a tearful young woman.

"Officer Carnelian." Anaala made everything sound like a rebuke. Even a greeting. She turned back to the shaking young woman, little older than a girl, her Maid Chaos costume tattered and bloody. "So, it was a woman who attacked you?"

"A wo – woman, yes," the girl managed, her voice shaking as an older woman wrapped an arm around her. "It was Maid Chaos."

"Maid Chaos?" Anaala lifted a single eyebrow, her expression bland. "Your attacker was dressed as Maid Chaos?"

"She wasn't dressed as Maid Chaos. She *was* Maid Chaos!"

Carnelian smirked but Anaala kept a straight face. "In moments of fear, it's easy to see things."

"I wasn't seeing things! It was a woman with flowing golden hair and a golden breastplate. She was tall and broad, and she swung a sword just like Maid Chaos in the stories. She was merciless. Merciless!"

"Thank you for your statement," Anaala said. "You are free to go. Next!"

But that was a good thing, wasn't it? Because if it was a tall blonde woman then it couldn't be Tamerlan, which meant that this couldn't be Marielle's fault for letting him go. And yet, the rock of worry in her belly felt heavier by the moment as if it might carry her through the street into the fires of hell below.

"And you saw?" Anaala prompted a man who was clearly a street vendor, his apron still stained with the brown smears of whatever food he had been selling. It smelled like meat pies.

"A young man. Tall. Strapping. Short blonde hair and a lean build. He fought with a small belt knife the length of my palm."

The stone in Marielle's stomach grew icy cold.

"He caused all this with a belt knife?" Anaala asked wryly.

The vendor shook his head. "Seemed like it. But then sometimes he looked like a woman with a sword."

"There were two of them?" Anaala clarified. "A man with a knife and a woman with a sword?"

The man shook his bald head like he couldn't find words for what he'd seen. "Two, yes. But also one. Like they were the same person, if you know what I mean."

"I really don't."

"Sometimes it was one. Sometimes it was the other. One would sort of fade out and then the other would surface. It was the oddest thing."

"How much did you have to drink last night?" Anaala asked the man.

"Well, my fair share, I suppose." The street vendor laughed nervously and Anaala gave Marielle a pointed look as if to remind her that she wasn't supposed to be hauling off everyone for public drunkenness. Marielle felt her cheeks heat. Even she could see this was no time to enforce that law.

No, right now was not the time for enforcing petty laws. Now was the time for Marielle to panic, because that description sounded a lot like Tamerlan. And last night she had let him go to save his sister. And now, today, there were over a hundred people dead because of her choice. Regret made the stone in her belly heavier as it pulled her down, down, down.

28: The Chase

Marielle

"I think we have enough to give chase," she said quietly to Carnelian.

Carnelian's eyes lit up. "Any other people described, Anaala?"

Anaala shook her head, waving the street vendor on. "They all mention either the man or the woman or both. No one else. It's not much to go on."

"But you can follow the scent?" Carnelian asked Marielle eagerly.

"With my eyes closed."

Carnelian pumped a fist, but at Anaala's severe look she colored, clearing her throat awkwardly. "Lead on, Marielle."

Once you had a scent, it was easy to follow it. Easy to block out the mother-wail of a nearby mourner and the agonized questions of a child. Or at least, it was easy to pretend you were blocking them out. It easy to forget the tragedy, the pain, the chaos. Easy to just give in to following your nose, to seeking the scent, to chasing that sensation.

There it was, leading up the side of that building. Had he really climbed up there? And there was still no divergence where anyone had broken off. If it had been both him and a woman you would think one of them would have gone a different way up the side of the wall. Not so.

She followed the zigzagging scent through the District, every shred of thought directed at the hunt, at the trail.

"That's right, Marielle," Carnelian encouraged. "Find them! Find them."

Marielle hurried, barely watching where she was going, she was so intent on the trail. Twice, Carnelian pulled her out of the path of a cart moments before she was hit. Another time, she'd physically picked Marielle up and swung her over a hole in the ground before she broke a leg falling in.

There was nothing but Marielle and the scent. And now she was no longer smelling the blood or death at all. In fact, she barely even smelled the pleasant call of the magic or saw its turquoise and gold. She was so narrowly focused that all she smelled was the honey gold of Tamerlan. She could have found him anywhere. She felt like she knew him. She could smell what he last ate, how he felt, who he was.

She stumbled, caught by Carnelian, and then recovered.

She could smell how he felt. She stopped for a moment, letting that sink in. He did not feel like a man on a killing spree. He felt panicked. Trapped. She could also smell horror in the golden smell, but when she drifted out of it again, she smelled glee in the turquoise magic.

Her mind whirled, confusion bubbling up. She'd never smelled anything like this before. It really was like there were two people she was following. Two people so close that they never left each other. Had the woman taken Tamerlan captive? Had she forced him forward while she killed all those people? That didn't make any sense. But neither did this smell.

She was barely watching her feet as she let herself drift on his scent. He was out there somewhere and either he had made her the accomplice to his evil when he convinced her to let him go, or he was somehow a victim, too.

Or maybe she just wanted to believe that because the alternative was too terrible.

Because if he had done this, then she was responsible for it, too. She was the one who had let him go. She was the one too cowardly to give her own life for the life of another. And these people had paid for that cowardice.

A hand yanked her back by the tail of her scarf.

"Fancy a swim?" Carnelian asked, pointing to the canal Marielle had almost walked into. For some reason, the railing was broken here.

"The scent goes that way," Marielle said.

"Into the water?"

She nodded.

"Come on, then." Carnelian led her along the shattered railing, through the access gate, and down the steps to the canal below. "Ho! Gondolier!"

They leapt onto the gondola as it pulled up and Marielle breathed deeply.

There it was. The scent.

The oar of the gondolier splashed merrily into the green canal – the only merry thing in a city of mourners – and then they were off, following the scent in Marielle's nose.

Was it possible that Tamerlan's scent was almost as addictive as the scent of magic? She was being foolish. Tamerlan had likely stained her soul with a black mark she could never expunge. She shouldn't be reveling in his scent.

They followed it down the canal and past where they had arrived, further and further out of the Temple District and across the river into the Trade District. The scent was growing fainter now, but the air was cleaner across the river and away from the tragedy. Here, a river away from the deadly rampage, trade continued as hagglers argued at the tops of their lungs along the packed streets and between the laden carts and crowded shops.

The Trade District was everything that Marielle usually hated – crowded, loud, and chaotic, it was the source of all of Jingen's wealth. And today it held their prize. They followed the canal under a bridge and then under a small inn – *The Laughing Gondolier.*

"Are you sure you still have the scent?" Carnelian whispered.

"Yes!" Marielle could still smell it and it still made her want more and more.

They slipped into the dark cavern. A small gondola floated, empty but for the oar and a bailing bowl, tied to a peg against one wall. The scent ended at the gondola.

Marielle looked around. There was nowhere else to go. No door nearby – the door to the storeroom of the inn was further into the cavern.

"Is there a trap door?" she asked.

Carnelian leaned out from their gondola feeling the bricks lining the canal. "I don't feel anything. What is a gondola doing here without a gondolier?"

She looked at their gondolier pointedly. He shrugged and she leaned forward aggressively.

"Don't just shrug. What is it doing here?"

"It's tied up," he said, with another shrug. "And look, it's little. Too little to be useful for trade or transport, yes?"

Carnelian grunted in agreement.

"Someone in the inn above us might own it. Maybe they use it to make it easier to unload barges," he suggested. "Or maybe someone pays to tie it here. Docking fees can be very expensive.

Another grunt.

But Marielle was distracted. How could the scent have just stopped? She could have sworn she could have followed it anywhere, but it didn't lead to the inn storeroom or out of the little docking area under the inn. It didn't even lead to the brick wall. It just stopped with the gondola.

"I've lost it. It's gone," she said disconsolately.

"Dragon's blood and ashes!" Carnelian cursed.

The stone in Marialle's belly grew again. The massacre in the Temple District there was her fault. She was the one who had let Tamerlan slip away. She was responsible for what he'd done. And now she couldn't even bring him to justice. His scent had grown cold.

And it was all her fault.

29: The Others

TAMERLAN

Tamerlan sucked in a long breath as Jhinn scrambled back into the boat. Sucking air through a hollow reed just wasn't the same.

"See?" he said, "next time I say 'strip', you strip fast! You don't want to get your pretty new guard clothes wet!"

Tamerlan sputtered, he'd sucked in some water with that breath. He wasn't used to staying submerged so long and that reed had barely brought enough air into his lungs to keep him from drowning. It had only been Jhinn's vice-grip on his shoulder that kept him underwater for as long as he'd been under.

"They might be back," he said, still gasping, handing the reed back to Jhinn who stashed them in his hidden compartment.

"I don't think so. If they knew we were here, they would have stayed. Waited us out."

Jhinn was almost fully dressed by the time Tamerlan pulled himself back into the boat, shaking the stinking canal water off and hurriedly dressing, too.

"Where are those scars come from, hey? Someone beat you good." Jhinn arranged a wide red cloth around his waist. It gave him a buoyant look that fit well with his wide loose pants, and bare feet.

"Not for years," Tamerlan said. He didn't like to talk about his father.

"My uncle used to beat me like that. 'No more stealing wood and rope,' he would say. 'That boat you built is stupid. It's too short to be a proper gondola and the bottom is too dished!'"

"But you still built it," Tamerlan said, tugging on the cloak that matched his uniform. "It's a pity this doesn't come with a sword."

"I have a sword in the hideaway. You need it?" Jhinn asked.

"I won't look like much of a guard without one," Tamerlan said with a laugh.

Jhinn pulled the gondola up to the side of the wall, opening his secret compartment again. "That red-haired Watch Officer couldn't find it. I bet she doesn't find much. All storms and no lulls."

"Why did you build your boat with a 'dished bottom' anyway?" Tamerlan asked.

"See how I built a cap over the stern and one over the bow? You can store gear in there and close the little door. If the boat flips, it pops right back up again. Your gear is safe. Yeah, you're wet, but you don't lose the boat. Good, right?"

"It is." Tamerlan's eyebrows rose as he took the sword Jhinn handed to him, strapping it onto his belt.

"Yeah, well, my uncle didn't think so." There was a long pause as they contemplated their scars. "Let's talk about tonight."

"I have to try to save my sister," Tamerlan said. He was already looking down the tunnel. Maybe he should be going already.

"Don't even think about it," Jhinn said. "They're looking for us. We should stay here until it gets dark. Do you think anyone saw you last night when you were in the world of the Satan?"

A lot of people had seen him. Not many of them had lived. But that wouldn't matter to Marielle. He'd recognized her as their heads slipped under the water when her gondola turned the corner. She'd been sniffing the air. She was clearly a Scenter for the Jingen City Watch. What must she be thinking this morning, knowing she'd let him go, smelling him all over the wickedness of the night before?

"Probably," he said.

"Then you need to wait here until it is dark enough to go. Then you will slip into the Seven Suns Palace and I will wait in the moat. You'll smoke that stuff rolled in paper. I'll show you how. Then, you grab your sister, get back to the boat and we row downriver to the stash, yeah?"

"Why are you helping me?" Tamerlan asked. His hands were shaking again at just the thought of trying the Bridge of Heavens again. He felt like he might be sick.

"I told you. I can see them. The others."

"What others?" Tamerlan asked.

"The night you saved me it wasn't just you. It was a man with a bow and a hood. And then when you woke up, he was still there, but fainter. And a woman with red hair and a wicked smile. And now there's one with golden curls and a cruel red mouth. They're looking over your shoulder like carriage drivers looking over the back of the horse. And I can't tell who is going to drive the carriage next."

"Then you should row away and leave me. You shouldn't be mixed up in this."

The boy shrugged. "I could. I don't want to."

"Why not?" Tamerlan asked. He felt so tired. He wished it was all over, that the worst had already happened. The waiting was the hardest part – the not knowing and the hoping it wouldn't be so bad next time. It was killing him.

"I want to see what happens next. This is more interesting than fishing or paddling people around for copper coins." He shrugged. "Maybe if I hang around long enough, I'll be in a story, too."

"You wouldn't like it," Tamerlan said gently. He hated it. He wished he didn't have to do it.

"You're just saying that because you're a nice boy and nice boys don't like doing wild things. I'm a wild boy. I don't like doing nice things."

Tamerlan snorted a laugh and Jhinn joined him.

"Now," Jhinn said. "Grind up those weird ingredients in your stone dish and I'll show you how to roll them up."

SUMMERNIGHT

LAST NIGHT OF SUMMERNIGHT

30: SUMMERNIGHT

TAMERLAN

The feeling of the city as the gondola slid down the canals was a strange one. The colored lights were still lit along the canals. Roses still hung in bunches, drooping a little now, their petals falling to float on the canals like red teardrops. The smells of toffee, fragrant teas, and fruit pies still drifted in the air, but the spirit of the city felt like nothing Tamerlan had ever felt before.

The celebrations in the streets above and spilling down into the canals and gondolas below were almost manic in their intensity, as if by jubilant celebration the party-goers could erase the turmoil cast over the city last night. Everyone was wearing their costumes tonight. Even the gondoliers and the Waverunners in their strange houseboats were decked in the garb of the Legends, honoring the spirits of the dead heroes.

But there was another strange note to the celebrations. A note of violence.

Tamerlan saw more than one wicked glare from a gondolier as they swept up the canals. When they passed the smoking wreckage of the Temple District and the heart-rending wails from above, the gondoliers rowed twice as fast with steely faces. Their passengers laughed doubly loud, their eyes glued to the water or each other but not, definitely not, to the wreckage in the streets above.

"The celebrations at the Seven Sun Palace are going to be the best of all time," a girl dressed as Queen Mer said in the gondola beside theirs.

Tamerlan rowed harder. Jhinn had given him an oar, too, and the tiny craft zipped up the canal like a thrown dart. They weren't fast enough not to catch snippets of conversations that Tamerlan wished he didn't have to hear.

"It's going to be lavish. The feast alone has emptied the Trade District of fresh fruits and I heard the Artificers have a special surprise!"

"Better than those golden cages? Those were sublime!"

Whatever the Lord Mythos had planned tonight was only a cover for the main event – the sacrifice of Tamerlan's sister. And no amount of fresh fruit or fascinating displays could distract Tamerlan from that.

He watched the crowd, though, as it made its way up the canals in a flotilla of gondolas as if the partygoers were laying siege to the Seven Suns Palace. He was invisible to them in his uniform, just another piece of the city.

Dragon-send that was true when he arrived, too.

He and Jhinn rowed in silence. They had their plan. And Jhinn was set on helping. Nothing Tamerlan had said could turn the boy around. In all likelihood, Tamerlan would fail again. But this time if he failed, he would die doing it. And then, hopefully, Jhinn would get safely away.

And even though that was almost assured, he couldn't stop hoping that he would succeed and that in just a few hours they would be shooting down these channels with Amaryllis tucked in the little hollow in the front of the gondola.

They paused with the other boats, waiting for the lock workers to raise all the boats up to the next level of the canal. The hydraulic pumps worked in the background and they rose upward to the next level, the level that would bring them to the Seven Suns Palace.

Tamerlan's eyes drifted over the crowd, taking in the elaborate costumes. No expense had been spared on these. Dyed feathers, swaths of silk, ruffled tulle, bright shining glass-work – even some real gems – bedecked the party-goers and the overly-merry looks on their faces brought out a glassiness to their eyes and redness to their cheeks that was visible even in the twilight.

When, finally, the lock was opened again, they rushed forward, racers in an exhibition no one had planned.

Was that – ? No.

His mind was playing tricks on him. He had almost thought he'd seen someone dressed as the *other* Legend. The one no one spoke of. The one – if history was true- who had made all of this possible – the five cities of the Dragonblood Plain, Jingen itself, the peace of the five cities. None of it would be possible without him, and yet no one would speak his name. Not just because he had gone insane after his great deeds but because no one wanted anyone to get ideas. After all, in a city built on an ancient dragon – even a mythical one only true in the minds of the religious – a dragon slayer was a terrible thing.

They were in the moat now, jam-packed among the other gondolas. Tamerlan glanced back at Jhinn who lifted a single eyebrow. But the bare hint of a smile on his lips spoke of his excitement. They were there. It was now.

Tamerlan took a deep breath, patted his pockets, and this time when they slid through the portcullis with the others and skimmed to the dock, there was no Byron Bronzebow stealing away his chances. This time, he leapt from the gondola to the dock with a quick wave to Jhinn and joined the jostling crowd.

Jhinn eased his gondola into the shadows. It wasn't going to be easy for him to sneak into the Palace moat to wait.

Tamerlan's heart was racing. His breath coming so fast that he had to fight it back to a normal rhythm. He was here. He was further than he'd managed to get before. No one noticed him as he strode through the crowd, his blue cloak and guard uniform making him just a usual part of the celebrations.

Now, he had to find the tower, free his sister, and end all of this.

He followed the crowd to the entrance of a Grand Hall. On either side of the entrance, musicians dressed like the Legends played a tune so frenetic and wild but compellingly beautiful that the crowd pressed ever forward, ignited by the music.

Tamerlan pressed forward with them. He wasn't looking at the soaring pillars or the scenes painted on the ceilings. He wasn't marveling at the polished marble beneath their feet or at the frescoes and inlays. His mind was racing on what to do next.

Once he reached the Grand Hall, there would be more chaos. Perhaps there he could slip away through one of the doors and find his way to the Sunset Tower. He took a deep breath as he reached the entrance.

"Landholds Chee G'hing and Sha'lain G'hing!" the steward announced, his voice ringing into the Grand Hall – as if anyone in the party could even hear it over the roar of voices.

Music poured out from the orchestral arrangements, and couples danced in the ballroom, while on the edges of the dance floor the other party-goers feasted at over-laden tables or viewed the wonders staged around the room – set in alcoves or hanging from the ceiling on golden chains. There were strange birds with plumage that rivaled the Legend costumes with their bright colors. There were caged creatures with sharp claws and sharper fangs. Statues that sprang to life when people passed, tattooed fortune tellers, panes of colored glass in diamond patterns with light shining through while dark silhouettes behind the glass mimed the stories of the Legends. It was more than a man could take in with a single glance – and it made it hard to see the entrances and exits of the room. It obscured where his attention should be focused.

At the very center of the room, a massive, gilded grandmother clock – a diamond shaped face and gem-encrusted hands, held up on four gilded pillars – was encased in a glass dome. Around it, whirled and spun gears of every size and shape, a massive tribute to the Timekeeper religion and a reminder to Tamerlan that time was short. There were more gears than he could count ranging from the size of a gondola to the size of a marble. It glowed in a way that suggested magic was at work in the careful tick of the sparkling hands as they danced around the face of the clock.

Shaking himself, he dragged his gaze away from the clock and tucked in behind a group of five people in costumes so flamboyant that no one would notice a mere guard behind them. As the steward announced them, he slipped into the Grand Hall, skirting behind a golden cage occupied by a very life-like Deathless Pirate and a dozen colorful birds with magnificent plumage. Smoke and secrets seemed to drift out of the cage as if by magic, whispering to Tamerlan of the gold on islands far beyond the horizon.

The pirate winked as he hurried past and he jumped with surprise, dodging behind an elaborate gear-and-weights display that moved in a steady metronome rhythm as if it, too, was a time-telling device. Maybe it was, though it rose so high in the vaulted ceiling that the tip of it was completely obscured by the darkness above the chandeliers.

Laughter from golden balconies above the Grand Hall spilled down into the room as waving silhouettes pointed down at the wonders below.

He needed to find a place to wait where no one would be suspicious.

There. At the other end of the room a row of guards stood in front of a massive black curtain covering most of the back wall and reaching as high up as Tamerlan could see in the shadows above the chandeliers. On either side of the curtain, open braziers – as wide across as Tamerlan was tall – were alive with leaping violet flames and popping sparks. Dragons cast in metal were wrought around the sides of the braziers, standing as tall as he was, and the flames inside their silhouettes made it look like they danced and swayed. They also cast long shadows.

Tamerlan strode through the partiers, standing aside politely for anyone in his path until eventually he found one of the dark leaping shadows behind the brazier to the right of the curtain and carefully stood so that it swallowed him up.

He patted his pocket with the rolled-up spices – the recipe for the Bridge of Legends. When the time came, he could use the brazier to light it. Patience was key. It was not midnight yet. He had time to wait for the right moment if he didn't act too soon.

This was his last chance.

Somewhere, behind that black curtain, was Tamerlan's sister.

And somehow, he was going to get her out of here.

31: Silk Dresses and Swords

Marielle

Marielle's mother loved pretty dresses. When Marielle was small, her mother would sometimes dress her up in them and paint her face with bright colors to make her "pretty" and they would take canal rides through the Trade District with all her mother's friends 'to remind people we exist' her mother had said. Marielle still blushed at the memories. And when people insisted that she wear a dress, she still wondered if they were trying to remind people of something.

"You'll wear the dress he sent, and you'll go to the party at the time the card says, or so help me, I will throw you out of the Scenters," Captain Ironarm had said when the dress arrived at the Watch House. "We have a District half-burnt to the ground, hundreds of dead, a band of killers on the loose who have disappeared and left no trace, and Jingen Watch Officer funerals to plan. This is not the day to test me."

"I'm a Watch Officer," Marielle had insisted for the third time, "not a doll to be dressed up and sent to parties on the whim of a noble."

"You were fine with it last time."

"Last time was different."

Captain Ironarm had sighed. She'd been up all day sifting through the Temple District, just like Marielle and Carnelian. And just like them, she'd come back to the Watch House to find the wrapped box with the dress and the invitation.

"Marielle, I'm a fair Captain. I keep a fair rota. I don't give out punishments lightly or turn a blind eye to bribes. But Marielle, when the leader of the city asks for assistance from a Watch Officer, I don't say no. I don't care if he wants you to dress up as a rat and run through a maze, you put on the clothes he sent and you go and do what he asks you to do. And you do it because you are grateful to help the city. It's not like he's asking for anything that might ..." she had waved her hands as if looking for words, "disrespect you. The note clearly says he wants you there close to the Lady Sacrifice in case you can smell a hint of the people who rampaged through the Temple District last night."

"In a dress? Why can't I at least wear my uniform?" Marielle had felt her lower lip trembling. There was something wrong about this. You didn't ask a girl to wear a pretty dress to investigate a crime. You didn't send it with rose petals thrown on top to make it smell nice. The whole thing made her skin crawl. Besides, if she had to stand next to the Lady Sacrifice then she'd have to see with her own eyes the one crime she wasn't brave enough to stop.

"Maybe he doesn't want people to know you're a Watch Officer. A disguise will help you go unnoticed – give you a chance to notice the people you are looking for without being noticed. Or maybe he just doesn't want to cause a panic on a night where the whole city is this," she had snapped her fingers, "close to exploding. Or maybe he just likes girls to wear pretty dresses. Insulting? Maybe. But you could be doing worse things for your keep, and on a night where I have to go tell *five orphans* that their father is never coming home, I don't really care if a junior Scenter isn't being shown the full measure of the dignity she feels she deserves. Is that understood?"

It had been understood. Marielle had dressed in the clingy silk dress, resentful of its pale purity and the way it clung to every curve. She still wore her leather boots under it, even though they looked ridiculous. No one had left any orders about shoes. It was her one small rebellion. She also had raided the armory, strapping a knife the length of her forearm to her inner calf, tucked partway into the boot. In the other boot, she stuffed her watch badge. It made walking uncomfortable, but it made Marielle feel a little less underdressed.

"Those boots look ridiculous," Carnelian said as they waited to enter the Grand Hall in the Seven Suns Palace. Carnelian didn't have to wear a dress. Carnelian had been allowed to wear her uniform. Just looking at it made Marielle want to spit. She felt naked in the thin dress. "And don't sulk. You look five years younger when you sulk, and you already look too young for this job."

Marielle shivered. It wasn't just that her dress was too light. It was also the strange atmosphere of this Summernight. The parties in the streets on the way there had been wild – but not in a celebratory way. Everywhere she went, she smelled whiffs of the crackling lightning-blue and acrid smell of fear tinging thoughts of the people around her. It mixed with their festivities in a way that washed everything in the frenetic smell of magenta and lemon. It agitated Marielle, making her nose itch and her skin crawl. This city was on the edge of exploding into violence. One wrong word tonight. One wrong action, and the pretty front of costumes and lights and music would be torn away by the rabid animal within.

"You worry too much. We were invited by the leader of our city. We should be proud to represent the Jingen City Watch." Carnelian held her head high as she spoke, but Carnelian wore a Watch uniform – clean and polished, but still a uniform. She was not dressed like a sacrificial lamb – again.

And Carnelian had no idea what was happening in the crowd around them. Marielle knew this smell. She smelled it sometimes on the docks when they were unloading next to the slaughterhouses. It was the smell of a herd ruled by fear. The smell of animals sniffing the air and wondering why they smelt death nearby. It was the smell of nerves and waiting, the smell of close violence and pervasive fear.

There had been one other time that Marielle had smelled it. Right before last year's Autumntide when someone near the slaughterhouses had thought it was a good idea to cut corners on the new fence. The fence had come down and the result had been a stampede through the streets of the Trade District. She'd never forget that smell.

It was all around them here in the entrance to the Grand Hall, just like it had been all around them on their way through the streets of Jingen.

"Jingen Watch Officer Carnelian Fishnetter, and Marielle Valenspear," the steward said as they passed through the doors into the marvels of the room beyond. But Marielle was not amused by the woman who rode by at that exact moment, balanced perfectly on her unicycle and blowing shining sparkles into their faces. Because while those around her clapped with glee, all Marielle could smell was the thick scent of fear rolling over the mob, like waves over the sand.

She swallowed, her mouth suddenly dry as Carnelian tugged her past laughing, costumed partyers and smooth-faced servants with trays.

"This way, there is a place reserved for us," Carnelian said.

There was a burst of sparks from the ceiling and a wave of tambourines began to shake from the sides of the room and then colorful cloth fell from the ceiling with a *whump*.

Marielle flinched, sinking into a protective crouch, ready for a fight. Who had fallen from the ceiling so high above? How did they get there?

But the crowd was clapping and laughing. Carnelian pulled her back to her feet as dancers whirled through the silks and the music began to pulse from every direction. They swirled around the massive grandmother clock – taller than four people standing on top of each other, the diameter of the base wider than two people end to end.

"It's the entertainment!" Carnelian yelled to her over the voices and shouts from the crowd. "Didn't you see all the bright colors? It's like the inside of a gem-encrusted crown!"

Of course Marielle hadn't seen gem-like colors.

"You should see all the gold! This must have cost a fortune," Carnelian continued.

And Marielle didn't see that, either. The only color Marielle saw was frenetic blue-lightning fear sparking and flowing from one person to the next until she wondered how anyone maintained a smile at all instead of hunkering in the corner.

They were getting closer to a black curtain on the other side of the room, sliding between bodies of impressed people gaping up at the ceiling.

"Do you see him? He shot out of the chandelier! Have you ever seen anyone flip like that?" a woman she passed was saying. Acrobats had arrived.

Ahead of them, there was an eddy in the electric blue smell. A pulsing orange ginger laced with turquoise and sparkling gold. Marielle's eyes widened as Carnelian pulled her closer and closer. If she could just catch a glimpse to confirm … If she could just be absolutely sure that it was Tamerlan in the long shadow by the brazier …

"Marielle Valenspear," the honey-thick voice almost seemed to speak right in her ear and then she was overwhelmed by the smell of magic and musk as the Lord Mythos flourished his cape with a smile and took his hat off to her. "I've been waiting for your arrival."

The fear that rolled over the crowd intensified around him – Etienne Velendark, the Lord Mythos – forming waves so high and wide that they seemed to wash away almost every other emotion so that one person's too-bright eyes met another's nervous laugh which turned to watch the color drain from another's face.

Something was going terribly wrong in Jingen.

32: Hope Twists

MARIELLE

"You're late," Lord Mythos said, but his narrowed eyes were on Carnelian who seemed to shrug slightly.

Why would she do that? Perhaps it was only a trick of the light because a moment later she was bowing deeply, pulling Marielle down with her.

"Lord Mythos," Marielle said respectfully.

"The Canticler is about to begin, and I crave your company for the reading," Etienne Velendark, the Lord Mythos said, extending his arm in its perfectly tailored silk coat.

Marielle froze. The Canticler was already about to begin? How late was the hour? Fear knotted in her belly. She wished she'd been able to see if that eddy in the tides of the crowd was Tamerlan. After the destruction he'd caused yesterday – after the lives he'd taken – she knew he was a danger to them all. She was here to watch for trouble, wasn't she? She was here to enforce the law.

Carnelian elbowed her in the ribs and with a start, she realized that the Lord Mythos was still waiting, arm held out for her to take. One of his eyebrows was arched like he found her discomposure amusing, but the look in his eyes was not amusement and his beautiful features were razor-sharp and almost otherworldly as they flared with pops of colorful magic residue.

His scent, oddly enough, was the smell and color of garlic – uncertainty. Like he was re-evaluating something. Perhaps he regretted singling out a Watch Officer like this.

Marielle hastily took his arm, surprised when Carnelian followed closely behind her. She hadn't been invited to join Lord Mythos and it wasn't like Carnelian to be presumptuous to Landholds – never mind the ruler of their city. Marielle shot her a warning look, but when she met Carnelian's eyes, the other woman didn't seem to notice her at all.

They walked with the Lord Mythos as the crowd parted and the dark curtain ahead of them loomed. Was the Lady Sacrifice behind that curtain? She felt a little hot at the thought – sweat breaking out under her pretty dress.

This was the moment when Marielle should be walking behind the curtain and to take her place. Because despite everything that Tamerlan did, his sister was still an innocent girl and she was going to be sacrificed. Marielle smelled magic behind the curtain – a magic so powerful that it made it hard to smell anything else, hard to smell the blue fear driving the crowd or the clove and mint smell of Lord Mythos, or Carnelian's boot polish and beer. Hard to smell the girl who must be back there.

Hard to smell anything but the pop and sizzle of living, breathing magic. She wanted more.

The black curtain was framed by a golden frieze of roses and lotuses and to one side was a raised three-tiered pulpit – each tier a little smaller than the one below – and sounding board. It was a strange contraption that looked foreign in a Grand Hall, but it could carry a voice over the crowd.

The Canticler climbed the stairs up to the pulpit, his white Timekeeper clergy robes spotless despite the chaos in that District. As he climbed, the Lord Mythos pulled Marielle to the pulpit, taking his place on the ground level of the tall, spindly structure. Applause filled the air as he took his place, gesturing for Marielle to stand beside him.

She felt her cheeks growing hot as she looked out at the eager faces, flushed with excitement and bright-eyed in the throes of their celebration. They turned her stomach. They were going to watch as an innocent girl died. She was going to watch.

She leaned against the wooden rail – certain she might empty her stomach. Her head felt light.

How far was she going to let this go before she did something about it? Her mouth was dry. Her tongue thick, curling with nausea.

She needed to speak. She needed to offer herself for the other girl. Why wouldn't the words come when she felt so desperate to speak them? Her heart pounded in her chest and she gripped the rail of the pulpit with sweat-slicked palms. And tears formed in her eyes as her tongue stayed silent. She didn't have the courage to give herself for another.

She was too cowardly to do what was right.

When the Canticler reached the top, he opened a leather-bound tome. He was younger than she thought he would be – barely graying at all – but what did she know of religion? She'd never been a part of the class of people who spent time in the temples. All she knew about Canticlers was that they knew the laws of Jingen backward and forwards and they knew the holy texts. They could quote any of them at will.

And now, as the Canticler's chant carried out over the Grand Hall, the music faded, and the last sounds of the party stopped as Marielle fought against the mounting shame of her choice to stay silent. Even the spectacles were quiet, the actors freezing in position and the wild beasts calming.

The sound of thousands of throats drawing in breath filled the air. They waited, watching the curtain and the pulpit.

The Canticler began his recitation, "The Pact between the five cities of the Dragonblood Plains was signed and sealed under King Abelmeyer the One-Eyed and the Lords of the Five Cities. And it is from this pact that Jingen derives her laws and from it that we find our purpose, our prosperity, and our pride."

"Our pride," the people echoed by rote and as they spoke, the black curtain began to part and the guards who had been stationed in front of it surged forward.

For a moment, Marielle's eyes grew wide as lamplight flashed off their gleaming armor and blades. Were they under attack? Was it Tamerlan? Had he really been in the crowd?

But it was only part of the show. The guards whirled in careful choreography, sword blades flashing, and then settled in place on one knee, swords held up in a salute. They were still guarding the curtain, but now the crowd could see easily over their heads.

There was a gasp as the slowly parting curtain revealed a wall with a mural of King Abelmeyer holding his sword aloft, dragons swirling in the sky above him. On the hills behind him, sword in hand, Marielle almost thought she could pick out the painted shape of the *other* Legend – the unspeakable killer of dragons. The wall began to slowly move, rotating the image. Marielle looked at the floor below the wall. Unseen clockwork gears turned and it was as if the entire Grand Hall were rotating – or perhaps it was just that wall with the mural.

"The Legends stood watch over the signing of the pact," the Canticler intoned and there were gasps of delight as the shifting wall revealed the Legends painted in their most memorable poses. "And by our catechism, we know that for blood, we give blood. For the lives of our city, we must give life. For the wrongs of our people, we must do a wrong."

The red of the crowd – the fear and violence began to pulse with his words as if the people resonated. Yes, they seemed to say, let someone else die for us. Let them take the pain and horror and leave us free to dance.

But how could Marielle judge that raw selfishness in their eyes? Marielle, who could take all that away from the innocent victim with just a few words?

Her head began to swim as the scent of magic grew stronger, reaching through the room like tentacles. It made it harder to think, harder to reason, like she was drunk on it.

The people who died in the Temple District had been her fault. She was no innocent. Not like the girl they were going to sacrifice. If she really respected tradition, wouldn't she want to uphold it? And if she really respected the value of human life, couldn't she admit that her guilty life should be the one forfeited, not this innocent girl's? It all made perfect sense as the magic swirled through her lungs, making her dizzy with the pleasure of the scent, washing away her nausea with the scent of lilac and vanilla, a scent that made her suck in gulping breaths to draw in as much of it as possible.

"On Summernight, at midnight each year, we give our Lady Sacrifice. She is blood of the Dragonblooded, sacrificed for us all, to bind magic to Jingen, to save our city from the wrath of the dragon, and to grant to her people one more year. As the laws of Jingen state, 'Each year a Dragonblooded woman of twenty-five years or fewer, unmarried, having borne no children, will be chosen from among the city and surrounding districts. She shall be purchased with blood money from her family and her blood shall be spilled upon the spine of the dragon. Any who hinder this shall be subject to prosecution and execution by Jingen City Law II A and their names shall be stricken from the books of births and remembered no more."

It was the law. And the law was clear and easy to understand. Marielle should have realized that when Tamerlan asked her to break it. She should have realized that there would be consequences. And now, there were hundreds dead because she had chosen to put herself over the law.

It was so hard to think with the magic swirling through her mind. So hard to grasp what was happening, but that part was true. She could see it so clearly now – almost as if someone was speaking into her mind. How had she failed to see it before? It had been her selfishness that killed those people. And only her selfishness could make an innocent die here tonight.

"It is for this purpose that we gather. We honor the Lady."

The crowd roared in appreciation as the wall mural finally showed the Lady Sacrifice, grim-faced but lovely, her head raised high as the Lord of the city – the Lord Mythos – raised his knife.

Someone would die tonight.

And that person would be Marielle.

"Lord Mythos," she said, urgently. "Take me instead."

His dark eyes were like pools of sympathy as he gently smiled. "I thought you might ask for that, Marielle." He bent in close until his breath raised goosebumps along her bare arms and across her neck. "I knew you were exactly what you seemed – pure of heart and noble. I knew you could never let someone else die while you lived."

The crowd still cheered, and the scent of magic swelled ever stronger – filling her, intoxicating her, making it all feel so unreal like a tide sweeping her away.

"But trust me when I tell you, I didn't want to do this," he said and his hand clamped around her arm, iron tight.

33: BREATH OF ASH

TAMERLAN

"It is for this purpose we gather," the man at the lectern said, speaking as if it was just another day of murdering innocent sisters.

Tamerlan's hands shook as he pulled the rolled paper out. It was time. Any moment now they were going to drag his innocent sister out from where they held her, and they were going to slaughter her here in front of everyone and he had one chance to stop them – this chance.

But he couldn't stop the shakes that rippled through him, making his fingers clumsy. He dropped the paper, quickly scooping it back up from the ground. The ends were still twisted. He hadn't lost the precious materials within.

Images flashed across his eyes. Images of people fleeing for their lives while he watched himself kill them, brutally discarding their broken bodies like tattered rags flung from a workshop.

What if that happened again? What if he slaughtered innocents again? He'd heard their mothers wailing and their fathers weeping in the streets. He still felt raw inside, like he bore a wound across his heart that would never heal. But if he didn't at least try to save Amaryllis, he would have done all of that for nothing, right? It was a simple choice – either try again and make all the evil he had done worth it for the good he could achieve, or don't try and it would still have been done but now Amaryllis would die, too.

Simple – but still not easy. He bit the inside of his cheek as the images rippled across his mind's eye, biting harder at the pain that ripped through him, triggered by the memories. He could taste blood. The inside of his cheek felt ragged against his tongue, but it was hard to stop, hard to wrench himself away from the memories of that horror.

This one thing was all that was left. He just had to do this one thing – save his sister. The thing he'd been doing all of this for. And then he could deal with the memories and the guilt. Then he could bury himself in shame, drink away the memories, hide himself from friends, slide into decrepit death.

But first this.

He drew a long, tremulous breath, glad that it was hard for anyone to see him. He reached over to the brazier and lit the roll of paper, bringing it to his lips to draw in the smoke. It flowed over his ragged cheek, across his tongue and sucked deep into his lungs. He stifled the cough, letting the smoke drift out his nose.

There was nothing yet. He pulled again on the smoke, scanning the sights before him, ready to charge.

The moving mural was still slowly spinning and the Canticler was still speaking, "We bless the sacrifice, placing on her our debt. Placing on her our hopes."

The mural spun into the wall and now a lattice of gold and roses was revealed as the wall continued to turn. Was that the whole base of the Sunset Tower spinning beside the Hall? Or was the Hall spinning around the tower? The ground beneath Tamerlan rumbled from the movement of weighty stone on weighty stone. Red light spilled from the lattice, flooding the front of the room as the crowd drew a wonderous breath together.

What was wrong with them? They were treating this travesty like entertainment! Their eyes sparkled, raptured looks painting their grotesque, made-up faces, their costumes looking utterly ridiculous – or maybe it was more pitiable, like children come to witness a beheading. Lost, broken children. What was wrong with Jingen?

The Legend still hadn't come for him. Maybe smoking the ingredients this way didn't work. Maybe he wasn't getting enough smoke. He puffed madly on the roll of paper, his hands shaking like leaves in a thunderstorm, and his heart beating so hard that his pulse pummeled his eardrums. Come on, Tamerlan! Come on! Open that Bridge!

His eyes flitted along the rapt faces, watching them, seeing them in the crowd, trying to cement in his mind an image of who these people were who so glibly sacrificed the life of another for their own.

Wait.

He ran his eyes back through the crowd to the girl dressed like the Lady Sacrifice – the one with long blonde hair arranged in elaborate curls and the virginal white dress dipped in pink at the edges. The girl with flushing cheeks and excited eyes. The girl who was standing right beside his father.

Oh no.

No, no. no.

He was wrong. The Lady Sacrifice wasn't going to be Amaryllis at all. His sister was safe, here only to attend the celebration. They must be guests. They must have come, as Landholds sometimes did, to attend the party.

But those had been her eyes on the barge, looking at him through the curtain. That had been her desperate, tear-stained face.

How could he have been so wrong?

He felt light-headed, suddenly, and his feet tingled as if all his blood had rushed away from his head and to his feet. They were glued in place, unable to run away from the events he had already set in motion.

Because it was too late for Tamerlan. Too late. The smoke filling his lungs was finally working its magic.

What had he done? What would he *do*?

The roll of paper dropped from his hand at the same moment that the moving wall finally opened to reveal the heart of the Sunset Tower. The bright glow coming from the base of the tower filled the Grand Hall, making the bright braziers and glowing chandeliers seem like candles on a summer afternoon. The rock of the floor – shaped like dragon scales, seemed to pulse to the same rhythm as Tamerlan's racing heart.

At the very center of the room, a horrific metal contraption – like the ribcage of some beast of prey – stood open, the straps to hold hands and feet were loose and ready to receive a victim. The drains that ran beneath it led to the glowing chasm on the other side of the tower base.

"Accept our sacrifice, dragon!" the Canticler said as Tamerlan's hands reached for his sword – no longer directed by him at all. "Spare us from your wrath!"

DRAGON! a deep voice in Tamerlan's head roared.

The massive clock at the center of the Grand Hall began to strike.

34: LADY SACRIFICE

MARIELLE

The Lord Mythos had her arm in his hand, his eyes narrowing as the Canticler continued, "We bless the sacrifice, placing on her our debt. Placing on her our hopes."

"The blessings of Jingen are upon her," he said, his face grave.

Marielle swallowed. She'd chosen this. She'd chosen to take someone else's place so that they wouldn't have to die. She couldn't back out now. She had to be strong.

As the mural faded and was replaced by a metal lattice, she strained to look through the lattice. Where was the girl?

Carnelian pushed a path through the spectators from the lower level of the pulpit and the Lord Mythos strode through it – Marielle's arm still clamped in his hand. Seven Suns Palace guards formed up around them, obscuring Marielle's view as she strained to see the girl whose life she would save. Where was she? A niggling voice in the back of her mind said, 'Are you sure she's worth it?'

Her mouth was dry, her limbs wooden and clunky. Why was Carnelian pressing in so close to her back? She glanced behind her to see her friend's firm expression and tight eyes. She'd expected more protest from Carnelian. Instead, that sweet smell she sometimes caught a whiff of when Carnelian was around suddenly burst into a puff of fleshy-pink. It was the smell of rotting fruit. And betrayal.

And then the lattice opened up as the wall moved.

"Fascinating, isn't it?" the Lord Mythos asked through a cold mask. "The tower walls spin on huge gears. A genius invention. I wish I could have shown you how it works."

And the room it revealed was the very one that the Lord Mythos had led Marielle into, but this time, as the light spilled out from the tower into the room beyond, it spread past the railing at the back of the tower and out to a black metal chair in the center of the room – a chair that looked like a giant squid, if squids had legs of blades and wickedness.

And it was empty.

There was no Lady Sacrifice in the chair. There was no Lady sobbing in the room, her eyes looking desperately for her salvation.

Marielle looked down at the dress she wore – the one that the Lord Mythos had insisted she wear – and then at the empty chair and then at Carnelian, stiff and blank-faced behind her. She felt the blood drain from her head so quickly that she stumbled, her vision clouding with popping black and white stars, the smell of acid and blood in her nose.

"Etienne," she said, her voice only a ghost of what it usually was. The voice of a child seeking reassurance.

"Marielle," he replied gently but still pulling her along, her booted feet dragging slightly as if her body was just now realizing what her mind had concluded.

"I thought you said you didn't want me to die." She hated how her voice wavered. She was a Scenter. A Jingen City Guard. She was strong and capable. She was a hunter of criminals, a lover of the law. She was not a helpless sacrifice.

Only, that wasn't true, was it?

"I also told you that I would do anything, sacrifice *anything* for Jingen," the Lord Mythos said.

"It's just a tradition. It's superstition."

"Oh no, sweet Marielle. It's very real. Your blood will save the lives of thousands."

She tried to pull away from Lord Mythos' grip, but she couldn't budge his hold. Carnelian stepped up and took her other arm in a firm hand.

"But there was never another Lady Sacrifice, was there?"

A look of pain flashed across his face. "Circumstances changed. Debts were called in."

"Accept our sacrifice, dragon!" the Canticler said as Carnelian and the Lord Mythos pulled her into the opening. Her feet were on the scales of the dragon. "Spare us from your wrath!"

She could feel the ebb and pulse of something underneath her – something alive.

The massive grandmother clock began to strike.

Bong.

The scent of magic filled the air around her until it was all she could smell. It obscured her vision, painting everything turquoise and gold.

Bong.

The crowd was chanting something she couldn't make out. Her breath was coming in gasps.

"No," she whispered, fighting against the iron grips that held her.

Bong.

"Shhh … don't fight it," Etienne, Lord Mythos said, his young face twisted with pity as he pushed her into the horrific chair. "Remember that impulse you had to give your life for someone else? Cling to that."

Bong.

They strapped her wrist in place.

Bong.

She could only hear the sound of the clock and the fervent cries of the worshipful crowd and a low purr in her mind like the largest cat in the world was happy.

Bong.

Both her hands were tethered now. She fought the bonds, tears streaming down her face.

Bong.

She could measure her life in seconds as she drew in the magic-laced air around her, choking on her stuttering breaths. She had five *bongs* of the grandmother clock left to live.

35: RAM THE HUNTER

TAMERLAN

Dragon. Dragon. Dragon.

It was as if that was the only thought that the Legend had as he took over Tamerlan's body, raising his sword high and leaping from the shadows.

No! Tamerlan tried to shout as he leapt into the screaming crowds, surging forward. At least whoever this Legend was, he wasn't slaughtering the crowd. A small mercy in a terrible mistake. He shouldn't have smoked first. He should have waited and made absolutely certain that his sister was the one being sacrificed. He sought her through eyes no longer under his control – saw her screaming and darting behind his father, saw his father draw a blade to defend her.

But the crowd was not in danger. Tamerlan was the one in danger. A ring of Seven Suns Palace guards surrounded the base of the Sunset Tower. No longer kneeling, they sprang to their feet, swords flashing.

Screams erupted from the crowd and loud curses. They shrank away, distancing themselves from the spectacle. But there was curiosity there, too. There were looks that told Tamerlan that they still wanted to be entertained. Was this fun for them? Watching a man rush with cold steel against other men was a delight? Didn't they realize that steel could bite and rend, could shred muscle and cleave bone. Didn't they realize that pain and mutilation weren't just things that happened to other people?

Tamerlan rushed toward the guards – the seconds seeming to take as long as drawn out minutes.

By the second *bong* his sword arm was raised and the unprotected neck of the guard – still fumbling for his sword – filled Tamerlan's vision. He wanted to screw his eyes shut. He wanted to stop, but his body moved on its own, slashing across the guard's exposed neck, parting the flesh in a way too gruesome for words. Bodies were meant to be whole and strong – vessels for the spirits they housed. They were not meant to be torn like rags.

By the third *bong,* he was sailing over the dead guard, like a grasshopper in midsummer, landing in a perfectly-balanced crouch on the other side and sliding under the boar's tooth sword position of the guard who brandished his sword with a grim face. His sword slipped up under it like a darting snake, flicking out to sever the artery in the man's leg.

As blood spurted across Tamerlan and the floor and the surrounding guards, the clock *bonged* a fourth time and now there were five opponents, sliding over the arterial blood, leaving curving red trails where their feet skidded over polished marble. These guards weren't surprised anymore. They weren't fumbling. Their nods and finger gestures spoke of discipline and team training.

It was time to die. Tamerlan didn't mind so much. After all, Amaryllis was safe. And he had sins to pay for. Perhaps, in death, there might be mercy.

Be a man. Cowards shame us all.

Encouraging words. This Legend sure had a sweet spirit.

It does me good to once again dance with death.

The fifth *bong* rang in Tamerlan's ears, almost drowning out the continued screams of the fleeing crowd. By the sound of things, people were getting hurt in the madness. He hoped his father was protecting Amaryllis. He hoped that the Legend didn't make him turn on them.

Not with a dragon near.

He kept saying that like it was true.

The nearest soldier lunged at them – clearly a feint and yet they had to dodge. If it had been Tamerlan controlling his body, he would have dodged the first blow only to be speared by the sudden jab from the left that one of the other soldiers executed with the slick precision of training. But it wasn't Tamerlan fighting. It was this Legend. And he chose to leap straight into the air – so much higher and faster than Tamerlan could even imagine. He leapt above both feints, spinning in the air with a muscle-popping maneuver that made the Tamerlan inside

Tamerlan gasp, and then landing nearly on top of one of the guards.

He leaned forward and bit, chomping down hard on the man's nose and while the Legend's jaw locked, twisting and pulling like a fighting dog, the Tamerlan inside screamed and screamed.

He tried to pull away, tried to close his eyes, but he already knew it wasn't going to protect his mind from the acid horror eating away at his sanity.

On the sixth *bong*, the Legend spat the nose out of his mouth, turning from the agonized cries of his victim and spun, taking in the scene around him. Tamerlan didn't know what he was looking at – what was important enough in his mind to warrant note, to react, to plan for.

But what Tamerlan did see, changed everything.

They were strapping a Lady Sacrifice to that torture chair anyway. It wasn't Amaryllis of the dark eyes and bright gold hair. It was a woman with long dark hair, deep purple eyes, and tears streaming down her cheeks. Her huge eyes seemed to plead with him for help. He knew that face.

Marielle.

They were going to kill the Scenter who had saved his life.

Bong.

The Legend spun him into a complicated spin, scooping up a second sword as he moved and wind-milling between the guards with lightning-fast strikes so that they fell so close on each other's heels that they seemed to die in a single stroke.

Perhaps, perhaps this bloodthirsty monster could be convinced to save Marielle.

The woman in white? Are they offering her to the dragon?

The voice seemed as disturbed as Tamerlan at the thought.

Yes! That was exactly what they were planning to do.

Bong

They finished fastening her last strap around her foot, tying her dress to the strap – strange that they still cared about how things looked with the crowd stampeding away like frightened animals. Her heavy boots, strapped in the chair, looked odd with her filmy white dress.

The Legend leapt to one side, narrowly dodging an attack and then spinning in a complicated defense that slapped the sword from a guard's hand with one sword while he ran the second sword under the arm of another guard.

Tamerlan barely noticed the moans and cries of the fallen men anymore. They were all someone's sweetheart or husband, son or father, brother or friend. And he took their lives like a child ripping daisies from the grass and he threw them away just as carelessly.

Bong.

But if they could just save Marielle…

I do not wish to see her die.

They'd have to hurry. There were only three more strikes and then it would be midnight and they would slit her throat.

The Lord Mythos gripped a handle at the top of the ribcage-like chair and then with a powerful pull, he turned the whole chair on a wheel so that Marielle hung upside down, her mouth open in a cry of terror and her long hair falling to the floor.

Bong.

The Legend swung away from the last soldier. When had they killed the others? Tamerlan must have been distracted. He dodged the guard's blow, kicking out with his foot and connecting solidly with the man's knee as they ran by. The crunch of his breaking leg was loud enough to be heard even in this chaos.

Bong.

They leapt the rest of the way to the chair in a single bound.

No one stands in the way of Ram the Hunter.

Ram? Ram the insane? The Legend who was not to be spoken of? The dragon hunter?

He reached out, snatching the knife from Lord Mythos's hand with Tamerlan's left hand and grabbing a lunging red-haired guard by the throat with the other hand.

Insane? I don't think so. Everything I do makes perfect sense to me.

He broke the redhead's neck with a crack.

36: Flight from the Seven Suns

MARIELLE

Marielle felt thick bands of magic rising up from the floor, reaching for her. She could smell them – their intoxicating scent a mix of such strong lilac and vanilla mixed with a cedar musk that she could smell nothing else. They drew her so that even while she knew they were deadly, she wanted them to take hold of her.

She thought she might be screaming, but she didn't know anymore if she was screaming from fear, or rage, or from desperate desire to be swallowed up by the reaching magic.

Her pulse pounded in her head as it hung down, close to the drain, close to where her blood would leak out and satisfy the magic. Were those other screams she heard? Probably not. She was probably just drifting so far on the intoxication of the magic scent that she was hearing her own screams. So drunk on it, that she thought she even heard the clash of steel on steel and roaring battle cries.

Perhaps, this was what death felt like. Perhaps it wasn't a quiet slip into another world, but a riotous roar as the life rushed out of you.

She braced herself. Her eyes and nose were so flooded with magic that she could barely see or hear a thing. Her gift, in these last moments, was a mercy. She wouldn't see the knife coming.

There was a loud snap from beside her. Strange. Something must have broken. Whatever it was fell to the ground heavily.

And then the wheel was turning, and her feet fell loose.

Something must have gone wrong.

Something must have stopped the ceremony and she was still so blind from all the magic that she couldn't see it or hear it.

Her teeth rattled in her head as she began to shake, rattling against the metal chair like a seed in a dry gourd. The magic was too much. The power was too strong. She couldn't think, couldn't control her own body.

Another scent slid through the magic as her right hand was released. Gold. Gold and honey and cinnamon. She breathed it in, desperately trying to pull in anything other than the magic. It cleared some of the fog, and she saw a cloudy form wrenching the restraint off her other arm.

Through the fog of her vision, she saw a dark shape rush at the golden form but he was tossed aside like a dry leaf. Marielle tried to stand, but she was shaken off her feet, falling painfully against the metal chair. The ground rolled like the river in a storm, marble and stone rippling like the sea.

Her breath caught in her throat as she froze, uncertain what do next, but now she was being swept up and thrown over a shoulder. She blinked as something hard drove into her belly like a wooden beam. It knocked her breath out and just as she was gasping to try to release her spasming muscles it hit again. Again, it plowed into her and again and again.

Her savior was running, and his shoulder was knocking the air out of her body. She felt them soar through the air, felt his muscles bunch as he delivered blows and flung enemies aside. It was like being blind in the heart of a tornado. But her vision was clearing now that the tentacles were gone, and her scent was clearing, too.

Terror spiked bright and blaring from every direction. It pulsed harder when the earth shook – what was causing that shaking? Could it be an earthquake? – and seemed to spike wherever they passed.

They were moving upward as if they were climbing stairs. Crashes and crunches around them suggested falling furniture and masonry. What was happening out there?

And then fresh air hit her hard in the face and she could smell the open air. It cleared the worst of the magic and she could finally see clearly. She pushed up from where she was awkwardly slung across a shoulder. They were on the wall around the Seven Suns Palace.

"Put me down!" she yelled. She was no Jing urn to be stolen from a palace. No precious ruby to make off with – even by her savior.

The wall of the palace shook slightly, like a bowl wobbling after being set too roughly on a table. Below them, screaming crowds poured from the palace, screaming and fighting to leave, their decorations and costumes falling from them like the shed skin of a snake as they rushed from the palace. Wigs and hats, necklaces and capes, and trampled bodies fell in their hurried escape, landing on the moat below, under the feet of those fleeing, or flying through the breeze out across the Government District.

A boy in a little gondola on the palace moat ducked as someone's belt of skulls flew through the air, narrowly missing him.

Perched at the height of Jingen, the entire city could be seen from the top of the Seven Suns Palace and for Marielle, it was painted in the rainbow hues of terror, mourning, and ecstasy.

None of this made any sense. Why was the ground shaking so badly? Why was the city so full of terror? Perhaps she really had died, and this was the next life, and for her sins, she was paying in fear.

She twisted to look up. But she didn't need to guess who had saved her. She would have known his scent anywhere. Even without the glimpse of light-colored hair and broad shoulders as he whirled in a dance of death, sliding from one graceful sword form to the next, she knew exactly who this was –

Tamerlan Zi'fen, the murderer of the Temple District. The man who had been so desperate to save his sister.

He'd saved her instead.

Was it wrong that her heart soared with joy? Was it wrong that she was so happy to be alive?

There was some commotion she couldn't hear and then a breathless Lord Mythos called out.

"Put the sacrifice down. You can go if you do. But we need her."

"No." The answer was a growl – a growl she didn't recognize, but she knew this scent. She wasn't wrong about who had saved her.

"Put me down," she whispered. "I can fight, too."

He ignored her.

"Can't you feel the dragon waking?" the Lord Mythos asked. His voice was ragged with emotion, desperation carrying through the wind in orange ginger pulses. "Only her blood can stop it. Only her blood can save us all."

Tamerlan set her gently to the ground, shoving one of his swords into her hands while she was still gasping in surprise.

They were surrounded by guards, swords held out in a guard position. And at the center of the ring, a breathless Lord Mythos held a black-gloved hand up, his beautiful face torn with anguish and his dark eyes violent.

"Please," he begged.

She risked a glance at Tamerlan's face. He looked older, harder. His broad shoulders and strong chin jutted out like he was prepared to fight the entire world to save her.

"I don't appease dragons," he said in a low voice. "I destroy them."

"Then you will destroy us all," Lord Mythos said, and his voice sounded like a man who had just been set on fire. "Take her from him."

37: Wake the Dragon

Tamerlan

These fools will pay.

One thing about Ram the Hunter was that he didn't mince words.

This body and mind are adequate for dragon slaying. We will not assuage this dragon. We will let him rise and then we will make him fall.

It was strange how his confidence buoyed Tamerlan as the guards rushed forward. His sword spun expertly before him and he danced under their swords and over their reaching arms to lunge and slash and parry. Ram fought as easily as breathing, his movements almost a dance as he worked his way through the guards.

Tamerlan kept his concentration on watching what was happening around them. Was Marielle okay? Was Ram keeping her safe while he fought? He hadn't expected to be saving her today – but he wasn't sorry that he had. At least this time he hadn't killed innocent bystanders. At least this time he was doing something good. Or at least sort of good. The tremors in the earth were troubling.

A blast of fire as thick as his wrist plunged through the air toward them from the open hand of the Lord Mythos. His face was twisted up like he was concentrating, but Ram dodged the bar of fire easily and it disappeared with a blinding flash.

He took that fire from the dragon.

He could do that?!

Why do you think he keeps it chained here instead of dispatching it as any man of valor would? Have no fear. Magic is a deadly thing but no match to a sword, a strong arm, and courage.

Tamerlan's heart raced. That magic certainly looked like a match for him.

Marielle grunted from beside him and Ram spared her a look, noting that she'd slain the man attacking her and then returning to the battle. She *was* good with that sword. That was good. Right?

It is good.

And then everything shifted.

The landscape began to change. Out toward the sea, past the smoking wreckage of the Temple District and across the University District to the highest point of land there where the Queen Mer Library stood, the land seemed to lift into the air, curling up toward them. Tamerlan almost choked as the Temple District of Jingen shook, people, buildings, trees and paving stones falling off of it like scale from a rock. They were far enough away to appear small. Close enough to be seen in the full horror of what was happening.

The land looked as if it had come alive, as if a rock-crusted head had lifted up and was slowly looking back and forth as the buildings and roads that had once adorned it fell off, crashing down into the burnt Temple District and the yawning blue ocean. Canal water poured off like rain on a roof, flooding the canals below and making sudden wave surges that washed across the locks and out to the river, carrying boats and debris with the surge of water.

The world teetered awkwardly and a grinding sound of stone on stone drowned out every other sound.

Tamerlan's heart was pounding. This couldn't be real. It couldn't possibly be real.

Dragon.

The head *did* look like a dragon. And as he watched, the Queen Mer Library – stretching out horizontally from the ground instead of towering over it - popped off the surface of the rock, falling down the slope and bouncing off the ground, breaking into pieces as it tumbled. Tiny bits of debris – books, he realized – fell like dust into the Spice District. All those books, gone! All those priceless treasures and grimoires and carvings. Sian and the librarians and the book with his bloody thumbprint in it. Gone.

Where the Queen Mer Library had been there was only a dark hole in the rock. And then the hole opened. A brilliant golden-irised eye with a pupil like a cat's opened wide and then blinked.

"It's too late," the Lord Mythos said, his voice quivering with horror. "Too late."

They needed to run. They needed to get into Jhinn's gondola and run!

Gondola?

In the moat!

Ram spun, jamming the sword in his sheath in a single fluid motion and scooping a startled Marielle up by the waist. He took three long strides and on the third stride, he leapt over the wall and fell through the air.

As they fell, Tamerlan heard him screaming.

Death to all dragons! Death to –

His voice cut off as they hit the tepid water of the moat.

38: Gondola Dash

Marielle

Marielle fell through the air, her breath catching in her throat. Her emotions were bubbling and surfacing so quickly that she couldn't process them. Had that been a dragon? *The* dragon?

Because now the pleading of the Lord Mythos – of Etienne Velendark – didn't feel so strange. He really hadn't been pleading for her death – though, of course, he had been. He'd been pleading with her to help him save Jingen.

She was shaking now, but not because the earth beneath them – the dragon beneath them – was, but because of the tiny distant people she had seen raining from the windows and doors and streets of the University District. They were only a tiny fraction of the people who were already dead there. How many more would be crushed by masonry, die from falls, or be washed away by the draining canals? Her heart felt like it was stuck in her throat, like she couldn't breathe. A hollow feeling – too empty to hold her sudden grief and shock – welled up inside her, choking out her life.

She was under the water, the sounds and smells of the disaster above insulated from her mind by the murky water. Bits of plant and algae floated in the thick murk. Safe things. Things unaffected by the frights above.

She could stay down here with them and wait until the world ended above.

A hand seized a fistful of her hair and dragged her painfully to the surface.

"I think the fall knocked her breath out," a young man's voice said, concern in every tone. She knew that scent. She leaned into it, breathing in the golden honey like it was her salvation, sucking in deep breaths of the wicked tinges of cinnamon and celery like they could scour out the terror of Jingen. She inhaled life and hope in his scent. She clung to it.

"Help me get her in," he said.

Tamerlan. Her salvation.

A second set of hands grabbed her under the arms – seaweed and cedar, flickers of strawberry genius. "What? You're stealing party girls now?"

"I'm not sure now is the time for joking, Jhinn," Tamerlan said mildly as they tugged her into the boat. She coughed, spewing water across the deck of a small boat. Her dress was too clingy. Her mind whirling too fast. "Look above us. Do you happen to see a large eye?"

"Mer's spit! Come on! We'd better hurry."

Marielle shook herself, pulling herself up to her hands and knees as the gondola lurched forward.

"Are you okay?" Tamerlan's voice was gentle – so different from how it had been on the walls of the Seven Sun's Palace that she paused for half a breath.

"Why did you save me?"

The muscle on the side of his jaw clenched and the golden honey scent of him flared so strongly that it seemed to overwhelm him for a moment.

"I went there to save a sister, but when my sister was safe, I didn't see anyone there to save you."

He quivered slightly, as if haunted by some awful memory and then he stole a glance behind him at the dragon head stretching in one direction and then the other in the distance behind them.

"Now is not the time for sentiment or explanations! Row!" the boy in the back of the boat – Jhinn – said.

Marielle stood up, searching for an oar when Tamerlan's fell to the floor. She stumbled as the boat rocked, dipping low enough into the moat that water trickled over the gunwales before it popped back up again.

"Maybe it's not too late," Lord Mythos said from where he balanced, gaining his balance after leaping onto the prow of the boat.

Tamerlan was already drawing his sword.

"Row!" Jhinn cried and Marielle stepped back, shoving the oar into the water and pulling against it.

But Tamerlan's amazing prowess with the sword seemed to fail him now. The Lord Mythos lunged forward and Tamerlan barely smacked his thrust aside.

Jhinn steered the boat as he and Marielle desperately pulled with the oars, and now Marielle could see why. The water around them was rising, a wave coming up from behind. The dragon's spine where the Seven Suns Palace perched was slowly rising. On one side of the little boat, the landscape fell away as they rose into the air.

Marielle's eyes were fixed forward as she worked the oar. Lord Mythos' next thrust was a hair away from piercing Tamerlan's side when he dodged it. Lord Mythos pressed in closer.

What was wrong with Tamerlan? He'd fought like a master on the wall, but here he fought like an amateur, barely keeping his footing as he fought. Marielle could fight better. She gritted her teeth, hoping she was wrong and that he could recover and press the attack. She'd lost her own sword in the leap from the wall and the knife tucked into her boot wouldn't be enough against a sword.

"Row!" Jhinn roared.

Their gondola shot from the moat into the canal, gaining speed. There was something about the little craft that made it faster than the others around it and they shot past family boats and passenger gondolas moving at five times their speed as Jhinn worked his oar at the back like a rudder, artfully dodging other boats with less than an inch to spare. When they got to close to one, Marielle stuck her oar out, pushing off from the other boat and barely saving them from a crash.

They were picking up speed still as the waves behind them rose. They hit the first lock, sailing over it like a thrown javelin and landing hard on the water on the other side. Marielle and Jhinn were braced for it, but Tamerlan slipped and Lord Mythos' sword plunged into his shoulder just above his chest. He fell to the deck of the gondola with a moan.

Triumph flashed through Lord Mythos's eyes. Tamerlan's eyes were shut, face pale.

Marielle didn't wait for a breath before she dropped her oar in the floor of the boat and scooped up Tamerlan's sword, standing over him in the guard position she'd been drilled to take.

Lord Mythos kept his sword steady, but his eyes locked onto Marielle's. "I'm a better swordsman than you, Marielle. Don't waste your blood on this. Not when there's still time. We can still save the city."

"You must be joking!" the boy from the back yelled. "Look around you, fool! This city is gone!"

They passed the bridge that signaled the entry into the Alchemist's District at the same moment that a building slammed down onto the canal wall beside them, breaking into pieces as it came apart from the impact. Marielle threw her arms up, covering her face and head, but the shattering debris still lacerated her arms and torso as it blasted across her. The thin, clinging dress she wore did little to protect her.

The sound of a building shattering and of the screams around her blocked out all sound. Puffs of scent exploded in every direction, their colors so bright and overpowering that Marielle struggled to parse one from another. She reached down for her scarf, but there was no scarf. She'd lost it somewhere.

Lord Mythos dropped his guard, his face pale with shock and then an oar snaked out from behind Marielle, under her arm, and hit him straight in the chest, shoving him over the side of the gondola into the canal.

Marielle blinked at the spot where he'd been, stunned. It was only Jhinn's shout that brought her back to her senses.

"At any moment the locks are going to blow and we'll lose the water. Row! Row for your life!"

39: Flotsam Hope

Marielle

They shot through the masses of gondolas and family boats choking the canals. The water raced as quickly as they did, a flow of rapids like the tightening of a mighty river.

"The Dragon's wrath is upon us!" a woman in a neighboring boat wailed as they passed her frantic paddling.

People and furniture, horses and carts, homes and taverns and cobblestones rained from the sky like the wrath of the gods, narrowly missing them or hitting the tiny craft as they sped past. Like a rain of wrath from the Legends on high.

Marielle's stomach clenched in sick guilt as they barely dodged the plummeting body of an old man, already dead, his staring eyes telling the tale of horror all of Jingen felt.

"Shove him in the forward compartment!" Jhinn screamed.

Marielle looked back at him frantically and then at Tamerlan, lying still in the bottom of the boat, blood pooling under him.

A piece of masonry had fallen on him as he lay, unable to dodge, wounding his leg.

She dropped her oar and crouched down, lifting the masonry and throwing it overboard.

The boat rocked as a fruit shop hit the canal, plunging five boats underwater in the blink of an eye. Marielle gasped. Her hands weren't working. Her mouth wasn't working. It was like a scream was stuck in her throat.

"Hurry!" Jhinn called over the screams and wails around them.

"Legends preserve us! Dragon have mercy! Mercy!" the voices wailed.

Marielle shook herself. The panic around them was overpowering – the scent of it thicker than the scent of magic had been in the Seven Suns Palace. It clogged her nose and threatened to wash her sanity away in a tide of awareness. With effort, she opened the hatch, dragging Tamerlan to it and then shoving him inside and closing the small door.

"Are you sure he is safe in there? He will drown if water gets in the boat!"

As she spoke, water washed over the bow, soaking her dress and filling her mouth and nose. Marielle looked up, a cry ripping from her throat at the huge wave swelling toward them. It swallowed the edges of the Alchemist District, raising the canals to street level and flooding the streets with a roar of river water.

Marielle risked a look up, up, up past the curve of the city, rising up above them like a wave to where the spine of the dragon was showing as the Seven Suns Palace slowly fell off its back like limescale chipped from a basin. The Sunset Tower hung precariously from the rest, attached by a single thread of metal gears before falling from the Palace and tumbling down, down, down to crash into the Spice District – or what used to be the Spice District. Now, it was awash with water, the boats usually lining its docks jettisoning from land like a flock of birds taking off.

She gasped, almost choking on her own vomit before retching over the side of the gondola. Nothing felt real. Not anymore.

She shuddered, willing her hands back into submission and grabbing her oar again and digging into the swirling water. Broken crates and bobbing barrels, sinking debris and screaming people filled the water.

"We need to stop," she said through teeth chattering from the shock. Her hands shook and her heart pounded. "We need to rescue those we can."

"Rescue?!" Jhinn's cry sounded like a curse. "We stop and we die. Row! Row for your life!"

She opened her mouth to argue when the river erupted, sliding toward them and swallowing up everything around her in a massive swell. Their tiny craft bobbed to the surface, water splashing over the gunwales as it buoyed up on top of the swell.

"Drop the oar and bail!" Jhinn cried and as Marielle scrambled for a bailing bowl as what could only be described as a wing tore itself from under the river, mud, fish, human skeletons tied to heavy rocks, and sunken wrecks spilling from its leathery surface to pour back into the river.

Their craft was sucked into the depression in the water as Marielle bailed for all she was worth, filling the bowl with water and flinging it over the side again and again. She tried to focus on the motion and to block out everything else. It was too much. Too much for the human mind to comprehend.

The *Jingen's Glory Bridge* sailed over them, shaken from the wing like an unwanted vine ripped up by a gardener. Marielle's eyes rolled in horror as one of its massive girders passed inches over her head.

Thought had ceased. She could no longer plan, only react, no longer think about what she should do but only what she was doing. No longer hope for anything, not even to live. It was one breath to the next, one action to the next.

Water from behind them rushed into the depression, propelling them forward down the Albastru River. There were so many vessels on the river that it seemed to be its own city, alive with a crowd of people, but Jhinn's tiny gondola sped past all the others, riding the rising water like a horse racing down a track.

A huge river barge loomed in front of them, when suddenly it rolled, spilling into the sea as the tip of a tail bigger than a canal skimmed a hundred boats off the river with a single flick.

Marielle's eyes followed the length of it to where it pulled free of the Trade District, spilling docks and cargo, ships and businesses into the mud nearby. Please, Legends grant her mother safety in the Trade District! Her home was on the mudflats there. There was a chance it wouldn't be devastated by the tail uprooting from the ground. But even as Marielle thought that, the water of the river surged across the flats, swallowing the buildings up in the river's ravenous swell.

Her heart was in her throat and nausea swelled through her as the little boat shot out through the supports of the tottering hulk of the Sea Breeze bridge. On one side of it, the tail of the dragon swung, clearing buildings and ships in its path. On the other side, where once the Spice District had been was now nothing but muddy, swirling water.

She bit down hard on her lip, tasting blood as they cleared the bridge and spat out into the brackish water beyond where the Albastru flowed into the Queen Mer Ocean and the currents beyond.

Behind them, the city continued to fall, piece by piece, life by life, destroyed by the dragon her blood was meant to appease.

Lord Mythos had been right.

Carnelian – the traitor! – had been right.

If she had only died, none of this would have happened at all.

The moon shone brightly above them, lighting the debris, picking out the silhouette of the dragon as his wings finally pulled fully free and he flapped them, sending the little gondola spinning with the force of air from his wings while he lifted up from Jingen and into the air.

Legends help whoever was still alive in the houses and streets on his back! Gods above help any living souls still clinging to life there.

Marielle could not help. But she sobbed helplessly as if her many tears could fix the horror she had caused. Her tears fell into the sea and swirled with the brackish water and in the depths below, something stirred.

Epilogue

Marielle

"He'll survive," Marielle said. "I think."

She worked on Tamerlan's wound with gentle hands. He looked so young as he slept, his head resting on the blanket Jhinn had pulled from one of his hidey holes. They'd cleared the hull of debris and water before pulling him out of the air-tight cabinet at the front and cleaning his wound. It wasn't the first stab wound Marielle had tended or seen tended. Even before she was a Scenter there were wounds among her mother's friends. She had a deft hand for stitching and Jhinn was surprisingly well stocked.

Jhinn paused along one of the river banks as she sewed by the light of his small lantern, pulling a few carefully wrapped packages out of a hole along the bank and stuffing them into the space Tamerlan had occupied.

"What are those," she asked.

"The source of all that trouble," he said before tying a small bobbing craft behind them with a thick rope.

"A dragon?" Marielle teased. She was starting to like his intense manner and clear fondness for his friend.

"The magic that Tamerlan used back there. The magic of the Legends."

"Magic of the Legends?" she asked, preparing a poultice from the herbs in Jhinn's store. It was hard to do it well in the lantern light. Even from so far downriver, the sounds and smells coming from the city kept her on edge and ill. Her head swam with the licorice black despair wafting downriver and the heliotrope of agony swirling with it.

"He called it the Bridge of Legends. Smoke the right ingredients, and a Legend will take you over and use your body – for good or ill. He was using it to save his sister. Is that you? Are you Amaryllis?"

Marielle shook her head as she wound a clean cloth around the wound.

"Then he failed," Jhinn said. He cleared his throat. "Not that I'm sorry he saved you. But that sister meant everything to him."

They were both silent for a long moment as Marielle bandaged and Jhinn put his head in his hands, his first break in hours. He smelled of seaweed and cedar, of ash and salt, of hope and determination.

"I wish I had a brother like that," Jhinn said.

"So do I," Marielle agreed, trying hard not to think of her mother in the Trade District and of Captain Ironarm in the

Government District, of Carnelian who she thought was probably dead and of the Lord Mythos who was a better person than her – who, it turned out, loved the law like she never did.

She pulled the cloak Tamerlan wore over his body like a blanket, gently stroking his cheek. She wasn't his sister. He didn't need to risk everything to save her, and yet he had. And he was both beautiful and monstrous in her eyes because of it. Both the savior of her life and the demon who had ruined her city.

The sun rose in the east, kissing the water with glimmers of gold and shining warm hope over them. And far in the distance, it caught on hints of white on the horizon.

"Sails," she breathed. "Perhaps they bring help with them."

"I don't think so," Jhinn said, watching under a shading hand with tired eyes.

"Why not?"

"Those are Queen Mer's people."

"Waverunners?"

"What Waverunners wish they were. The Retribution. The scourge of the land."

That didn't sound like help at all.

"Prepare for the rise of the Legends," Jhinn said. "Prepare for the sifting of souls."

Marielle shivered, looking down at Tamerlan. She owed him her life. However much she might regret him saving it. She looked over her shoulder at the crumbled ruins of the city tumbled in ragged heaps far behind them and then back to the peaceful, innocent looking face of the sweet man lying on a blanket at the bottom of the boat.

She owed him. And whatever came next, she would protect him. Maybe together, they could repay the debt they owed to Jingen, to the law, to life itself.

***

I hope that you enjoyed reading Summernight as much as I enjoyed writing it. You can continue with the story here in *Dawnspell: Book Two of the Bridge of Legends* or chat with us about it in the Discord group.

APPENDIX

Diagram of the Sunset Tower in the Grand Hall many thanks to Harold Trammel for his work on the creation of this diagram of the Sunset Tower.

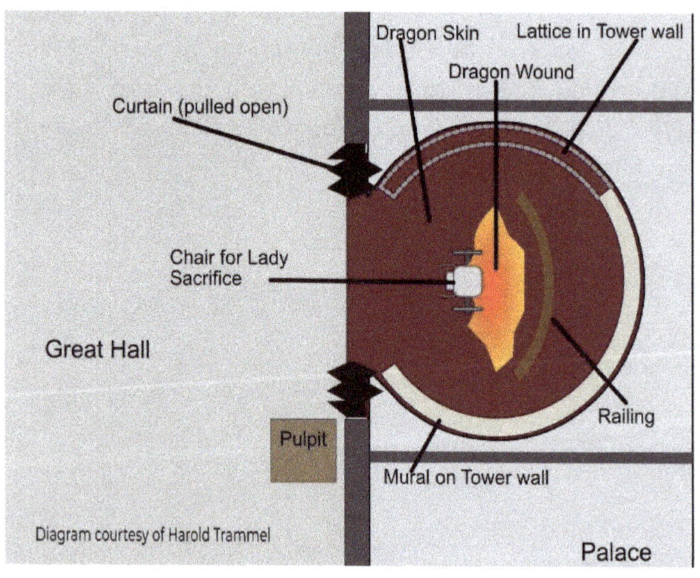

THE LEGENDS
BYRON BRONZEBOW
KNOWN FOR HIS GOOD LOOKS, BRONZE BOW, AND HIS CARE FOR THE POOR AND NEEDY.
DEATHLESS PIRATE
KNOWN FOR HIS LOVE OF TREASURE, INVULNERABILITY, HOOK FOR A HAND, AND BELT OF HUMAN SKULLS.
GRANDFATHER TIMELESS
KNOWN AS HEAD OF THE TIMEKEEPERS RELIGION, A HIGH HAT, LONG BLACK COAT, GOLDEN WAISTCOAT, AND FOR BEING TIME IN HUMAN FORM.
KING ABELMEYER THE ONE-EYED
KNOWN FOR HIS SINGLE EYE, BROKEN CROWN, AND UNITING THE FIVE CITIES OF THE DRAGONBLOOD PLAINS.
LADY SACRIFICE
KNOWN FOR HER LOVELINESS, INNOCENCE, SACRIFICE AND WHITE DRESS.
LILA CHERRYLOCKS
A MASTER THIEF AND TRICKSTER. KNOWN FOR HER LONG CHERRY-RED LOCKS, DEFT SKILLS, AND ADVENTUROUS SPIRIT.
MAID CHAOS
THE RIGHT HAND OF DEATH. KNOWN FOR DESTRUCTION, DEATH AND HER GOLDEN BREASTPLATE.
QUEEN MER
QUEEN OF THE SEA. MOTHER OF WAVERUNNERS, HURRICANES AND TYPHOONS. WEARS SHELLS, SCALES, AND SEAWEED.
RAM THE HUNTER
THE UNSPOKEN LEGEND. SLAYER OF DRAGONS. INSANE.
BRIDGE OF LEGENDS

BEHIND THE SCENES:

USA Today bestselling author, Sarah K. L. Wilson loves spinning a yarn and if it paints a magical new world, twists something old into something reborn, or makes your heart pound with excitement ... all the better! Sarah hails from the rocky Canadian Shield in Northern Ontario - learning patience and tenacity from the long months of icy cold - where she lives with her husband and two small boys. You might find her building fires in her woodstove and wishing she had a dragon handy to light them for her

Sarah would like to thank **Harold Trammel** and **Eugenia Kollia** for their incredible work in beta reading and proofreading this book. Without their big hearts and passion for stories, this book would not be the same.

Sarah has the deepest regard for the talent of her phenomenal artists – **Francesca Baerald** who designed the gorgeous map for this series and Lius Lasahido and his team at **Polar Engine** who created the gorgeous cover art that accompanies this book. Without their work, it would be so much harder to show off this story the way it deserves!

www.sarahklwilson.com